REINING HER IN

KATIE ASHLEY

Love,
Katie
Ashley

the
BOOKWORM
box

Helping the community, one book at a time

Chapter One

The squeaky soles of my Crocs echoed down the hallway. With my head down, my eyes scanned over the electronic chart of the patient who awaited me in the operating room. After presenting the familiar symptoms of a bowel obstruction, an X-ray had revealed a round foreign object in the stomach. The mystery object was too large for a laparoscopic removal procedure. Instead, I would be scrubbing up and going in surgically to remove it.

I'd just come back from briefing the family, which was never easy. I tried to put them at ease by assuring them I had done the procedure countless times. After taking their hands in mine, I stared reassuringly into their anxious eyes.

As I entered the anteroom off the OR, I stepped in front of the sink. After lathering up my hands and forearms with the medicinal soap, I rinsed them thoroughly. Once they were dry, I slid a surgical mask over my face before donning the surgical cap.

When I entered the OR, I found my nurse, Tasha, preparing the instruments. "Hey girl, how's it going?" she asked, her dark eyes twinkling behind her mask.

"It's going. Besides Barney, it's been a pretty noneventful day."

Waving a pair of surgical scissors at me, Tasha said, "I wouldn't hold my breath. It's a full moon tonight, and you know the crazies always come out of the woodwork."

I laughed and moved to the operating table. "That's true."

Lying on his back, my patient's limbs were strapped down to the table, leaving his abdomen exposed. A symphony of machines echoed around me as they registered the patient's oxygen intake and blood pressure.

At the sight of a set of low-hanging balls between his legs, I rolled my eyes in disgust. I was tempted to lop his sac off right then and there. At his age, it wasn't like he was going to get any use out of them. *Why the male species obsess over their sacs is beyond me.*

What? Did you think Barney was a human patient I had plans to castrate? I didn't mean to mislead you. Maybe it's because I take my job so seriously it might seem I'm a physician, rather than veterinarian. Turning away from Barney, I picked up the remote to the radio. Within seconds, an old-school Whitney Houston tune was piped in through the speakers.

Because I listened to music during surgery, one of my ex boyfriends loved to call me a wannabe Meredith Grey at *Fur's* Anatomy. I liked to call him a micro peen. Well, at least I did in my head. I wasn't bitchy enough to actually voice it. Instead, I quickly ended the relationship and vowed to never date anyone again who didn't respect my career or who had a moderately sized dick.

For those who are slightly squeamish, I'll skip the descriptions of the blood, guts, and gore that occur when you do internal surgery. We'll just move right on through that like you're fast forwarding on a DVR. To get you up to speed, my fingers had just enclosed around something that felt like a hard, round ball.

"What the hell?" I asked as I pulled the object out. As I turned it around in my fingers, I noticed it was larger than a marble but slightly smaller than a golf ball. The surface was smooth, and it gleamed silver in the light.

"Let me see that," Tasha said.

When I handed it over, Tasha widened her eyes before dissolving into laughter. "I-I can't b-believe it!" she sputtered.

"What?"

"You seriously don't know what this is?"

"If I did, would I be asking?" I replied.

"It's a Ben Wa ball."

I furrowed my brows at her. "Hold the phone. Ben Wa as in the sex balls?"

"Bingo."

"Are you telling me I'm going to have to go out there and tell the family that Barney ate one of their coochie balls?"

Tasha started laughing again. "Better you than me."

Sure, it wasn't the first time I'd dug slightly unmentionables out of a canine's stomach or intestines. Over the years, there had been a plethora of chewed up thongs, not to mention parts of a veiny dildo. There'd also been several condoms. Thankfully, the condoms had been eaten directly from the box.

Part of my apprehension came from the fact Barney's owners were a sixty something woman and her forty-something daughter. Shaking my head, I muttered, "Fucking full moon."

"You can say that again," Tasha snickered.

With the cause of Barney's blockage taken care of, I began suturing him back up. Once I was finished, Tasha and I wheeled him next door to the recovery room. As I was making post-surgical notes in his chart, a beep came over the intercom. "Dr. Beasley, your mother is on line two," a secretary related. Inwardly, I groaned. While I might've been knocking on thirty's door, my mother still treated me like I was a teenager. She insisted on almost daily texts or calls. She claimed it was because I lived so far away in the "big city".

With a roll of my eyes, I said, "I better go take this. Keep an eye on Barney for me?"

Tasha nodded. "Of course."

"Can you also have one of the floor nurses tell the family he came through fine, and I'll be out to talk with them in the next ten minutes."

A wicked grin flashed on her face. "Want me to have her tell them the happy news that their Ben Wa ball has been located safe?"

"Um, no. I'll take care of telling them the source of the blockage as well as the fact they don't have to search any of their orifices for the missing ball."

Tasha snorted. "Damn girl. That's a mental image I won't easily be able to forget."

"Tell me about it."

When I got into the hallway outside the recovery kennels, an arm snaked around my waist and jerked me into one of the supply closets. When I opened my mouth to protest, warm lips covered mine. I should say warm and *familiar* lips. Otherwise I'd be protesting very loudly at being manhandled.

After enjoying a few seconds of breathless lip lock, I forced myself to pull away. I stared into the jet-black eyes of the drop-dead-sexy vet tech I'd been hooking up with. Kieran was five years younger than me, which I suppose wouldn't necessarily qualify me for cougardom. But there was no future with him. He was just a distraction in light of the upcoming six-month anniversary of the breakup of my last long-term relationship. Instead of continuing to lick my wounds, I'd decided to lick Kieran's perfect washboard abs instead.

"I've been thinking about you all morning."

"You have?"

He dragged his teeth across his full bottom lip. "I've been thinking of all the ways I'm going to make you come tonight."

A bolt of white-hot lust zapped me between my thighs. "Is that right?"

"Mm-hmm

I slid my hand down the stubble on his cheek. "You sure are a naughty boy to be thinking those NC-17 thoughts at work."

Kieran gave me a wolfy grin. "What can I say? You drive me crazy."

An unattractive snort came from my nose. "In my scrubs and lab-coat?"

"Well, I know what you look like without them."

Oh yeah, he was killing me, Smalls. I could have stood there basking in his appreciation of me, but then I remembered my mother's waiting call. "Hold those risqué thoughts until tonight, okay?"

"My pleasure." He winked. "Or should I say *your* pleasure."

Why, oh why did he just have to be a fuck boy? Any other woman would probably not have had such a fatalistic view of a potential future between us. They might have reasoned that age shouldn't be an obstacle. After all, it was just five years. If the genders were on the other foot, so to speak, it wouldn't even have been an issue. He had drive and ambition—not to mention his own apartment so he wasn't living in his parents' basement or anything along those lines.

But I wasn't any of those other women. Life experiences—or love experiences—had altered me into a Pessimistic Patsy rather than a Hopeful Hannah. I could call a fling at fifty paces, and that was all Kieran was. A fling. But for the moment, I was happy flinging with him.

With a grin, I smacked his ass before heading out the door. Hustling down the hall, I made my way into the office allocated for us vets. After flopping down in a rolling chair, I picked up the phone before tapping the button on the flashing line.

"Hey, Mom, to what do I owe the pleasure of this mid-afternoon check-in?" I teasingly asked.

"Peyton, it's about Papa."

At the mention of my grandfather, my body tensed. Few people are blessed to actually know their hero personally, but I was a lucky one. My father was an only child, so his parents were especially enamored with me and my siblings. While grandparents don't really have favorites, I was the apple of my papa's eye because I was an animal lover. While my younger brother and younger sister loved our family pets, they had no desire to hang out at his vet practice or follow in his footsteps into veterinary medicine.

As my fingers dug into the headset of the phone, I demanded, "What about Papa?"

"He had a stroke this morning."

I shot out of my chair. My mind began free-falling with out-of-control thoughts. After a few seconds, the analytical side of my brain kicked in. "Which hospital? I'm hoping it's Erlanger because they have a better neurological unit than Memorial. They've done an MRI to assess the damage?"

When Mom sniffled, my breath hitched. "Mom?"

"Oh Pey, he didn't make it."

Air whooshed from my body, and I staggered back. Pain ricocheted through my chest. Thankfully, the desk chair was behind me to catch my fall. "Papa is..." I couldn't bring myself to say the words. A few seconds passed before I whispered, "Dead?"

"Yes, honey, he is."

Tears stung my eyes. "But I talked to him last night."

"I know. He'd had breakfast with us. Nothing seemed off with him at all. He went out to get in his car to go on rounds, but he collapsed in the driveway. It was very quick, and he didn't suffer." Mom's voice cracked, and she began to cry.

Hearing her weep broke me even further, and I began sobbing. As tears clouded my vision, a reel of sweet, happy memories played in my mind. A pint-sized me sporting a stethoscope that was almost as long as I was tall. Going on rounds through the Georgia countryside with him. Cups of brew that were ninety-five percent milk and five percent coffee.

The next thing I knew my father came on the line. "Hey, Peybug," he said.

At the sound of him using my childhood nickname, I cried even harder. "Oh D-Daddy, I'm s-so s-sorry." After all, my dad had lost his father. Even though Dad hadn't followed in his footsteps, Papa had always loved and supported his only son.

"He wouldn't want you to upset yourself like this at work. He would tell you to be strong for your patients."

Reaching for a Kleenex on the desk, I blew a grief-induced snot wad into the tissue paper. "I know he would. I just can't help it."

"I'm trying to be thankful for small mercies." Dad's comment was true to form. As a minister, he always tried to find the good in a situation or the greater plan. "It was quick and painless, and he died preparing to do what he loved."

"You're right. He always said he wanted to go quickly." After he'd watched my grandmother deteriorate from colon cancer, Papa often commented how he wished she hadn't had to suffer. He always lamented what a blessing it was to die in your sleep or to have a quick death. *But I'm not ready for him to be gone. It's too quick.*

"We've decided not to make any plans until you can get here."

Of my siblings, I was the only one who had left my hometown of Hayesville. My younger sister, Rebecca, taught first grade at the elementary school while my baby brother, Quinton, worked as a loan officer at the bank.

Before I could say anything, Dad added, "I know it won't be easy coming back, Pey."

He was right. My stomach churned at the prospect of entering Hayesville again. It had been almost a decade since I'd been within the city limits of the town where I'd grown up. I'm sure you're wondering how it was possible for me to be so close to my family yet never go back home. The truth was my family respected my wishes not to ever have to lay eyes on a certain person ever again. The certain person who had broken my heart into jagged shards when I was just twenty years old. Since the bastard's family went back generations in Hayesville, he wasn't leaving anytime soon. Instead, I'd limped out of town and never returned. *He'd run far until I left . . . bastard.*

Papa owned a lodge outside of the quaint Alpine-esque town of Helen, and we always met there for holidays and family events. You could say I was thoroughly spoiled that my family had allowed me to wallow in self-pity or self-preservation all these years. They probably should have told me to get over the bastard who had driven me away. The whole "Time heals all wounds" bullshit. But they got what it was like to live in a small town that fed off gossip like buzzards over a carcass.

Although I didn't want to return to Hayesville, my broken heart wanted the comfort only my parents could give. Even though I wanted nothing more than to run out the door that minute, I couldn't. I had post-surgery patients to check on, not to mention the other emergencies that might be brought in. I was one of the few vets who didn't have children, so it would be almost impossible to find coverage. "I'll leave right after work."

"No, honey, that isn't necessary. Just come up in the morning. We can tell Rebecca and Quinton to meet us at the funeral home around noon."

Part of me still wanted to hop in the car the moment my shift was over. I didn't like the thought of having to spend so much time alone with my grief. "Are you sure you don't need me?" Inwardly, I was hoping he would change his mind and demand I come home that instant.

"We're fine. You go take care of your patients, and we'll see you at noon."

I sighed. "Um, okay, if you're sure."

"Love you, Peybug."

A knife twisted in my chest. "I love you, too, Daddy."

My head pitched forward, and I buried my face in my hands. In spite of the cloud of grief overcoming me about the loss of Papa, my mind went back to a different time—one that wasn't completely tied to Papa. A time where I experienced a different type of loss and grief.

Chapter Two

The Past

In the past twenty years of my life, I don't think I'd ever been so focused on time as much as I was today. Maybe it was because I'd not only scheduled my wedding day with military precision, but I was barking out orders like a 4-star general. Everything from hair and makeup appointments to when to arrive at the church was meticulously timed. It was all part of my Type A personality. The loveable neurotic in me, as I liked to joke.

Six months ago when I'd announced my engagement to Declan St. James, time had also been on the minds of my family and friends. The question echoed most was, "Don't you want to wait until you get through veterinary school or at least your undergrad?" I'm sure to most people my wedding went against type. Valedictorians with full scholarships to the University of Georgia didn't get married at twenty, even if they were from a small town. The rumor mill fanned the gossip that I must be pregnant. But after a few months passed by without a baby bump, people finally abandoned the idea.

Since I wasn't pregnant, it made it even more problematic why I wanted to get married at twenty. People just didn't want to accept the answer that I was in love, or that my fiancé, Declan, supported my decision to finish school and pursue being a vet. As he often said, "There's no reason in hell why we can't achieve our dreams together,

Pey. I love you, and I want to marry you right now." Considering he was not only my boyfriend of the last two years, but the town catch, you could say I was easily persuaded. He'd been the quarterback of the football team as well as Homecoming King when I'd been elected Queen. He had plans of his own to earn a business degree and work for his father's contracting business.

Now as I stood in one of the preparation rooms at the First Baptist Church of Hayesville, I couldn't imagine my life without Declan. Not only that, the minutes couldn't fly by fast enough until I became his wife. Even better would be when we arrived in Aruba late this evening to begin our honeymoon.

As I was smoothing my fingers over the strand of pearls at my neck, I caught the reflection of my bridesmaids in the mirror. They were huddled in a clump by the door. With their heads bent, they spoke in low, frantic tones.

Turning around, I asked, "What are you guys doing?"

"We were looking for Declan," Becca replied.

My heartbeat accelerated at the thought of him in his tux. "How does he look?"

Becca gave a slight shake of her head. "He isn't out there."

I blinked at her. "What do you mean?"

"I mean, he isn't at the altar. He..." She threw a look at the others before she could finish. "He isn't even here at the church."

Unease pricked over my skin. "What do you mean he's not here? The wedding is in an hour. He knew we were going to take the pictures before." It had been his idea to get the photos out of the way so we could get to the reception earlier, which in his case meant getting to party quicker. In the back of my mind, I couldn't help feeling slightly suspicious that it might be bad luck for him to see me before the ceremony.

"He's probably just running late," Mom suggested.

With a furious shake of my head, I countered, "Declan is never late. He is irritatingly punctual."

"Any number of things could be preventing him from being here. A flat tire. An accident."

"He could at least call to let me know he was going to be late."

As if on cue, my phone began ringing. A relieved smile lit up my mother's face. "See there. He's calling."

Always the pessimist, I said, "It's probably a telemarketer."

Becca dove across the table to grab it. Once she recovered it, her eyes widened. "It's Declan."

While I tried to act calm, cool, and collected on the outside, I found myself screaming with relief on the inside. "Hey, honey," I said pleasantly. After whirling away from the others, I hissed, "Where are you?"

"The hunting club."

A maniacal laugh escaped my lips. "Now is not the time for jokes."

"I'm serious."

"That you're two hours away in the backwoods of Northern Alabama when you're supposed to be here at the church?" With my free hand, I swept my hand to the back of my neck to wipe away the beads of sweat.

"I'm sorry, Pey."

"I'm confused. Are you sorry you're not here at the church, or are you're sorry for something else?" His tone felt just as strange as it had last night at the rehearsal dinner. Well, as strange as one could sound when they only uttered four or five words. I'd chalked the somewhat sullenness up to him being exhausted from being out at his Bachelor Party the night before.

In his silence, I plowed on through. "I mean, excuse me for being slightly addled. I would imagine shell-shocked is a better description."

"I can't marry you."

"Well, obviously not today when you're two hours away."

"I can't marry you ever."

Oh God. Even though the tiny voice in the back of my mind had dared to utter it, I couldn't fathom Declan was actually verbalizing it. "You can't marry me," I repeated lamely.

"No. I can't." His ragged breath crackled through the phone. "More than anything, you shouldn't want to marry me."

"I'm wearing a two-thousand-dollar wedding dress while two hundred of our closest friends and family are on their way to the church. That should cement the fact I *want* to marry you."

"I'm sorry, Pey. I should have never let it go this far." *Let it go this far? What. The. Hell?*

My hurt and rage suddenly channeled Adam Sandler from *The Wedding Singer*, I screamed, "You know that information would have been a little more useful YESTERDAY."

"I know. I'm a bastard, and I don't expect you to forgive me."

"You're lucky you're in Alabama because so help me God if you were close, I would break every bone in your body!"

"And I would deserve it."

Damn it, how was he being so resigned and calm while I felt like I was being shattered into thousands of tiny pieces? How long has he been thinking this? That's when I was assaulted with a nauseating thought.

"Is there someone else?" An image formed in my mind of him with another woman. A blonde with bigger breasts and a smaller ass.

"God no. It's nothing like that."

His response had the opposite effect on me. Instead of feeling relieved that he hadn't strayed emotionally and physically, a hollow feeling echoed within me. "Then what is it?"

His ragged sigh rattled in my ear. "It's hard to explain. It's been coming on so gradually, but I didn't want to acknowledge it."

"What has been coming on gradually?"

"Doubt."

"About us getting married?"

"Yes. And everything else."

"I don't understand."

"Since you moved back from college this summer, I've had these suffocating moments. Like my entire life was already all planned out for me at twenty years old. There were no what-ifs. No curves in the road. Nothing but a straight line from now until I dropped dead."

"That isn't true. Neither of us know what the future holds. There could be lots of crazy curves, but we could navigate them together."

"I'm sorry, Pey. I just can't. It's like we just drifted apart these last few months you were at school."

"Bullshit. The last two years of our relationship have been long-distance. Why didn't we drift apart then?"

"I don't know. Maybe we did, and you just didn't realize it."

"Oh no. I'm not the delusional one jilting the man I love at the altar."

"You're right. You'd never do that. You've always been too good for me, and you always will be."

"That's not true, and you know it."

"It is. Even though I hate myself for doing this to you, I know it's the right thing. It's better to walk about now before it costs us more emotionally and monetarily."

Rage burned through me. "Yeah, well, I bet I hate you more. May your dick rot off before you die a long, painful death!" I then hung up on him.

The overbearing silence of the room crept up on me. Slowly, I turned around to see my bridal party and mother staring wide-eyed and open-mouthed at me. Pity radiated back at me from their eyes. Sure, there was anger mixed with it, but for the most part, it was overwhelming pity. After all, how else are you supposed to look at a jilted bride? No one would be looking at Declan with pity. He was probably heading to the beach now to relax in the sun and *feel guilty and horrible* about himself. But no one nearby would know. He was blissfully anonymous. *The coward.*

"Get me out of this dress," I commanded.

My five bridesmaids lunged forward, and a flurry of hands and arms began to dismantle me from my satin prison. Instead of dissolving into weeping and gnashing of teeth, I just stood there, staring ahead. I didn't even flinch when one of their nails poked me in their frenzied pursuit. My heart should have been aching in grief, but instead, I felt numb.

"Why isn't she crying?" my cousin, Sarah, whispered—both concern and fear vibrating in her voice.

"She's...in shock," Becca replied.

Once I was freed from the yards of beautiful satin and beading, I took a few slow steps away from the dress. When I got to the mirror, I stood in nothing but my white bustier, gut-sucking-in spanx, and my lacy garter. As I'd slid the garter on, I'd giggled at the thought of Declan removing it with his teeth just before he tossed it to his awaiting groomsmen. Instead, it was my French manicured fingers that slid it down my thigh before tossing it into the trash.

"Honey, what do you want us to do?" Mom asked.

I want you to get a backhoe in here so I can erect an actual hole in the floor for me to crawl in and die. "The guests will be arriving soon. Someone needs to stand at the door and tell them not to waste their toasters or flatware on me because the wedding is off."

After giving me yet another pitied look, Mom nodded. "Your father and I will take care of it. Why don't you go on home and rest?"

"That sounds like a great idea. Just as soon as I stop off at the liquor store." I winked at my bridesmaids. "Our house is dry as a bone since Daddy is a preacher."

Inside of dissolving into laughter, the girls remained silent. I cocked my head at them. "Oh, come on. Don't tell me your sense of humor has died just because I'm a jilted bride?" I widened my eyes at Kara, my best friend. "Do you know what I just realized?"

She slowly shook her blonde head. "What?"

"I'm Granny Weatherall."

Her brows furrowed. "Who?"

With a roll of my eyes, I replied, "Oh my God, don't you remember? *The Jilting of Granny Weatherall* that we read in eleventh grade. We had to write an essay about it, and we both felt so bad for Granny because the worst thing in the world that could ever happen would be getting left at the altar?"

Tears sparkled in her blue eyes. "I don't remember the story."

"Aw, Kara, don't cry about it. It's okay if you don't remember."

"But I'm not crying about not remembering."

Right. "Oh, I get it. You're crying because you just realized I'm Granny Weatherall."

Mom stepped between us. Placing both hands on my shoulders, she then spoke slowly and evenly like I was a little girl. "Peyton, we're going to get you dressed. I'm going to have Becca and Kara take you home, and then I'm going to get Dr. Preston to come by to give you a sedative."

When your dad was a minister with a straight line to the big guy upstairs, he reaped certain VIP benefits. One of those was the local family doctor would make a house call to administer some happy juice to knock your jilted daughter out of her misery.

Words escaped me, so I merely bobbed my head in agreement. For the next few minutes, I was a dress-up doll as my mother and sister put me back into the button-down shirt and capris I'd worn to the church.

Once I was dressed, Mom nodded to Becca. "Go ahead and crank the car."

As I watched Becca leave the room, I whispered, "I don't want to see anyone."

"You won't. Papa pulled the car up to the back door. Everyone else will be at the front."

"Good."

A knock came at the door, which caused me to jump out of my skin. At what must've been my panicked look, Mom gave me a reassuring look. "Don't worry. I'm not letting anyone in here."

"Thanks."

After cracking the door, she peered into the hallway with a steely look of determination on her face. I was pretty sure in that moment she would have physically taken out anyone who tried to bust in the room, which was saying a lot considering her diminutive frame. When her expression softened, a relieved breath whooshed out of me. "Come on in, Harris."

At the sight of my grandfather's face, the dam holding my emotions together imploded, and I once again began to cry. "Oh, Peybug," Papa murmured. When he opened his arms to me, I gratefully fell into them. From the time I was just a little girl, I'd always felt safest in his arms. Although I couldn't ask for better parents than my mom and dad, there had always been something special between Papa and me.

"I'm so sorry, honey."

"I keep thinking I'm going to wake up to find it's been a horrible dream."

"I wish it was just a dream, too. It breaks my heart to see you in this much pain."

I shook my head against his chest. "How could he do this to me?"

A ragged sigh rumbled through him. "I don't know, Pey. I honestly don't know."

Pushing back, I stared into his wise brown eyes. "If you'd asked me twenty minutes ago if I ever thought Declan would jilt you, I would have said no with absolute certainty. But sometimes in spite of how well we think we know someone, we don't, and no matter how hard we love them, we can't save them from failing."

"Oh Papa, what am I going to do?"

His hands left my back to come to cup my cheeks. "This day won't define you, Peyton. You're far too strong for that."

"No offense, but I'm pretty sure getting jilted by the love of your life isn't just a little blip along life's road. It's more like getting hit by a semi."

"You will overcome this. It won't be easy. There are many tough hours and days ahead of you. But at the end of your life, this will just be a faint memory in retrospect to all you have overcome and accomplished."

Cocking my brows at him, I countered, "How can you be so sure? I could start drowning my jilted sorrows in alcohol, which would become the gateway drug to heroin."

Papa shook his head. "The only addictive tendency you have is pleasing people and working your butt off to succeed at everything you do."

"Yeah, well, I didn't succeed at being a bride, did I?"

"We are only accountable for the wrongs we make in life, and today isn't your fault. You did everything within your power to be a wife. I mean, you showed up and got in a poofy white dress, didn't you?"

The corners of my lips quirked slightly. "I did."

"Then you succeeded."

"I'm pretty sure no one else is going to see it that way. To everyone in town, Peyton Beasley wasn't enough to *keep her man*. Peyton Beasley *failed*."

"To quote another exceptional woman, Eleanor Roosevelt, 'No one can make you feel inferior without your consent.'"

I didn't quite share Papa and Eleanor's resolve. The thought of seeing anyone outside my family sent a crippling panic through me. That panic caused my stomach to churn, and I fought my gag reflex. Since I couldn't find my voice, I merely shook my head.

"Peyton, I don't speak with certainty about a lot of things. But I can say without a doubt in my mind that you're going to become a damn good veterinarian. You're going to save the lives of animals, and by saving those lives, you'll enrich the lives of their human counterparts. Your life *will* have purpose. And one day when the time is right, your Prince Charming will come along."

It wasn't just his words that gave me a renewed sense of purpose, but it was also the conviction in which he delivered them. I knew he wasn't just blowing smoke up my ass in my time of distress. He honestly believed every word he had said. And that fact alone gave me the strength I desperately needed. Maybe I would find a Prince Charming, but even if I didn't, my life would matter. *I* would matter.

With tears clouding my eyes, I whispered, "Thank you."

Papa smiled. "No need to thank me. We'll get through this together."

I nodded. "Yes. Together."

Chapter Three

The Present

It was a little after nine in the morning when I drove past the hand-carved *Welcome to Hayesville* sign as I coasted down Main Street. It probably should go without saying that I hadn't slept well the night before. Although Kieran had given me two doses of sexual healing, I'd found myself on edge, rather than being relaxed. Sensing there was something wrong, he'd offered to stay the night, but I'd assured him I was fine. The last thing I needed was for my grief to override one of my principles that hookups didn't get extremely personal details or stay the night. Oh shit. I was starting to sound like a man.

With a disgusted groan, I twisted my hands tighter around the steering wheel. My disgust came from both my behavior about Kieran and the fact I was even thinking about him considering what I'd come home to do. The only man I should have been thinking about was Papa. I was in mourning for fuck's sake. I shouldn't have been thinking about Kieran wrecking my vagina the night before, least of all Declan who had wrecked my life, not my vagina.

Well, that wasn't entirely true. Even though we'd been young, there had been passion and heat between Declan and me. Although he'd already sowed some wild oats by the time we got together our senior year, he was my first. Over the years and after many lovers, I could still say with certainty he knew what he was doing.

Throwing my hands up, I shouted, "Dammit, Peyton! Would you focus?"

When I threw a glance to my right, a man in a pickup truck was staring at me like I had lost my mind. Or maybe he thought I was just another weird out-of-towner. Ducking my head, I sank down in my seat. My foot slammed on the accelerator the moment the light turned green.

When the brick building on the corner came into sight, I began slowing my car. Even after all these years, it was just as I had remembered it. After a quick glance in my rearview mirror, I whipped my car into one of the parking spaces. With my heart beating like a brass band in my chest, I threw the car into park and grabbed my purse. After searching for my key chain (I had one of those "fancy button cars" as Papa would say), I flipped to the gold one.

Although he knew I didn't plan on entering town anytime soon, Papa still insisted on me knowing the alarm codes for both of his houses and his practice. He also kept me up to date with a set of keys. I guess in a weird way he probably thought it was another way of giving me a tie to Hayesville. Like one day the fact I had the key to his practice would make me want to abandon Atlanta and come back home for good.

Since my parents weren't expecting me until later, I felt like I had time to go inside. I didn't know if one of the vet techs had already come to do the morning feedings for the surgical patients or the dogs being boarded. Keeping my head down, I hustled across the sidewalk and up to the front door. My hand shook slightly as I slid the key into the hole.

After unlocking the door, I stepped inside. With a smile, I realized the alarm keypad was still in the same place. I punched in the code and disabled the alarm. As I turned back around, I took in the warm red, blues, and greens of the waiting room. While the furniture had changed, the color scheme had not. The giant saltwater aquarium was still in the back corner. With my face pressed against the tank, I'd spent hours as a kid watching the fish swim.

Walking past the reception desk, I opened the door leading to the examining rooms. Papa always had the canine examining rooms on the left and the feline on the right. After poking my head in one of the doors, I smiled that it was still the same. I shouldn't have been surprised. Papa was an extreme creature of habit.

As memories swirled in my head, I continued purposefully walking. One room in particular was drawing me. When I turned to the left down the other hallway, I stopped at the first door. For a moment, my hand hovered over the knob. I wasn't sure I could handle what was inside. Shuttering my eyes, I sucked in a deep breath before opening the door.

Before I took a step inside, a familiar voice echoed through my mind. "Peyton Anne, what are you doing standing there in the doorway? Come on in here and tell me all about your day."

Tears streaked down my cheeks at the sweet memory of how Papa always greeted me. When I opened my eyes, I wished more than anything to find him sitting in his chair. But it was empty. Slowly, I stepped across the oak floorboards as I made my way over to his desk. The same worn, high-back chair was in front of the mahogany desk that had belonged to my great-grandfather.

Pulling the chair back, I eased into the seat. As I scanned over the framed photographs on the desk, tears once again overflowed. Some of the photos were of my grandmother, who had been gone for fifteen years. Others were of my father when he was a little boy. The knife of grief twisted further in my chest at the picture of me in my cap and gown at my graduation from vet school. With an arm around my waist, Papa was leaned in, kissing my cheek while I smiled at the camera.

As the emotions overwhelmed me, I buried my head in my hands. For the second time in twenty-four hours, I sat at a desk sobbing uncontrollably. When I finally came back to myself, I was a snotty mess. After reaching for a tissue, I swiped my eyes before blowing my nose. I didn't know how long I'd been sitting there crying at Papa's desk. In some ways, it felt like forever and in others, it felt like I had just sat down. If just being in his office had this effect on me, how would I make it through the next two days of the visitation and then the funeral?

With an agonized sigh, I pushed the chair back and rose to my feet. Just as I turned to start to the door, the phone rang. The moment the shrill ring echoed through my ears I felt a strange pull to answer it. For the life of me, I didn't understand why. Before it could go to voicemail, I reached over and snatched the receiver. "Hello?"

"Hey Mandie, this is Roy Wallace. I need Doc Beasley out here. I gotta breech calf, and I can't for the life of me get it turned."

The request sent the knife of grief twisting further in my chest. I cleared my throat. "This isn't Mandie, and Dr. Beasley isn't here."

"Well, if he's out on rounds, can you get word to him to come?"

I shuttered my eyes in pain. *I'd give anything in the world if I could.* "No. I can't. Papa—I mean, Dr. Beasley passed away yesterday."

"Oh no. I just got back in town this morning from a cattle show, and I sure hate to hear the sad news. Harris wasn't just a wonderful vet —he was a fine man."

"Yes, he was."

"Please pass along my thoughts and prayers to the family."

"I will."

"What about Doc Kisick?"

"Unfortunately, he's on vacation at the moment. He won't be back until tomorrow evening."

At the loud baying of a cow, Roy let out a juicy curse. "I just don't know what I'm going to do. This heifer has got to be seen about. You wouldn't happen to know of any other vets, would you?"

I bolted upright in the chair. "As a matter of fact, I do."

"Oh good. I hope he isn't too far away."

"Actually, you're talking to *her*."

Silence echoed on the line. I could only imagine Roy was contemplating whether or not he wanted to subject his cow to a "lady doctor". Female veterinarians faced the same narrow-minded prejudices that women did in the medical field. Especially in backwoods areas like Hayesville.

Just as I was about to ask if he was still there, Roy coughed. "I ain't been to town for a few weeks, but did Doc Beasley hire a new vet?"

"No, he didn't. I'm Peyton Beasley, his granddaughter."

"Little Peyton that used to run around his office with a stethoscope around her neck?"

I smiled at the image. "That was me."

"Well, I'll be darned. I don't think I've seen you in ten years. You were supposed to marry the St. James boy, weren't you?"

At the mention of Declan, I tensed. "I was," I bit out. I don't know why I was surprised Roy mentioned my infamous jilting. It was one of the top three things Hayesville residents seemed to remember about me after being Valedictorian and Homecoming Queen.

"I think your grandfather told me you were a vet in Atlanta."

"I am. I work at one of the top animal and surgical centers there."

"Isn't that somethin'? I sure would be honored for you to come out and look at my cow."

Shifting the phone between my shoulder and cheek, I reached for the notepad on Papa's desk. "What's your address?" As Roy related it to me, I scribbled it down. "Give me about twenty minutes.

"Okay. I'll see you then."

When I hung up from Roy, a renewed sense of purpose filled me. *Thank you, Papa. Roy would be honored for me to tend to his cow. All because of you.* I hustled out of Papa's office, and went straight to the supply closet. Although it had been at least ten years since I'd been inside, nothing had changed in his meticulous organization. Some of the tools and medicines had been updated, but I knew exactly where to go to find the necessary materials to deliver a breech calf.

Once I had gathered everything, I plopped it all down on the counter. "Okay, let's see. Halter and rope? Check. OB gloves? Check. Lubricant? Check. Roll cotton? Check. OB Straps and Handles? Check." I turned and went over to the medicine cabinet. After taking out some oxytocin and epinephrine, I surveyed the room for an extra medical bag. I knew Papa's would be at home or in his car since he always liked to be prepared.

After finding an extra bag in the corner, I packed up the materials. On my way out of the storage room, I grabbed an empty bucket. Satisfied that I had the necessary tools, I started for the back door. At the sound of my heels clicking down the tile floor, I froze. Glancing down at my feet, I shook my head.

There was no way my heels would make it. I'd be sinking in the pastureland the moment I stepped out of my car. Sitting the materials down, I headed back into Papa's office. Thankfully, he kept a few pairs of Wellies. Although they would be a little big, I grabbed a pair and tucked them under one of my armpits. With my free hand, I punched in the alarm code before grabbing the medicine bag and bucket.

A feeling of heightened anticipation washed over me as I punched in Roy's address on the GPS. It was quite unexpected considering the last eighteen hours had been spent smothered in a cloud of grief.

Roy's farm was about fifteen minutes north of Papa's office. Once I began making the familiar curves and turns along the country road, the high of anticipation left me. In its wake was choking bitterness. I knew this area all too well. It was where Declan had grown up.

Glancing out the window, I could almost envision me sitting on the back of one of his ATVs as we kicked up clouds of dirt while tearing through the pasture. Other times I would be astride one of their horses as we rode along the sixty acres his family owned. We'd fallen in love on that land.

Fuck. This was a bad idea. It was one thing to have to come to Hayesville to deal with my grief. Since I'd grown up a town kid, my area of interaction would have been regulated to a five-mile radius of Main Street. Taking Roy Wallace's call had thrown me right into Declan's world.

Once the GPS directed me to the faded mailbox at the end of a long, gravel drive, I eased my car off onto the shoulder. Swinging my legs out of the car, I deposited my heels and then slid on the Wellies. As I was gathering my materials, a voice to my right bellowed hello.

I jerked my head up to search for the voice. An older man leaned against the gate. In his faded denim overalls, Atlanta Braves baseball cap, and jaw full of tobacco, he appeared every bit the stereotypical backwoods farmer.

"Mr. Wallace I presume?" I asked as I lumbered up to him. The oversized boots were not helping my gait on the uneven terrain.

"Yes, ma'am." He grinned as he extended his hand. "But call me Roy."

"Peyton Beasley. Nice to meet you."

After shifting his chaw of tobacco, Roy's gaze dropped from mine to trail down my body. Just when I thought he was getting slightly pervy, he motioned to me. "You gonna do this in your fancy clothes?"

Now it was my turn to glance down. Shit. In my haste, I'd forgotten to bring an apron to protect my clothes. My black pantsuit wasn't exactly "fancy" as Roy called it, but it was one of my more expensive outfits considering I lived in scrubs.

"I suppose I am."

He jerked his thumb to the driveway. "I could get you an extra pair of my overalls. Maybe even a pair of the coveralls I use when I'm working on the farm equipment."

Normally, I would have dismissed his suggestion, but considering the fact I had to be at the funeral home later, the last thing I needed to do was show up with bovine blood spatter or amniotic fluid on me. "You know, I think the coveralls would be wonderful. Thank you."

Roy nodded. "Be back in a jiffy."

While he went after the coveralls, I checked in on my patients back in Atlanta. I was grateful to hear everyone was doing well, including Barney after his tango with the Ben Wa ball. I chose to ignore a text from Kieran asking me how I was doing.

When Roy returned, I stepped into the faded blue coveralls that were dotted with grease and motor oil. Once I zipped them up, I found Roy grinning at me. "Not my style?" I asked.

He laughed. "No, I'd just been thinking you look a sight better in those than I do." He patted the slight bulge of his belly. "I'm not as fit as I used to be.

"While I appreciate the compliment, I'm sure you totally rock these."

Motioning me with his hand, I followed Roy into the pasture. After hauling about a half a mile, we came to the top of a hill that ran along the woods. Although several cows were milling around, I noticed the pregnant heifer right away. "Let me take a closer look," I told Roy. A "closer look" in veterinarian speak meant an internal exam, and between the two holes to choose from, I was going in the ass.

It had been a considerable amount of time since I'd worked with cows, or in this case been up to my shoulder in a cow's ass, but some aspects of veterinarian medicine you never forgot. I was in middle school the first time I'd slid on one of the industrial sized OB gloves that looked like a giant condom. Under Papa's tutelage, I had delivered my first breech calf. I'd learned it's best to go through the rectum first to assess the situation before rooting around in the vag. The fact I didn't lube the glove up enough and took a back hoof to my mouth full of braces also helped me to remember the proper procedures.

Today I made sure to pour plenty of lube across my condom-clad arm. After easing my way inside, I noted the signs of distress. After pulling my arm out, I looked at Roy. "Okay, first, I'm going to give her an epidural to stop her from straining so she's not pushing against me. I also think some epinephrine couldn't hurt because it'll help her uterus to relax."

Roy nodded. "I knew I could keep pulling on the calf's leg all day, but I was worried about tearing her womb."

"You made the right call," I replied, as I dug the medications and needles out of my bag. After measuring out the proper doses, I administered the medicines. Now it was time to get down to business birthing the calf.

To keep from spreading bacteria, I put on a clean pair of gloves before I went in the birth canal. As I was turning the calf, I heard the sound of something coming through the brush. At the sound of conversation coupled with the snort of a horse, I surmised it must be some riders on horseback.

"Peyton?"

Fuck me with a chainsaw. I recognized that voice. I'd know the deep timbre anywhere. It had haunted me all these years. At the sound of the voice, I became a full-fledged Peyton statue. All of the pain and mortification and anger converged in that moment leaving me paralyzed. I couldn't blink, least of all move. I just stood staring at the cow's ass with my arm buried in its vagina while wishing I could sink beneath the grass and manure.

With my arm still engaged, I threw a glance over my shoulder. "Declan," I acknowledged. There was no way in hell I would dare say it was nice seeing him. To be polite, I could lie about a lot of things, but that wasn't one of them.

Sadness, tinged with regret, flashed in his blue eyes. "I was very sorry to hear about Harris passing. He was a good man," he said sincerely.

"Thank you."

"I assume his funeral is what brings you back to town after all these years."

"Yes, that's the reason."

Peering curiously, he jerked his chin at me. "But what are you doing now?"

"I'm violating a heifer. What does it look like I'm doing?" I snapped.

Declan opened his mouth, but any sound coming out of it was drowned out by the agitated mooing of the heifer. Apparently, the tension I was feeling externally had correlated to my grip inside her. After vocally telling me off, she raised one of her legs and nailed me in the thigh.

The force sent me off balance. What happened next will remain a mystery to me. Maybe because I've never quite grasped all the laws of physics and motion. One minute I was upright, reeling from the pain of having a hoof to my thigh while trying to stay upright, and the next I was face-planting into a pile of cow manure.

Yes, you read that right. I was lying in a pile of literal shit in front of the man who had treated me like shit. I had just fallen one rung below the seventh ring of Hell.

Strong male hands came under my armpits and hoisted me upright. When I was once again on my feet, I swiped my face on the back of my arm. I could barely see since my eyes were still encrusted with a mixture of dirt and cow shit. Blinking through my clouded vision, I couldn't believe my savior had come in the form of Declan.

"Jesus, are you okay?"

After jerking my chin up, I flipped a strand of manure encased hair over my shoulder. "I'm perfectly fine, thank you. I certainly didn't need your help."

"Same old ball-busting Peyton," Declan remarked.

I jabbed a shit-covered finger at him. "You're damn right, I am. One might say I'm even more ball-busting. It's the one good thing that came out of your cowardly ass jilting me at the altar."

Regret flashed in his eyes. "Peyton, I—"

"If you will excuse me, I have a breech calf to deliver. Unlike you, I honor my promises." I then turned back to the heifer. When I dared a glance at Roy, his eyes were as wide as saucers. If he didn't close his mouth, he was going to catch flies.

"Nice seeing you, Mr. Wallace," Declan said.

As I attended to the cow, I heard his footsteps go back over to his horse. A few moments later he was racing through the brush. Inwardly, I wanted to crumple onto the pasture floor, roll into a fetal position, and bawl my eyes out. But I had a job to do and no man, not even the one who had shattered my heart into pieces, was going to stop me from doing that.

Nodding at Roy, I said, "Let's do this."

You know the old saying about how you can't go back home again? Well, you certainly can't go back home again covered in cow shit and stained with afterbirth. As soon as I'd dragged my wounded pride back to my car, I'd called Becca. Thankfully, she hadn't left for the funeral home yet. Since I figured it would be easier to explain what happened in person, I kept my story short.

Becca lived two streets over from Papa's practice. When I pulled into the driveway, I found her husband's police cruiser in the driveway. Unlike me, Becca's high school sweetheart, Anthony, had shown up on their wedding day, and they were going on two years of wedded bliss.

With my roller board trailing behind me, I limped up the front walk. When I got to the steps, Becca came out on the porch. "Oh my God! What happened to you?"

I was accosted by a ghost from my past. "A heifer with a breeched calf."

Becca furrowed her dark brows at me. "Huh?" Narrowing her eyes, she asked, "Are you limping?"

Where the heifer had nailed my thigh was throbbing, so I ended up hobbling up the front porch steps. "As a matter of fact, I am." I then related to Becca what had happened when I'd gone by Papa's practice.

"Only you would go deliver a calf two hours before we were due at the funeral home."

"What choice did I have? Roy could have lost both the calf and the heifer."

She gave me a sad smile. "I know. You would have made Papa so proud." Although she opened her arms to hug me, her nose wrinkled at both my shit smell and soiled clothes.

I held my hand up. "We can forgo the official homecoming until after I've had a shower."

Becca giggled and that small sound warmed me. "Come on. Let's get you inside and cleaned up." She turned and opened the front door so I could pass through. Although I'd seen pictures, it was the first time I'd ever been inside Becca's house. That fact made me feel both selfish and guilty. Like I should have swallowed my pride regarding Declan and come back to Hayesville to see her first home.

Compared to my streamlined townhouse in the city, it was much more understated. But every inch of the farmhouse décor and homey feel was Becca. She was the quintessential small-town girl. "Your house is just as beautiful in person as the pictures."

Beaming with pride, Becca said, "Thanks." After eyeing my shit-stained form again, she said, "Anthony's getting ready in our bathroom, so I'll get you set up in the guest bath."

"At this point, I'll take a water hose out back or even a pressure washer. Anything to get the manure off."

Throwing me a wicked glance over her shoulder, Becca said, "I could take you over to Macland's Car Wash. They're still old school with the brushes."

I laughed as we started up the stairs. "I might take you up on that if the shower doesn't work."

After we reached the landing, I followed her down the hallway. When we got to the bathroom, Becca turned on the light for me. "It's all yours."

Nodding, I pulled my suitcase inside with me. When I caught a glance at myself in the mirror, I grimaced. While I might've looked pretty damn good before my face-plant, my current image was the one Declan would be left with. I'm not sure why I cared what he thought of me. After all, he hadn't thought enough of me to show up on our wedding day ten years ago.

"Can you bring me a trash bag for this suit?"

Becca's eyes widened. "You're not throwing it away, are you?"

"Actually, I planned on soaking it at Mom and Dad's before I took it to the cleaner's." I cocked a brow at her. "Unless you want me to do it here."

Holding up a hand, Becca shook her head. "Nope. That's all right." She jerked her thumb at the door. "One trash bag coming up."

"Thanks, little sis."

Once Becca started down the hallway, I closed the door. After stripping out of my clothes, I slid under the scalding hot stream of water. I didn't start to feel human again until I'd washed my hair three times. I also scrubbed up and rinsed probably five times. Sure, I came in contact with animal feces on a daily basis. It was unavoidable. However, your average dog or cat didn't produce the quantity that cows did.

While I was busy outwardly cleaning myself, my mind was still sullied with the memories of what else had transpired. As hard as I tried, I couldn't scrub myself of the image of seeing Declan again. Or what I imagined was the image of me lying face-first in cow shit. I was pretty sure I was never going to be able to cleanse myself of the horror that was our encounter.

Once I finished my shower, I wrapped a towel around my hair. After hoisting my suitcase on the closed toilet lid, I pulled out a mid-knee black skirt and paired it with a black silk blouse. If you took a peek in my luggage, you would surmise I was either in mourning or paying homage to the man in black aka Johnny Cash.

As I was drying my hair, Becca came in with a fresh cup of coffee. "I thought you might need this."

I smiled at her reflection in the mirror. "Aw, you're too good to me." After taking the cup from her, I inhaled the delicious brew before gulping down a fiery sip. "Mm," I murmured in pleasure.

"I know it's not your usual."

"My usual?" I questioned.

"You know, one of those fancy latte things from Starbucks."

Ah, there it was. The old city girl who was a coffee snob stereotype. As close as we were, sometimes I got the impression Becca somehow felt inferior to me. Since we both got a college education and we were both professionals, I could only imagine it had something to do with the fact I lived in Atlanta and not Hayesville.

"For your information, I don't drink highbrow coffee."

Becca's surprise was evident. "You don't?"

"Nope. I usually make my own at home or drink what they make at work."

"Interesting."

With a smile, I said, "I'm not as citified as you think."

Becca grinned. "Maybe."

As I fluffed and styled my hair, we fell into silence. After a few seconds, I shook my head at her reflection in the mirror. "I can't believe he's gone, Becs."

With a sniffle, she replied, "It's unreal."

I couldn't help the sob that left my throat, because being here, being in the arms of my family, just made it so much more real. We clung to each other, and it felt so good to be held by someone who loved you unconditionally. Who grieved with you, and understood the pain you felt through every bone in your body.

"When was the last time you saw him?" I asked.

Becca pulled away a little, trying to compose herself. *This sucks ass.*

"On Sunday at church. He was his normal self."

"Strong and resilient as hell," I chuckled.

Becca grinned. "Exactly." She grabbed a tissue from the decorative container on the sink. After dabbing her eyes, she said, "There was no warning. But in some ways, I'm glad too. I can't imagine watching him slowly die like we did with Grandma."

"Yes, I thought that, too. I know it's so sudden and so out of the blue, but I am glad he didn't suffer." Papa would have hated that and not deserved it either. I took a deep breath and tried to put on a brave face. I didn't want to be a basket case when I saw my parents.

Winking at Becca, I said, "Speaking of Grandma, it's time I put on my face." Our grandmother was one of those women who never went out in public without her hair perfectly coiffed or her makeup on. She often told Becs and me, "If you have to leave the house without putting your face on, you make sure to at least paint your lips to make sure you have some color."

"Yes, please don't disgrace the Beasley name."

"I wouldn't dream of it."

As I pulled my makeup bag out of my suitcase, Becca backed into the bathroom and closed the door. I threw a glance at her over my shoulder. "What's with closing the door? Are you afraid for Anthony to see me without my face on?"

"No. It's nothing like that."

I tilted my head at her. "Then what is it?"

"How does it feel being back home again?"

With a laugh, I replied, "I'm not sure I can accurately answer that question considering I've only been here three hours, Becs."

Becca nibbled on her bottom lip. "You know what I meant."

"Right. You want to know how I'm handling finally being in the same zip code as Declan." Now it was my turn to nibble on my lip. You could say it was a family trait. Papa did the same thing whenever he was surveying a difficult case. At Becca's earnest expression, I sighed. "There's something I didn't tell you about delivering the calf."

"What?"

"I delivered the calf out at Roy Wallace's."

Becca's dark eyes widened. "Isn't the Wallace farm next to the St. James property?"

"Yep. It is."

"Did you see Declan?"

"Oh yeah, I saw him."

Sweeping her hand to her mouth, Becca gasped. "What happened?"

I wanted so much to be able to tell her I held my cool. That I merely ignored his presence. That I had showed Declan I had matured in the ten years since I'd seen him. In the end, I couldn't lie to my sister. "I face-planted into a pile of manure, which he pulled me out of."

Horror came over Becca's face. "Oh Peyton."

"Yep. That pretty much sums it up."

Slowly, she shook her head. "I don't know what to say."

"Yeah, I know. It wasn't how I saw things going down between us when I finally saw him again." As I downed a hot gulp of coffee, I wish it was laced with whiskey. "At least I told him off."

"You did?"

"Yes. I sure did. Of course, I'm sure it would have come off a lot more badass if I hadn't been reeking of cow shit."

Sighing, Becca leaned back against the bathroom door. "I wish I had some words of wisdom or comfort, but you've pretty much floored me."

"Trust me, I get it." I ran my fingertip over the mouth of the coffee cup as I contemplated asking the one question that was burning in my mind. Over the years, my parents never willingly volunteered information about Declan. Becca was the one who kept me in the loop. She'd been the one to break it to me when Declan had gotten engaged five years ago. The weekend of his wedding she'd come to Athens to be my DD after I got shit-faced. While the engagement had been hard, the wedding had stung worse. I think it was knowing he *could* marry another woman but not me. It had been equally painful a year later when I'd heard he'd had a child. A son.

Biting the bullet, I asked, "How are he and Bailey doing?"

"They've been separated since right after Christmas. Rumor is they're finally getting a divorce."

Whirling around, I narrowed my eyes at Becca. "He's been separated that long, and you didn't tell me?"

"You were with Brady and doing well. I didn't want to dredge all that shit back up."

With a groan, I replied, "Brady and I've been over for six months. Hearing bad news about Declan would have cheered me up."

Becca held up her hands. "I'm sorry. It just slipped my mind."

"Apparently, it slipped everyone's. Mom and Dad didn't mention it, nor did Papa."

"Maybe we hoped that after all this time, you didn't need to hear anything about him because you were over him."

Ignoring her expectant gaze, I unzipped my makeup bag. When I righted myself, I stared defiantly at her reflection. "I am over him."

Cocking her head at me, Becca gave me a look. "Are you?"

"Yes. I am."

"You just freaked out and face-planted in cow manure over him."

My eyes bulged. "A cow kicked me."

"Probably because your arm tensed because you were freaking out."

"Whatever." Focusing on my reflection in the mirror, my fingers worked furiously to blend in the makeup. After a few moments, I caught Becca's eye in the mirror. With a sigh, my shoulders sagged in defeat. "Fine. I'm not over him. After ten years and what feels like a lifetime apart, he still has the ability to wound me." I threw a glance at her over my shoulder. "Happy?"

"I could never be happy hearing you're in pain," she countered.

And I knew that. No one supported me or had my back more when it came to Declan than Becca. As tears filled my eyes, I shook my head. "God, I hate myself. What kind of asshole am I to be back home for my grandfather's death and getting all emotional about the bastard who jilted me?"

"You're not an asshole." At my skeptical look, Becca added, "You're human. We can't always control our feelings. All we can do is try to control our behavior."

Swiping my eyes, I nodded. "Right. Soldier on. Declan is out of sight and out of mind. Most of all, be strong for Papa."

"Exactly."

With a smile, I reached over to hug Becca. "Thanks, Little Sis."

"You're welcome." As she pulled back, love shone in her eyes. "More than anything in the world, Peyton, I want you to find someone who loves you as much as you deserve."

My chin trembled at her words. "Would you stop? I'm going to be a blubbering mess."

"Fine. How about a subject change?"

"Works for me."

"Is there anyone you're seeing back in Atlanta?"

I groaned. "Jeez, kick me when I'm down why don't you?"

Becca giggled. "I had to ask."

"If you must know, my physical needs are being met by a young vet tech with a body like a Greek god."

"Very nice."

Wagging a finger at her, I said, "Before you ask, there's no future for us."

Disappointment flickered in Becca's eyes. "Are you absolutely sure?"

"Positive."

"I think city men are wrong for you. Maybe you'll find your prince right here in Hayesville."

I snorted. "Oh, my sweet summer child," I chided.

At the reference to our favorite show *Game of Thrones*, Becca grinned. "Stranger things have happened."

"Unless there's been a huge influx of new Hayesville residents, I don't see it happening."

"Scoff if you like, but I'm not giving up on the idea."

"Fine. Just promise me you won't try to play matchmaker during Papa's viewing and introduce, or reintroduce since this is a small town, me to anyone."

"Please, I'm not that uncouth." With a wink, she added, "I'd only slip him your number."

Staring up at the bathroom ceiling, I replied, "Kill me now."

Chapter Five

The next two days saw a proper and respectful send off for Papa. From the scribbled signatures in the funeral home ledger and the long lines during the viewing, the town of Hayesville really stepped up to show their love and appreciation. Their love also came in the form of Mom and Dad's kitchen table and counters overflowing with homemade cakes and casseroles. As a minister's daughter, I had a sixth sense on how to spot the tastiest desserts. Whenever an impeccably dressed church lady arrived with an offering, I mentally catalogued the plate. In my experience, the bigger the hair, the better the food. There was just something about teasing your hair to the heights of glory while cementing it in place with a can of Aqua Net that made you a better cook.

In a matter of forty-eight hours, I came in contact with practically everyone I had spent a decade away from. People seemed genuinely glad to see me. Although it pained me to admit it, I was glad to see them too. Well, at least under the circumstances. Dare I say that I had missed them? Like Mrs. Neighbors my first-grade teacher or Howard Ross who managed the Piggly Wiggly. Most knew what I'd been up to because of my parents and Papa. I did notice a couple of the town gossips eyeing my left hand to see if I was engaged. To their credit, they didn't ask if I had a boyfriend. Thankfully, I appeared to be old news now.

Of course, all the sweet words and goodwill in the world couldn't have prepared me for the moment I turned to see Robert and Pauline

St. James before me. My lungs compressed and all the air in my chest whooshed out of me at the sight of my almost mother- and father-in-law. They'd been so kind and supportive of Declan and me when we were dating. Their support continued after he jilted me. For the first few years after the breakup, I received care packages at college from them. Like the good Southern girl I was, I always sent them a thank-you note, but I never gave them much more than my gratitude.

After we all stood there staring and blinking at each for a few seconds, Pauline gave me the most Southern of greetings: she hugged me. Even though so many years had passed, I still remembered what it felt like to be in her embrace. As she pulled back, I saw tears sparkling in her eyes—the very crystal blue ones Declan had inherited from her. "While I'm so terribly sorry about Harris, it really is so good to see you, Peyton."

When I finally managed to find my voice, I said, "It's nice to see you, too."

Since Robert had never been much of a hugger, we merely shook hands. "My deepest condolences."

"Thank you."

"Nana," a tiny voice whined from somewhere behind the St. James's.

Surprise filled me when a panicked look flashed on Pauline's face. Before she could say anything, a dark-haired little boy peeked out from behind Pauline's waist. Once again, I fought to breathe because I saw Declan in that face. I'd grown up with that face since we'd gone to elementary school together. Because of that fact, I didn't have to ask Pauline who he was.

I knew.

He was Declan's son. In an alternate universe, he could have been *my* son. The child Declan and I conceived in love within the confines of our marriage. An agonizing series of images flashed before my mind. Declan rubbing my swollen belly. Declan squeezing my hand as he spoke words of encouragement as a contraction wracked my body. Declan and I watching him learn to crawl and then walk.

Since I was a little girl, I'd always wanted to be a mother. In spite of wanting to be a vet, I always imagined I'd be a mother by now. For some reason, the emptiness of my womb seemed particularly agonizing tonight. Maybe it was because the sting of grief already encompassed me, and when coupled with seeing my former fiancé's son and imagining what could have been, it became unbearable.

Realizing I'd been staring for too long, I whipped my gaze back to Pauline. She appeared almost apologetic. Like she knew seeing him would be painful for me. "Normally, we wouldn't have brought him, but his daddy had to go check on a job over in Cleveland today. He wasn't going to be back in time to get him." In any other situation, I would have found it comical she couldn't even bring herself to say Declan's name in front of me.

"I thought Greer was getting you a drink," Pauline said to the little boy.

"She did, but then she went to talk to her friends."

Pauline pursed her lips. "Greer is Danielle's oldest daughter," she explained. The mention of Danielle took me back to my past. She was Declan's oldest sister, and she'd been one of my bridesmaids.

Waving my hand absently, I said, "Oh, it's fine. Mama had me at the funeral home when I was half his age."

I'm pretty sure Pauline didn't buy my avoidance. Instead, she bent down and took the little boy's hand. She eased him out from behind her. "Cameron, can you say hello to Miss Peyton?"

After staring up at me, Cameron buried his face in Pauline's waist. "Hi," he finally said, his voice muffled.

"Hi there." Bending down, I smiled at him. "Your daddy and I were friends a long time ago."

He instantly perked up. "You were?"

"We sure were."

Robert and Pauline appeared both relieved and touched that I had taken the high road. I'm not sure why they would have expected anything different from me. They knew me well enough that even in my grief, I wouldn't have taken out what Declan did to me on his son.

"It was Peyton's grandpa who took such good care of Bentley." Pauline smiled at me. "After we lost Buckley, we got a puppy who looked just like him. Of course, we had to take him to Harris. No one was a better vet than he was."

As sweet memories of the St. James's Golden Retriever, Buckley, filled my mind, I nodded. "He certainly was the best."

"From what we've heard, you're not so bad yourself," Robert said.

Smiling at his compliment, I replied, "While I learned from the best, I'm not sure anyone is better than Papa."

"We sure are going to miss him," Pauline added while Robert nodded.

"Thank you. We're going to miss him as well."

Only a moment of awkward silence passed before my mother hopped out of line to barge in front of me. "Pauline, Robert, thank you so much for coming."

I'm sure she thought she was saving me, but I was fine. At least I thought I was. I was glad Becca had spilled the beans about Declan's son before tonight. It would have been far worse to have had his existence sprung on me when I stood three feet from Papa's casket.

With the "Ghosts of My Almost In-Laws Past" now away from me, I turned my attention to the next mourner. But for the rest of the night, I couldn't get Cameron's face out of my mind. When I thought of him, I inadvertently thought of Declan.

In the end, it was just too emotionally taxing. I knew if I didn't get out of there and get some fresh air, I was going to lose it. Even though there was still a line of mourners, I mumbled my apologies before power walking out of the room. I nodded hello to several people in the hallway. Instead of heading out the front where I might run into more people, I sprinted towards the back.

As I blew out onto the back stoop, I knocked into someone. "Oh, excuse me—"

At the sight of Declan standing in front of me, I froze. Just like in Roy Wallace's pasture, I became a perfect Peyton statue.

"Hello again, Peyton."

Slowly I began to thaw from my repeated shock. Pursing my lips at him, I replied, "Hello, Declan. I'm rather surprised to see you would show your face here."

His expression darkened. "In spite of what happened between us, I admired and respected Harris. He was the only vet I trusted with my horses."

I jerked my gaze away from his to try to hide my surprise. Papa had never mentioned caring for Declan's horses. I just assumed that after what happened, Declan found a new vet or saw Papa's partner Hank Kisick. Somehow it felt like a betrayal on Papa's behalf. All the years he supported me never seeing Declan again yet at the same time, he was caring for his horses. "He was a forgiving man," I finally muttered.

"More than his granddaughter."

My gaze snapped back to his. "Excuse me?"

"Before I asked Harris to care for my animals, I went to him to make things right."

"You apologized to my grandfather for jilting me."

"Damn straight."

I held up one of my hands in front of him. "Did it ever occur to you that while you were making things right with him, I was the one who was owed an apology?"

"How was I supposed to apologize to you if you never came back home?"

With a contemptuous snort, I rolled my eyes. "You must be joking. I mean, have you ever heard of the phone?"

"I thought what I had to say was a little too serious for the phone."

"You didn't seem to have a problem breaking up with me over the phone."

"I was a stupid kid then. After growing up and actually becoming a man, I realized what I had to say should be said in person."

"You act like I moved to Antarctica, not Athens and then Atlanta. You could have found me if you really wanted to."

"Yeah, well, I figured since you stayed away all these years, you didn't want to hear from me. After the years passed, I figured it was better just to let it go. You had your life in Atlanta, and I had mine here."

"Seems like you're still deluded about relationships and love. I can see why your marriage ended," I snapped.

My words caused Declan's head to snap back like I'd slapped him. "My marriage ended because Bailey was cheating on me. It wasn't the first time it happened either."

Oh shit. Way to go, Pey. I felt horrible. No one deserved to be cheated on. "I didn't know."

"I'm surprised considering how the rumor mill has been churning for months about it." He glowered. "You'd think they'd try to respect my kid. The separation and now impending divorce has been hard enough on him. Now he has to grow up with people whispering that his mama chose another man over him."

I swallowed hard. "She did?"

"Yeah, she did. She's shacked up with the man she left Cameron and me for."

Oh God. What a mess. Poor sweet Cameron. Poor... Declan. Even though I had every right to treat Declan like shit, I still felt horrible. "I'm sorry that happened to you."

"I'm sure you are," Declan retorted sarcastically.

"No. I really am. I'm very sorry for your son. I know it can't be easy on him." Glancing at my black heels, I replied, "Or you."

"It hasn't. Karma can be a real bitch."

I jerked my gaze up to meet his. He exhaled a ragged sigh. "It was terrible what I did to you, Peyton. I know I apologized to you that day, but I still owed you a hell of an apology all these years later. I should never have embarrassed you like that. I should have manned up and taken responsibility that day by addressing the church myself instead of running off to the hunting camp."

And there it was. The words I'd never expected to hear. "Thank you," I finally said. Although it pained me to say it, I added, "After all this time, it means a lot to hear you genuinely say that."

"You're welcome."

Did his apology mean we were made up? Did a few words mean a decade of pain had been erased? How could it possibly be that easy? It felt like putting a Band-Aid on a gaping wound.

As I was still processing my thoughts, Declan jerked the rug even further out from me. "You know, when it's all said and done, I think we can both agree I did us a favor that day."

"What do you mean?"

"I'm sorry about *how* it happened, so please don't confuse that. But regardless of how much we were in love, we had no business getting married at twenty."

"Um, I thought we did."

Cocking his head at me, Declan asked, "Even after all these years, you really would have wanted to marry me then?"

It was a question I'd never really asked myself. I'd been too focused on the hurt and humiliation to ever fathom if it had been the right thing for both of us. "Are you trying to say your actions helped me, rather than hurt me?"

"In a way."

"How?"

"What were the odds you would have actually finished veterinary school if we'd gotten married?"

"How dare you even make that assumption? I've finished everything I've ever started."

"Married life would have eventually gotten in the way. Especially if we'd had a child."

"You promised me we would wait until after I finished school to have a baby," I countered.

"We both know I wouldn't have really wanted to wait six years, not to mention it would have been hard for you considering how much you love kids."

"Maybe you're right. According to you on our wedding day, you didn't know what you wanted out of life since it was already planned out for you."

Throwing up his hands, Declan argued, "It was all planned out. I'd never seen it like I did at our rehearsal dinner. If we had gotten married, I never would have finished college. I would have gone to work for my old man at the surveyor's office because I would have wanted to be better able to support us. I would have given up on *my* dream of becoming a developer, and in the end, I would have cost you *your* dream."

I shook my head at him. "That's a convenient realization you've arrived at."

"You have to be able to see it."

There was a part of me that did. I knew Declan well enough to know he would have given up on his dreams to try and see me achieve mine. At least the Declan I once loved would have. In the end, what did I really know? I would have never in a million years thought he would have left me at the altar.

But I wasn't giving him the satisfaction of agreeing with him. I was still far too petty to do that. "No. I don't. Your view of what our potential future could have been goes against my character. I wouldn't have given up. *Ever.*"

"If you say so."

"Oh, I *know* so."

"Same old Peyton," Declan mused with a faint smile.

"Yes. I am. Unlike you, I've always known just who I am."

Intensity burned in Declan's eyes as he closed the distance between us. My heartbeat suddenly accelerated. I hadn't been this close to him in a long time. While he'd had his hands on me in the pasture when he helped me up, we certainly weren't close. His noble gesture hadn't extended to getting covered in manure.

The smell of his cologne assaulted my senses. It was the same smell I always identified with him. I didn't know how it was possible after all these years he hadn't changed colognes. His stare was so intense I felt it go straight through me.

"Why didn't you ever come back to Hayesville?" he questioned, his voice unusually husky.

"Is that a serious question?"

"Yes."

"I would think it was obvious." I narrowed my eyes at him. "I didn't want to see you or even be within ten feet of you. I loathed you that much."

"I understand you feeling that way at first. But after all these years, I don't get it."

"Last time I checked, you don't get to validate or deny my feelings. It's all on me."

"So, you've hated me enough the last ten years that you refused to step foot in your hometown or go back to your childhood home?"

"Ding, ding, ding! We have a winner. That's exactly why."

"But why not come back and confront me? Give me a good slap or knee to the balls."

There were many times I'd debated confronting him. I'd discussed it at length in therapy. My therapist had suggested me seeing him again just to bury the past. But instead, I'd opted for a more mature response: I'd just ignore his existence by going out of my way to never see him again.

"Your suggestions would have been beneath my character."

Declan chuckled. "I seem to remember you punching the shit out of that man you saw abusing his dog."

"That's different," I argued.

"Do you want to know what I think?"

"No. But I'm sure you're going to tell me."

As Declan loomed over me, I took a tiny step back. "I think you still have feelings for me."

"Excuse me?"

"Oh, I'm sure you heard me."

"I didn't think I could have considering how delusional you sounded." When I jabbed my finger into his chest, I momentarily lost my train of thought. His pecs were rock-hard. Damn, he was even more built now than he was back when he was playing football in high school. Once I regained my senses, I spat, "Of course, I have feelings for you. Murderous, angry feelings."

"I hate they're all still so negative. I still consider you one of the smartest, best-looking, and kindest women of my acquaintance."

"Wait...you what?"

"Why is it you haven't come back home in ten years?"

"Don't be pedantic."

He grinned. "You always loved using those big words."

"I'm serious."

"So am I. Call me crazy, but I always found your intelligence sexy."

"Sure you did."

"I did." He waggled his brows. "It kinda turned me on when you used that extensive vocabulary of yours."

What the hell? Was this real life? "Are you drunk?"

Shrugging, he replied, "No. I'm just stating facts."

"I would think you would have to be drunk or high to stand before the woman you humiliated and flirt with the finesse of a teenage boy. We're at my grandfather's funeral for God's sake."

That seemed to sober him up a little. I had no idea where this was coming from. Only a few minutes ago he was angry at me.

"You're right. I'm sorry."

"Look, Declan, I need to get back inside. Thank you for apologizing. That helped. But if we need to rehash the past can it not be today?" I took a deep breath, hoping it would give me the courage and strength I needed to get my game face back on. *I need this day to be over.*

But then his eyes focused on my lips, and too many odd sensations ricocheted through me. I had to get the hell out of there. I took a step back and my foot came down on air instead of concrete. Flailing, I started to fall back when Declan grabbed my hand. As I tried to pull myself toward him, I ended up jacking him toward me. A high-pitched scream escaped my lips as I tumbled backwards off the porch and into the shrubs below.

Although it should have been a soft landing with all the brush, the branches scraped and scratched like agony, causing me to shriek with pain. Of course, it didn't help when Declan's body crushed onto mine.

For the second time in twenty-four hours, Declan asked, "Are you okay?"

"Can't. Breathe," I wheezed.

"Shit. I'm sorry." When he started to get off of me, he bellowed in pain. "Fuck. I think there's a branch up my ass," Declan grunted.

A laugh burst from my lips at his statement and the absurdity of the situation. "Oh, you think me being victimized by a shrub is funny?" Declan demanded.

"It sure as hell is."

The porch door burst open before people came spilling out. Apparently, my screams had been loud enough to carry inside the funeral home. "I don't see anyone," a man said.

"Maybe it was a ghost," another man said.

"Seriously, Harold?"

"Hey, this is a funeral home. If ghosts are going to be anywhere, it's gonna be here."

Just when I was hoping we could hide out and not be seen, a man's head peeked over the railing. "Declan, is that you?"

"Yeah, Harold, it's me."

"Wait, is that Peyton Beasley down there with you?"

Busted. "Yes," I squeaked.

"Well, I'll be damned. Never would have thought you two would be together again."

"We're *not* together," I quickly corrected. Declan remained silent, probably because he was trying to get unpinned from the branch.

"Then what are you doing down there in the bushes together?"

Rolling my eyes, I said, "I tripped, he fell, and here we are." This was so bizarre. Too stupid to be real life. I'm not sure how escaping for a simple breath of fresh air had spiraled so badly.

Declan cleared his throat. "Technically, Peyton fell, I tried to help her, and she pulled me into the bushes with her." Now I wanted to slap him. Seriously? Where was his chivalry?

Once Declan finally freed himself from the branch, he was able to roll off me. Once he got to his feet, he hopped back up on the porch. He reached down to help me, but the last thing I wanted was to touch Declan again.

"What? You don't want me to help you?"

I blinked in disbelief at him before shaking my head. I was back to angry. This day needed to be done. "No. I didn't expect you to help me. I expected you to do what you do best when it comes to me: leave." Oh yeah, the claws had epically come out.

As Harold held out his arm to me, the frantic whispering of conversation of those on the porch assaulted my ears. Great. I'd been home one whole day before giving the gossip mill something to talk about.

Once I was back on the porch, I nodded my head at Harold. "Thank you."

"My pleasure," he replied with a smile.

Without a word to the others, I smoothed my skirt down before plucking a few leaves off my blouse. Just as I was about to start inside the back door, a hand smacked my ass. Gasps of shock rang around the porch.

When I whirled around, amusement burned in Declan's dark eyes.

Holding up his hand, he waved a leaf in front of me. "I would have hated for you to go back inside with this on your backside."

Ignore him. Be the better person. He needs Jesus.

With those phrases echoing through my mind, I did something ten years overdue. After closing the gap between us, I gave Declan a sweet smile before kneeing him in the balls. As he doubled over in pain, I said, "Oops, my bad. I thought I saw a leaf."

My actions left the group on the porch positively shell-shocked. No one said anything. I don't think they even drew breath. Instead, they just stared at me with wide eyes and gaping mouths.

"Good evening, gentleman," I said demurely before heading back inside the funeral home. When I got to the viewing room, I made a beeline straight for Becca. Cutting in front of the next mourner, I whispered into her ear, "I have to go. Now." As teenagers we had often enacted that statement many times when a situation went south. No questions were asked about the how or the why. We just got the hell out of there.

She stared into my eyes when I pulled away. "I'm right behind you."

After saying a quick goodbye to her husband, Becca grabbed her purse and hustled with me out the door. "By any chance does this have to do with Declan?" she asked in a low voice.

"Unfortunately, yes."

As we started by a group of people I didn't recognize, I heard, "She actually kneed him in the balls right there on the back porch."

When I cut my eyes over at Becca, she wore a slightly horrified expression. "Was that—"

"Unfortunately, yes," I repeated.

Becca groaned. "I think we're going to need wine. Lots and lots of wine."

After a quite conspicuous ending to the first day of Papa's viewing, I drank myself into a wine stupor before passing out on Becca's couch. I'd hazily come around to find Anthony draping me with a handmade quilt before carrying Becca upstairs. In the morning when he made us a greasy hangover breakfast with a side of Advil, I had to give my sister props for marrying such a thoughtful guy.

When I arrived home to prepare for the day ahead, Mom and Dad did their best not to ask too many questions. I could tell they were going to draw blood if they didn't stop biting their tongues. Although they were used to counseling people and asking all the right questions to start healing conversations, it would seem they were keeping to their usual handling of the Declan situation, which meant mum was the word unless I volunteered the information. I planned to come clean about everything, but for the moment, I only wanted to focus on Papa.

After arriving at the funeral home, I hoped my somewhat glassy-eyed appearance would appear more of a form of grief and not because I'd gotten shit-faced after my epic showdown with Declan. Damn him! I loathed him even more for taking my focus off of Papa and making it about him and our past. Thankfully, he didn't make another appearance. Due to last night's porch tango, his specter was all around me in the form of hushed whispers and knowing looks from the mourners. I merely righted my big girl panties and ignored them.

When the day of Papa's funeral dawned, I wasn't sure I could make it through. How could I possibly say goodbye to the man who had meant everything to me? I felt like a hollowed-out gourd—just a flimsy little shell left. Although it was emotionally annihilating, I'd also found strength in the words of praise for Papa. He was truly beloved in Hayesville, and that meant so much.

It was for him and his memory that I dove deep to harvest a reserve of strength I didn't realize I had. Although teary, I stood behind the oak pulpit at my father's church and delivered Papa's eulogy without breaking down. In fact, I kept my emotions in check until after the burial. I even managed to get through lunch in the fellowship hall of Dad's church without losing it.

But when I was finally alone in my childhood bedroom, it was as if the walls I'd been hiding behind came toppling down, and I was completely and thoroughly exposed. With nowhere left to hide, I finally allowed myself to cry.

A gentle knock at the door interrupted me easily an hour later. It was Mom. Without speaking, she came in and eased down on my bed. When she opened her arms, I fell into them. The same scene had been repeated the day of my wedding.

After everyone left and I was finally alone, the floodgates had opened. Mom had come to my room that night and held me until I drifted off to sleep.

After sitting in silence for a few minutes, Mom pushed a strand of hair behind my ear. "When are you planning on going back to Atlanta?"

It didn't slip my notice that in spite of me being gone for ten years, she still failed to call Atlanta home. In her eyes, Hayesville would always be home. "The hospital told me to take the week."

Mom stared knowingly into my eyes. "But you won't do that."

I shook my head. "I figured I would go back on Wednesday." I probably would have left today if I didn't think my parents needed my help going through some of Papa's things.

"Since Quinton and Becca are going back to work on Wednesday, your father and I thought it would be best to have the will read tomorrow."

A wry smile curved on my lips. "The town gossips will say we aren't wasting any time burying Papa one day and reading his will the next."

Mom laughed. "They can talk all they want. We've had some church members whose families read the will while they were still on life support."

Tsking, I replied, "Vultures."

"I would agree."

"What time were you guys thinking?"

"Mason set aside time for us tomorrow at ten."

Mason Zeller had been our family attorney for years. Not that he had needed to handle anything salacious in our family other than wills and the partnership papers when Papa took on Hank to help him with his patients.

"As much as I would rather skip it, I'll be there," I said.

"Good. I'll let your father know." Instead of rising off the bed, Mom took my hand in hers. "With all the business of mourning, I haven't had the chance to speak to you about Declan."

I groaned. "I would prefer we didn't."

"Not even what happened at the funeral home?" Mom pursed her lips at me. "I can assure you I didn't appreciate having to hear from some of the church busybodies how my daughter kneed her ex fiancé in the..."

Of course, she couldn't bring herself to say balls. When we were growing up, Mom never cursed. Instead, she spelled it. Like we really knew we were in trouble for something when she would threaten to beat our *a-s-s*.

Since I let my cursing flow freely, I had no trouble helping her out. "Balls."

Wincing, she replied, "Yes. Those."

"I'm sorry you had to hear it from other people. I just couldn't bring myself to expend the energy to tell you about it."

"Did you really have to get so violent with him?"

I rolled my eyes to stare at the ceiling for a moment. "Don't you mean why did I have to be so vulgar?"

"Well, yes, that too," Mom replied, as she fretted with the hem of her skirt.

As a minister's wife, I suppose I couldn't fault Mom too much for being mortified that her daughter nailed a guy in the balls with a bevy of witnesses. It wasn't ladylike in the least, which my mother prided herself on being. Besides pushing a strong background of education, Mom wanted Becca and me to be ladies.

"It was warranted under the circumstances." Before she could protest, I held up my hand, "Yes, I realize we were taught that it should only be used in self-defense. In my case, I was using it as an emotional self-defense tool." My mind flashed to Declan smacking my ass. "And somewhat physically as well."

Mom gasped before sputtering, "D-Did he make a p-pass at you?"

"He was removing the dirt from my backside." When Mom furrowed her brows in confusion, I explained, "From when we fell off the porch into the bushes."

"I see." The corners of her lips quirked up. "One might argue he was being somewhat chivalrous."

"Oh yeah, he's a real gentleman." With a wink, I then quoted one of our favorite movies *Steel Magnolias*. "I'm sure he takes the dishes out of the sink before he pees in it."

Mom giggled. "You're terrible."

"He's terrible."

Tilting her head, Mom asked, "He didn't even apologize?"

"Well, yeah, he did, but—"

"He wasn't sincere?"

"It's complicated."

A forlorn expression came over Mom's face. "I hate to hear that. I was hoping that once you saw him again, things would go back to the way they once were, and you would be okay with coming back to Hayesville.

I reached out to take Mom's hand in mine. "Regardless of my less than stellar reunion with Declan, I *will* come back to Hayesville."

Her brows disappeared into her salt and pepper hairline. "You will?"

With a nod, I replied, "It's time to put the past in the past." It was time for me to see my family more, because if there is one thing I'm certain of now, it's this. You never know how long you'll have with those you love. Most of all, I'd spent far too long letting the ghost of Declan affect me.

"Oh Peyton, you don't know how happy I am to hear you say that."

"Now I'm not saying I'll be here every weekend, but I'll come back for more than just the holidays."

Mom held up her free hand. "I'll take whatever I can get."

Warmth overcame my chest at Mom's reaction. It was good to be the recipient of such love. Mom broke the moment by rising up off the bed. "It's getting late. I better go and let you get some rest."

"Thanks, Mom. You know, for everything."

She smiled. "You're welcome." When she got to the door, she turned back to me. "Maybe if I play my cards just right, I can get you to move back here."

I snorted. "Don't hold your breath on that one."

With a wink, she replied, "We'll just have to wait and see."

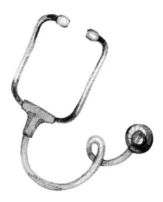

After Mom left me, I took a quick shower before collapsing into a deep sleep. The past grueling couple of days had drained me of energy, and I ended up sleeping until almost nine-thirty. Like my former teenage self, Mom had to rouse me from bed. The one bright spot in all the sadness and grief was having someone to look after me again. It wasn't that I really needed looking after per se, but having someone who loved me unconditionally made me feel less alone. Not only was she my alarm clock, but she also did my laundry without me asking. Maybe I would start coming home more often.

I slid into the backseat of Mom and Dad's Buick to ride along with them to Mason's office. Rebecca and Quinton were waiting on us when we arrived. Our somber group was then ushered down the hall to an office with an enormous oval table.

Like most of the people in Hayesville, Mason hadn't changed much in the last ten years. There was a little more silver in his blond hair, and a slight bulge of his stomach that hadn't been there previously. Once we had taken our seats, he slid a pair of reading glasses on. "This shouldn't take long. It's just one of the many facets of the business of death."

Papa's possessions were laid out in several "bequeathing paragraphs". "I leave my house at 239 Wilmington Way in Hayesville to my son, Timothy, as well as the lodge in Helen. The twenty acres with commercial property potential are to be split between my grandson, Quinton, and my granddaughter, Rebecca."

Although Mason read that line out loud, I had to go back and reread it myself to make sure I really hadn't read my name. I mean, it had to be an oversight. Papa wouldn't knowingly leave me out. But after rereading it twice, my name was still not there.

At what must've been my apparent surprise, Mason shifted his glasses up the bridge of his nose. "Peyton, I believe the last paragraph will be of interest to you."

Embarrassment prickled over my skin at being somewhat called out for my confusion. As my gaze dipped down the page, Mason began to read again. "As for my practice located at 181 Main Street, I leave the entirety of the business and dwelling to my granddaughter, Peyton."

My lungs compressed, sending air wheezing from my lips. "H-he left me his p-practice?"

Dad reached over to rub my arm. "I can't say I'm too surprised, Pey."

Yeah, well, I sure as hell am. Like I could've been bowled over with a feather kinda surprised. Why would Papa leave his thriving practice to someone who didn't even live in town? Someone who had absolutely no desire to live in Hayesville, least of all work there. "But my job is in Atlanta," I protested. *My life is in Atlanta.*

Mason tapped his pen on the table. "I can assure you he was of very sound mind when he dictated that clause."

Slowly, I shook my head back and forth. "But he never even mentioned it to me. He never even planted a thought in my mind that he would leave it to me. I just assumed he would pass it on to Hank Kisick."

"Originally, that was the plan. But after having a mild heart attack last spring, Hank's looking at taking an early retirement at the encouragement of his doctors."

"Then Papa's practice would cease to exist?" The thought alone was almost too much to bear. The pets and livestock of Hayesville had been under the care of Beasley Veterinarian Hospital for almost a century.

"You could always lease the building to another doctor or set of doctors."

Unease pricked over me as I shifted in my chair. The idea of keeping the practice going should have given me comfort, but it didn't. The thought of strangers working in Papa and Granddaddy Beasley's practice turned my stomach. Sure, Hank Kisick wasn't a member of our blood family, but he'd worked with Papa since he graduated vet school. That made him family.

At my hesitation, Mason cleared his throat. "There is another option."

"Oh?"

"Harris's corner office is a prime piece of real estate. I know a developer has been eyeing the tract of buildings."

I furrowed my brows at Mason. "What would happen to the building?"

Easing back in his chair, Mason replied, "As far as I know, they plan to gut and restructure the space to bring more businesses back to main street."

Gut and restructure? The thought of a wrecking ball anywhere near Papa's practice caused my stomach to lurch. "That sounds like a terrible prospect," I choked out.

"You could always move back here and take over Daddy's practice," my father suggested. His hopeful tone picked off a few more pieces of my already shattered heart. I hated to have caused him pain and disappointment. I'm sure Mom shared his hope.

"I wish it were that simple. But I've made my career at Blue Pearl as well as my life in Atlanta."

"But this was your home for twenty years, Peyton. It could be your home again." When I opened my mouth to protest further, Dad shook his head. "You may have practiced at Blue Pearl for the last three years, but you can't possible know it as well as you do Dad's practice."

He had a point. I'd grown up in Papa's clinic. It had become a part of me—like a second skin. My first day back in Hayesville had proven I still knew it like the back of my hand. The scents, the filing system, the pictures on the wall. I knew where everything was, every nook and cranny of the office. *It also felt like home,* but I wasn't ready to properly acknowledge that. But it missed a crucial element: *Papa.*

Oh God. *Not now. Take a deep breath, Peyton.* Black spots were entering my vision. The room was closing in on me, and all I could do was hold on to the arms of the chair, hoping that would keep me upright. *I can't do this. I can't do this without Papa. I can't breathe.* I shot out of my chair. "I'm sorry . . . need some air," I choked out.

Before anyone could stop me, I barreled around the table and fumbled for the handle on the door. When I burst out into the hallway, I slammed into a hard body. "I'm so s—" My apology died on my lips when I saw who I had run into. It was Declan.

I narrowed my eyes at him. "What are you doing creeping around out here?"

Declan scowled at me. "I'm not creeping."

"What the hell would you call it? Skulking about? Snooping? Eavesdropping?"

"Skulking? Who the hell says skulking?"

"Those with a broad vocabulary," I replied.

With a roll of his eyes, Declan replied, "You and your big words."

"Stop deflecting and answer my question."

"Fine. I'm here protecting my business interests."

"Excuse me?"

"Look, Peyton, it's not a secret around here that Harris was contemplating retiring."

"Funny since he never said a word to me about it."

"While he might not have vocalized it, he was easing himself out of practicing. It was assumed he would sell the practice to Hank until he had his heart attack."

I really loathed the fact Declan seemed to know more about Papa's business than I did. Although it was fleeting, I didn't like the feeling of betrayal I experienced towards Papa. I couldn't believe he had shut me out of some of the most important decisions of his life.

Crossing my arms over my chest, I countered, "Regardless of whether Papa was planning on retiring, it doesn't answer the question of what business you could possibly have here."

"I needed to know the course of action your parents were going to take with the practice."

"Why would you possibly need to know that?" And then it hit me. It hit me so hard a violent shudder ripped through my body. No. This couldn't be happening. The universe couldn't despise me this much. "*You're* the developer who wants to buy the building?"

"Yes, I am."

Another shudder rippled through me. My hands flew back to brace myself against the wall's textured wallpaper so I wouldn't collapse into the floor. The man I despised most in the world was going to gut and restructure my beloved grandfather's veterinarian practice. How could he? How could he betray Papa like that? Or me? I struggled to wrap my mind around it. Although the past three days had been a nightmare of epic proportions, this felt like I had stumbled into an alternate universe or a really bad Soap Opera plot.

"Look, Peyton, I know because of our past you think I'm going to take advantage of your parents by lowballing them. I would never think of doing something so despicable. I promise to make them an above market offer."

I blinked at him. There appeared to be one part of Papa's business he wasn't aware of: the part where he left the business to me. Drawing my shoulders back, I stared him down. "Papa didn't leave the practice to my parents."

Declan's brows shot up in surprise. "Wait a minute. He didn't sell it to another developer, did he?" With a shake of his head, Declan added, "He swore if he ever sold, it would be to me."

E tu, Brute, or in my case, E tu, Papa? Talk about feeling knifed in the back. How could Papa have possibly entertained selling his beloved building to the soulless bastard who broke my heart?

"Excuse me?" I choked out.

"We had a really good talk about it a couple of months ago. It's why I'm here today. I assumed he had left provisions in his will about me buying it."

What the...Papa had had a "good talk" with Declan and failed to tell me. I don't know what was worse: the fact he'd talked to him period or the fact it had been amicable. Well, at least in Declan's eyes. But knowing Papa as well as I did, I knew he would be civil to Declan regardless of what had happened. "No. He didn't tell me about talking to you, and he certainly didn't mention you in his will."

"Then who bought it?"

"Nobody. He left the practice and building to me."

Declan appeared crestfallen. "He did?"

I nodded. "Trust me, I'm just as surprised as you are."

"Wait, you didn't know?"

"Nope. I was completely blindsided."

Running his hand over his face, Declan muttered, "Huh."

"You could say that again."

"That certainly changes things."

Drawing my shoulders back, I replied, "I'm sure it does."

"Look, Peyton, if you would rather deal with one of the other guys at my company instead of working directly with me, I'll understand. "

"Wait, do you think I'm going to sell it?"

"Of course, I think you're going to sell it. What are you going to do with a veterinarian practice two hours from where you live?"

"Maybe I'm going to rent it to some other vets?"

With a smirk, Declan replied, "You would never allow a bunch of strangers to work on the sacred ground that your grandfather and great-grandfather did."

Damn him and damn our shared past that enabled him to know

exactly what my thoughts would be. I'd hate anyone else working within those walls. And it wasn't about control either. But I hated that Declan dared to smirk at me in this moment. To think he truly had no respect for me at this moment . . . To think he understood the importance of this place yet still only thought of lining his own pocket. "That's rich you speak of sacred ground when you want to send a wrecking ball through it."

"I'm not planning on destroying the building. Considering it's a historical site, my grandmother and all her old biddy friends on the Historical Society would have my ass."

"Mason said you were going to gut and restructure."

"Only interior." He gave me an earnest look. "You have my word I would treat it with the best care possible to ensure the integrity of the original while making it more accessible for new businesses and shops."

I rolled my eyes. "Right. That makes it so much better."

"It makes it a hell of a lot better for the working people of this town. This isn't Atlanta, you know. We need more opportunities."

"And you're the savior who is going to bring them?"

"I'm going to sure as hell try. I just need you to work with me."

"You flatter yourself if you would think I would ever sell to you or any of your partners."

Declan glowered at me. "Any other developer is not going to give two shits about the historical merit. They won't care about my grandmother and her Historical Society friends making a fuss—they eat old ladies like that for breakfast. They'll mow everything to the ground without a second thought. I'm the only one who will try to preserve some semblance of what Harris had. Unlike you, he appreciated my vision."

At that moment, the door to Mason's office cracked open, and my dad poked his head out. With our raised voices, I'm sure he and everyone else had heard most of our conversation.

I held my hand up. "I'm not selling to anyone, and I'm not renting the building."

"So, you're just going to let a perfectly good building rot and decay?" Declan shook his head at me. "That's not what Harris would have wanted."

"I would never let it fall into disarray, nor would I trust anyone else working in there."

"Then what exactly is it you're going to do?"

My gaze flickered over to my dad. At the hope burning in his eyes, I knew exactly what I was going to do. "You're looking at Hayesville's newest veterinarian!"

Chapter Seven

Three Weeks Later

"Oomph," I muttered as I hoisted an over-packed moving box labeled *Bedroom* into my arms. With another grunt, I stumbled down the hallway and into the master bedroom. After depositing the box on the floor, I glanced around the chaos surrounding me. Two weeks ago when I'd stood in this room, Papa could be seen in every nook and cranny. After all, it had been his bedroom. But now all semblances of him had been wiped away and replaced with my possessions.

While I was in Atlanta working a two-week notice for Blue Pearl and packing up my condo, my family had prepared Papa's house for my arrival. Even though it made me feel guilty, I was glad I didn't have to help dismantling Papa's possessions. The thought of emptying his closets and going through his drawers made me nauseous. Of course, I hated it for Mom and Dad and my siblings. I'm not sure how they managed to complete the arduous process in just two weeks. In between patients, I'd often get a text with a picture of a piece of furniture asking me if I wanted it. What wasn't divided between us was donated.

It had been necessity, not nostalgia, that had led me to take my parents' offer to move into Papa's house. Since I didn't want to stress Dr. Kisick's heart condition with a heavy patient load, time was of the essence to get me to work in Hayesville. A tiny part of me felt somewhat relieved I wasn't buying or renting. It made me feel like moving back home wasn't so permanent. Like, I had an escape clause if things were just too much.

The announcement that I was moving to Hayesville had been met with shock and horror by my Atlanta friends and coworkers. "What the fuck?" had resonated most with my best friends. Most thought I should have waited a year since you're not supposed to make any big personal or professional life decisions the first year after loss. Since my close friends knew my true aversion to Hayesville, they couldn't believe I would actually put myself in the position of potentially seeing Declan every day. But I thought of what my therapist had said in regards to what she perceived as me constantly running from my past. There would never be true healing until I could coexist with Declan.

For the past week since I'd gotten back home, I'd been spending my mornings in the clinic. It was a way to ease in to the practice, introduce myself to my four-legged patients and their owners. After lunchtime, I'd come home and tried to put my new life in order at the house. Considering the amount of boxes littering the bedroom, I still had a long way to go.

The clanging of the doorbell interrupted my work. Throwing a glance at myself in the mirror, I winced. After coming home from the clinic, I'd stripped off my bra and replaced my scrubs with yoga pants and a ratty T-Shirt. Whoever was at the door wasn't going to see me at my best. After heading down the hall, I opened the door. To my shock, Pauline standing on the porch with a hesitant smile on her face. "Hello, Peyton."

"Hey there. How are you?" I quickly crossed my arms over my braless chest while I tried to wipe away any shock that might've been on my face.

"I'm just fine. I hope I'm not interrupting."

"Oh no. I was just doing a little unpacking." A nervous giggle tumbled from my lips. "I mean, I'm sure that's obvious considering how I look like a bum."

"You look just fine. Besides, the unpacking is the reason why I'm here."

"Oh?"

Pauline nodded. "I figured you had your hands full with trying to settle in to Harris's place." It was then I noticed the picnic basket by her side. When I met her gaze again, she said, "I wanted to do a little something to welcome you back to Hayesville."

"That's so sweet of you. Please come on in." It shouldn't surprise me really. Pauline St. James had always been generous in so many ways. I'd missed her over the years. As I pushed the door open wider, Pauline stepped into the foyer.

After sitting the picnic basket down on the coffee table, Pauline opened it up and began emptying its contents onto the coffee table. "Robert and I both think it's wonderful you've come back home. We know how much it means to your parents. I know it would mean a lot to Harris as well."

My chest constricted slightly at the mention of Papa. "Thank you. I hate it took his death to get me back."

"Sometimes fate works in mysterious ways," Pauline replied knowingly. An uncomfortable silence filled the air. "Anyway, I made you one of my chicken casseroles. I remember you really liked them."

The pain in my chest ratcheted up again at the mention of the past. Forcing a smile to my face, I replied, "Oh, I didn't like them; I loved them."

Pauline laughed. "I remember you always ate seconds, and it wasn't just because you were trying to be nice."

"A lot of time might've passed, but I've never forgotten what an amazing cook you were."

"You flatter me, but I appreciate the sentiment."

"You're welcome." Pauline motioned to the bag. "There's also a salad and some of my chocolate chip cookies."

"Seriously, you are way too kind. I mean, I already feel indebted to you."

"For what? A little casserole and some cookies?"

"I mean, how you went above and beyond with your care packages when I was at UGA."

With a frown, Pauline asked, "Care packages?"

"You know, the goody boxes you and Robert sent me every month for my first year of school. I can't tell you how much it meant to me. Each and every one was so thoughtful." When Pauline continued staring curiously at me, I added, "I know I sent you guys a thank-you note back then, but I wanted to tell you in person as well. Even after all these years I haven't forgotten them."

"Peyton, Robert and I never sent you any care packages."

An awkward laugh tumbled from my lips. "What do you mean you didn't send them? I got a package with your return address every month. Even my roommate knew who the goodies were from. I used to have to fight her for the homemade cookies."

"I'm not doubting you received them. But I can tell you with absolute assurance that we didn't send them."

Unease pricked its way up my spine. "If you didn't send them, who did?"

"I think I have an idea."

Since Declan's sister, Danielle, and I weren't particularly close, I couldn't imagine who else from the St. James household would have sent them. And then it hit me. "Are you telling me that after jilting me at the altar, *Declan* sent me monthly care packages?" She winced at that one. She'd never been proud of Declan for that move.

"That's the only explanation I can think of."

The shock cascaded over me, causing me to shudder. Unable to form a coherent thought, I uttered, "Wow."

"I feel the same way."

"You really had no idea?"

Pauline shook her head. "He never said a thing to us."

Once again, all I could say was, "Wow."

Closing the distance between us, Pauline took my hand in hers. "Peyton, I will never, ever condone what Declan did. Both Robert and I were deeply hurt and ashamed by his actions, which we vocalized to him back then. But I want you to know he has grown and matured so much. I worried after what he did to you, that he might be lost. For many years, he was. But something wonderful happened to him when Cam was born. I'm so very proud of the father he is, and the man he has become."

Being rendered speechless was becoming par for the course in this conversation. With my emotions so jangled, I desperately wanted a drink although it was far from five o'clock. Had learning Declan sent me care packages in college changed my perception of him? Somewhat. At the same time, it couldn't fully erase the pain he had caused. Hearing a glowing review of his character from his mother in a small way affirmed the idea that he had changed. But a tiny, petty part of me argued that Pauline was Declan's mother, and of course, she would give him her approval.

Desperate to break the awkward silence around us, I squeezed Pauline's hands. "I'm glad to hear that."

With a tentative smile, she said, "I hope now that you're home for good you can forgive him and maybe come to see he isn't the enemy anymore."

The tide of good feelings towards Declan abruptly ended, and the petty bitch in me bristled at her words. *Yeah, maybe I wouldn't have seen him as the enemy had he not shown such disbelief that Papa had left the practice to me. Arrogance and I had never been friends.* Thankfully, the somewhat genteel Southern lady residing somewhere inside me reined me in. "We'll see," I responded diplomatically.

Before Pauline could reply, the front door blew open, and Becca came hustling inside with a box of Dunkin Donuts in one hand and drink container filled with two coffees in the other. The one almost semblance of civilization Hayesville could boast is we had a Dunkin Donuts. Well, it was ten minutes outside of town, but we didn't sweat the small stuff. "All right slave driver, you have my help for two hours, but then I have to go home to cook dinner."

At the sight of Pauline standing in my living room, Becca skidded to a stop. "Um, hi. I didn't know you had company."

Pauline waved her hand dismissively. "She doesn't. I just ran by to bring Peyton a welcome back meal."

Becca grinned. "That's a pretty thoughtful gift since Peyton can't cook."

"Har, har," I muttered. Sure, it was the truth I wasn't known for my culinary skills. At the same time, I didn't need my almost mother-in-law hearing any of my shortcomings.

Glancing between us, Pauline said, "Anyway, I'll get going so you two can get to work."

As we started to the door, I said, "Once again, I can't thank you enough for the food."

With a smile, Pauline replied, "You're more than welcome. Let me know if Robert and I can do anything else."

"I appreciate the offer, but you have already gone above and beyond."

"Just know we're here if you need us."

Looking past me, Pauline said, "It was good seeing you, Becca."

"Good seeing you, too, Mrs. St. James."

After walking out onto the porch with her, Pauline gave me a hopeful smile. "Please think about what I said."

"I'll try." While it might have been a noncommittal reply, it was the most diplomatic thing I could think of to say. My emotions were far too jangled to say anything else.

When I went back into the house, Becca had a glazed donut in one hand while she rifled through the containers on the coffee table. "Excuse me, but that's mine, thank you very much."

She rolled her eyes at me. "Like Pauline would care if you shared a bite or two with me."

I swatted her away. "She's a better person than I am," I teasingly replied.

Although there were a million things I should have been doing to unpack, I was both emotionally and physically spent after Pauline's visit. I grabbed a chocolate frosted donut and collapsed onto the couch.

Becca furrowed her brows at me. "Is this the portion of unpacking where you play the role of supervisor and boss me around?"

"I'm sorry. I just needed a break."

"Having Pauline here was hard, huh?"

"Not really. It's not like I've ever had a beef with her."

"Then what is it?"

After inhaling the rest of my donut, I proceeded to relate the saga of the care packages. When I finished, Becca shook her head. "I really don't know what to say."

"So, it's not just me wanting to make something out of nothing?"

"No, I'd say it's pretty momentous Declan did that."

I swiped a napkin off the table. "I seriously don't need this right now."

"Because you need for Declan to stay the villain in your narrative?"

With a scowl, I tossed my napkin at her. "Whose side are you on?"

"Yours. But I wouldn't be a very good sister if I didn't play Devil's Advocate."

"Trust me, I'm already doing it enough in my head." An exasperated growl came from deep within me. "Why do I let this man have so much power over me?"

"Because he was your first love. He broke your heart and your trust," Becca answered diplomatically.

"Right. That's it."

"But you are a different person now and so is he. You've both grown and matured. Maybe it's truly time to bury the hatchet." When I opened my mouth, she shook her head. "And no, not in his back."

"I was going to say his balls but whatever." At my wicked grin, Becca laughed.

"Since I've been teaching, I always have one or two really pain in the ass kids. In the beginning of the year, I don't see how I'll make it through without losing my sanity. But then as time goes on, little things start to change, and they show me a different side of them." She gave me a pointed look. "While there may be the odd psychopath or two, no one is really all good or all bad."

Damn, my little sister had just emotionally owned me. "You're absolutely right."

"Although you hate to admit it," she teased.

I laughed. "Yes, I am, but I'm also proud of how wise you've become."

"I would say you were a great teacher, but we both know you're an emotional mess."

"Okay, that does it," I grunted before smacking her in the face with a throw pillow.

"Oh, it's on!" she cried before grabbing a pillow.

The next thing I knew Becca and I were engaging in an all-out pillow war like we'd had when we were kids. Of course, we didn't quite have the stamina we had back then, so it ended rather quickly. Huffing and puffing, we lay on the couch trying to catch our breath.

"I've...seriously...got to start...working...out...," I heaved.

"Ditto," Becca panted. Turning her head towards me, she grinned. "I'm so glad you're back home."

The familiar pang of guilt crept back on me. "I'm sorry, Becs."

She furrowed her brows at me. "For hitting me with the pillow?"

I shook my head. "No. You totally deserved that." I paused because this was something I had really struggled with. She'd lived without her big sister being present at home for so many years, and nothing made that okay. Not by a long shot. "No, for being such a petty dumbass by staying away so long."

"You didn't just stay away because of Declan. You were chasing your dreams of becoming a veterinarian. Last time I checked, you couldn't do that here."

"I could've made time."

Becca smiled. "You didn't need to make time to be here. You did the most important thing which was make time for us. Sure, I couldn't drive five minutes and see you, but I always saw you."

Her words should have made me feel better, but they didn't. As tears pricked my eyes, I swallowed down the rising sobs. "I could've had more time with Papa if I'd come back home."

"Come on, Peyton. I went away to school thirty minutes from here, and it was still hard finding time to see him. It's the natural progression of things—the baby birds fly the nest. The most important thing was you were off making him proud by following in his footsteps. He loved his weekends in Athens and Atlanta with you."

"He did?"

"He used to say it made him feel young again going to the football games at UGA, or to go to the Big City, as he called Atlanta."

The guilt-ridden part of me always feared Papa was just pretending to enjoy coming to Atlanta. It felt like I was inconveniencing him by taking him away from his home. But I know he'd loved seeing me too.

I swiped my index fingers under my eyes. "I still can't fight this feeling I've wasted years of my life letting Declan have such a hold on me."

"If you were living in a van down by the river, I might agree with you."

I snorted at the thought. "Professionally I might have escaped the van, but I can't help feeling like I'm there personally."

Appearing thoughtful, Becca replied, "I wouldn't say personally since you have great friends and a wonderful relationship with your family."

"Then I'm romantically in a van down by the river?"

"Potentially."

With a groan, I replied, "Damn, that's grim."

"You can always turn the van around." She grinned. "Trade it in for a house with a picket fence."

"Trust me, I'd love to do that."

"Mind over matter. The past is just the past. Declan isn't the Big Bad Wolf creeping around to sabotage your future relationships."

Becca was right. Of course, it's always so easy to hear or say the words. It's implementing them that's an entirely different story. But I knew for both my sanity and my future I had to try. With a confident smile, I replied, "The past is just the past. I'm going to focus on the present and the future."

Nodding, Becca replied, "I'm going to hold you to that."

"How do you propose doing that? A pinky swear?"

"By allowing me to fix you up."

While my gut reaction was to groan and tell her hell no, I realized that wasn't focusing on the present. If I was truly going to move forward, *here in Hayesville,* I needed to believe I could forge my own future here like I did in Atlanta. I'd dated. I hadn't felt . . . rejected . . . for years. *But was that just because I'd left my heart here?* No. I had to swallow my pride.

Reluctantly, I replied, "Okay."

Becca worked to hide her surprise at my lack of protesting. "Okay."

"Just promise me it won't be with anyone from my past."

"I wouldn't dream of it." *And there was* that *smile on her face, the one so much like Papa's when he had mischief on his mind.*

It was because of that smile I didn't believe her.

Chapter Eight

The morning of my one-month anniversary back in Hayesville found me seated on a barstool at the counter of the Main Street Café. During the past few weeks, I'd fallen into a routine of stopping by for breakfast before heading to the clinic. Not only did they boast the best coffee in town, not to mention their famous pancakes and cheese grits, but it was less than a five-minute walk to the clinic.

While I could have easily just prepared something at home, there was something to be said for eating at the café. The owners of my current patients, as well as prospective patients, were a part of the breakfast crowd. Although I'd grown up in Hayesville, my decade long absence somewhat made me a stranger. I dare say an outsider. Hanging out with the locals helped to remedy that.

As much as I'd feared the humiliation of returning home to Hayesville, my anxiety had been unfounded. I'd come to find most people were genuinely glad to have me back. Most noted that they knew it meant so much to my parents while only a few dared to mention Declan. While they might not have been mentioning him, my thoughts were certainly on him. I kept going back to Pauline's visit. Part of me wanted to confront him about it while the other part want nothing more than to pretend he didn't exist.

On this particular morning, I was enjoying a rather large stack of blueberry pancakes when someone plopped down on the stool beside me. Without looking up from my phone, I knew who it was the moment the familiar cologne assaulted my nose.

Fuck me.

"Good morning, Dr. Beasley," Declan said, in an annoyingly cheerful voice for seven o'clock.

"Morning," I reluctantly grumbled. Even though I was prepared to live and let live when it came to Declan, it was way too early in the morning to have to deal with him. In my mind, I hoped to only sporadically see him. Like that odd person from high school you run into every Leap Year. Up until today, I was doing pretty well.

Pointing to my plate, Declan said, "Mm, are those some of Mrs. Conroy's blueberry pancakes? They look delicious."

"Yep."

Cissy, who was my equally cheerful waitress, appeared before us. "Can I get you your usual, Declan?"

Shaking his head, Declan replied, "You know what, Cissy. I think I'll have what Peyton is having."

"It'll be right out."

"Thank you, ma'am." After Cissy left, Declan leaned closer in to me. "How are you settling in?"

"Just fine, thank you."

"Good. I'm glad to hear it."

Jerking my gaze up, I narrowed my eyes at him. "Somehow I don't believe that."

He shrugged. "Believe what you want. It's the truth." Turning towards me on his stool, Declan said, "Honestly, Peyton, I really don't know what else to do to show you I'm not the man you think I am. I've apologized profusely. I'm not sure what else I need to do to change your negative opinion of me."

"Is there a reason you sat down here besides aggravating me?"

"Do I have to have a reason to be friendly? I mean, you are new back to town. It's the cordial thing to do."

"There is no reason you need to be cordial to me. We can pass and repass without acknowledging each other." Of course, that wasn't going to be easy considering he looked practically edible in his crisp, white button-down shirt and electric blue tie. Some women loved men in uniform while others like me enjoyed suit porn.

"I don't think I could do that. Especially considering how close in proximity our offices are to each other."

I blinked at him in disbelief. "If you don't leave me alone, I'm going to give you another unladylike knee to the balls."

"Then I'll be sure to start wearing a cup when I come to work."

Then he had the unmitigated gall to wink at me. What was next? Groping my ass...again?

"Insufferable bastard!" I grunted. After taking a ten out of my wallet, I threw it on the counter. I slung my purse over my shoulder before giving Declan one last *rot in hell* look. I stormed through the café's doors and out into the sunshine. Considering my mood, it might as well have been pouring rain. As I stomped down the sidewalk, I clenched my fists at my side. God, I hated him. Like with a thousand passions from the depths of the darkest part of hell. I wasn't even sure that did my level of hatred justice.

Even though I was confused, one thing was absolutely clear. There was no way I'd let him get his mitts on Papa's practice. He could pry the deed out of my cold, dead hands!

Chapter Nine

After putting the last suture in place, I stepped back from the operating table. My gaze flickered from the Shih Tzu's tiny abdomen over to the machines recording blood pressure, heart rate, and oxygen levels. I breathed a sigh of relief into my mask. Although ovariohysterectomy aka spaying was a relatively easy procedure, it wasn't without risks. I'd completed hundreds over the years, but I always breathed easier once the procedure was over. "Everything looks good," I remarked as I swept the green surgical drape off of Miss Bailey—the pride and joy of the Dunlop family.

My vet tech, Jaycee, nodded in agreement at me across the table as she finished the final antiseptic cleaning before we moved Miss Bailey to recovery.

It had been a week since my altercation with Declan at the café. To avoid running into him, I'd started leaving the house thirty minutes earlier. By the third day, he'd somehow caught on. He appeared just in time to claim the stool next to mine. Although I'd ignored him as I devoured my pancakes, Declan had continued right on talking to me much to the amusement of the other patrons.

The next day I decided it was best to arrive thirty minutes *later*. When I swept through the café doors, I froze at the sight of Declan sitting at the counter grinning at me. *What the fuck....*

Although I thought about turning around and marching out of there, I decided I wouldn't let him have the pleasure of aggravating me. There was also the pesky fact my growling stomach was pretty insistent on me getting a hearty breakfast, especially since it was a half an hour later than when I usually ate.

"Are you stalking me?" I demanded as I took my seat.

"And good morning to you, too."

Scowling at him, I replied, "Answer the question." When he opened his mouth, I threw my hand up. "No. Don't bother. I'll just have Anthony file a report for me at the station."

Declan chuckled. "Christ, Peyton, I'm not creeping outside your house in the bushes. I'm merely patronizing the same café as you are."

"If you're not stalking me, then how did you know I'd be here when I changed my routine?"

The amused look in his eyes changed over to one so intense it caused me to shiver. I'd seen that look many times in our past. It usually meant he was about to tell me something deep about his feelings for me, or I was soon going to end up with his dick deep inside me.

"Because I know you." His deep voice hit me straight between the legs, which caused my mind to immediately go to the sexual connotation of his comment. He had certainly known me in the biblical sense many, many times in many, many different positions. At the moment, I knew he was speaking more to the fact we'd grown up together before our relationship had deepened when we'd begun dating.

After taking a moment to recover, I drew my shoulders back to glare at him. "You might've known the old Peyton, but you certainly don't know me now and you never will."

"Hmm, my ability to accurately anticipate your next move would say I do know the old and new Peyton." When I waved Cissy over, Declan leaned in to where his body touched mine. I swallowed hard as I fought my body's reaction to having him so close. "You want to know what you're going to do next?" His breath warmed my earlobe, and I felt the hairs on my arms rise.

"Not interested," I gritted out. *But I'm very interested in the prospect of dribbling maple syrup over what I can only imagine is your six-pack abs. What? Peyton, stop right now. We don't want to see Declan's sex...no, Declan's six-pack abs.*

"Since you're hungry and won't let me screw you out of your daily pancakes, you're going to ask Cissy to make yours to go."

I swiveled my head to stare at him. Holy hell, he really did know me. Now that he'd called my hand, I didn't know what to do. Did I go ahead and get a to-go order because I couldn't stand being near him one second more, or did I go ahead and dine in rather than letting him be right. Talk about an epic conundrum.

But at that moment, I was rescued by some divine intervention in the form of my father and some of the deacons from church. Thrusting my hand into the air, I furiously waved at my dad. I then turned to Declan with a sickeningly sweet smile. "Actually, I was just waiting to join my father for breakfast."

A cocky grin slunk across Declan's face. "You had plans to join your dad's weekly deacons' meeting?"

Crap. Was that a thing? While I wouldn't have had a clue since I hadn't been in town that long, Declan would have been privy to that knowledge. *Think Peyton.* "Yes, I planned to discuss with them my idea for a blessing of the animals."

Declan snorted. "Sure you were."

"I'm sorry that you don't know everything."

"I stand corrected. Now you have a good one, Peyton." Using two of his fingers, he made the "eyes on you" gesture. "I'll be watching," he teased.

"Jackass," I muttered under my breath as I made my way over to Dad's table. Although they'd initially been surprised, Dad and the deacons welcomed my company. From time to time, I'd throw a glance over my shoulder at Declan. Every single time he anticipated me and would wink.

Since I'd grown tired of playing the "breakfast roulette game", I'd decided to stop going to the café the last two mornings. This morning as I choked down a McDonald's biscuit in my car, I'd cursed Declan with every chew. *Who the hell actually enjoys these things anyway?* At the same time, I knew how ridiculous I was for just not ignoring Declan and enjoying my usual breakfast.

But getting back to Miss Bailey and the present. Jaycee had just transferred her off the operating table before wheeling her over to the recovery bay. Back at the operating table, I started to put the organs into a medical waste bag when Jaycee's gasp caused me to freeze. "What? Is it Miss Bailey?" I called over my shoulder since my hands were currently cradling a tiny uterus.

"There's no water."

Forgetting the uterus, I whirled around to see Jaycee standing gloveless in front of the sink. "You mean it's running slow?"

She turned on the faucet. "No. There's nothing there at all."

Her answer caused me to fumble with the slippery uterus, which in turn sent it bouncing off the table. It pinged against my thigh before sliding down one of my legs.

Hell. Fucking. No.

After bending over, I snatched up the uterus and then tossed it into the bag. I crossed the room to Jaycee. Her expression was horror stricken, which I imagined was not from the water shortage, but from the escaping uterus.

Once I removed my gloves, I moved the handles back and forth. But just like with Jaycee, nothing came out. For a moment, I could only stand there wide-eyed and open-mouthed. We'd paid our bill, so it wasn't like we didn't have water from being disconnected.

And then it hit me. The only reason why our water wouldn't be running is if a line had been disturbed, and the best way for that to happen would be through construction. *Declan's* construction to be exact.

Since I wouldn't sell to him, he was resorting to underhanded techniques to sabotage my business. Rage rocketed through me. "Fucking bastard!" I screamed.

I must've looked as scary as I felt because Jaycee took a step back from me. "Who is a bastard?" she tentatively asked.

"Declan."

Her eyes bulged. "You think he's the reason why we don't have water?"

"Can you think of anyone else who is gutting and jackhammering and bulldozing?"

"That's the contractor's doing, not Declan's. He's just in development."

I snapped my fingers. "Bingo! He's the one calling the shots, and I will no longer allow him to undermine my business simply because I refuse to sell him the building!"

"What are you going to do?"

"Give Declan a piece of my mind."

"You want me to have Sylvia get him on the phone?"

"Oh no. I'm going to march myself down to his office."

Jaycee's gaze trailed down me. "You're going looking like that?" I knew she wanted to screech, *"You're going out in public with blood-stained scrubs?"*

"Do you know of a better way of getting his attention?"

"Oh, I'm sure it's going to get his attention. I'm just not sure that's the best course of action. Especially considering your history with him."

I wagged a finger at her. "This is *not* about my history with Declan. It's about him continuing to be an unimaginable asshole because I won't give in to him like I used to when we were dating."

"You know it could be just a misunderstanding."

"Clearly, you don't know Declan like I do."

"No. But the Declan I know would never sabotage a business that takes care of animals. Cam is crazy about their dog, Moose, not to mention all of Declan's horses."

"Any love he has would be clouded by his overpowering need to stick one to me."

"If you say so," Jaycee warily replied.

"Oh, I know so." Jerking my chin over to Miss Bailey, I said, "Can you do me a favor after you get her into recovery and call the family?"

"Of course."

"Good. I'll be back as soon as I can."

The corners of Jaycee's lips quirked up. "I'll be here in case you need bail money."

"With my rage, that's a distinct possibility."

While my resolve was firm to make a spectacle in order to get Declan's attention, I didn't intend to do that in front of any of my patients in the waiting room. Instead, I hightailed it out the back door. I stayed in the alley until I reached the side of Declan's office building.

Normally, I might've received a catcall from the hard-hat horndogs working construction. But not today. They stared wide-eyed and open-mouthed as I crisscrossed in front of them. Ian Plummer, who not only was the construction foreman but had graduated with Declan and me, said, "Christ almighty, Peyton. Are you all right?"

"I'll be fine once I get a piece of Declan."

He shook his head. "From the looks of it, you've already had a go at him."

"Oh no, I would look worse if I had."

With Ian blinking in disbelief, I powerwalked to the ornate office door bearing the name, *St. James Development*. When I entered the office, the overwhelming smell of essential oils assaulted my nose. My eyes narrowed on the receptionist. Of course, she would be incredibly young. God forbid, he hired an older woman. Not only did she barely look twenty-five, but she was platinum blonde, heavily made up, and incredibly thin. *You're just pissed because she's the complete opposite of you.*

When she glanced up from the computer, her eyes bulged. "M-May I help you?"

"I need to see Declan."

"I'm sorry, but he's on a conference call right now with some investors. Would you like to make an appointment?"

I waved a dismissive hand. "No. I don't have time to wait. I have to see him now."

"I'm sorry, but that's just not possible. If you'd like to have a seat—"

"Which room is he in?"

"I'm not—"

"You can tell me, or I can find out."

The wheels appeared to be furiously turning in Receptionist Barbie's head. "He left word not to be disturbed," she repeated more for herself than for me.

"Oh, he's going to be disturbed." I then walked around the front office desk and started down the hallway.

"Ma'am, please just wait for me to let him end the conference call!"

"Nope. I don't think so." I threw open the first door I came to and found an empty office. After leaving a blood smeared doorknob behind, I started for the next door. I froze when I heard voices coming from down the hallway. As I grew closer to it, I made out Declan's voice over the others. Bingo.

I burst through the door so hard it flew back on its hinges and banged against the wall. Declan's gaze snapped up to stare at me. Without taking his eyes off of mine, he said, "Excuse me, gentleman, but I'm going to have to put our call on hold for a moment."

I stalked over to his desk before jabbing my finger at his telephone. "Don't even think you're going to silence me and try to save face. Your investors should know what kind of underhanded means you use to try and pressure people into selling."

"I've already muted the call. What are you talking about? I haven't pressured anyone into selling."

Receptionist Barbie came sprinting in. "Mr. St. James, I'm so very sorry. I asked her to wait or make an appointment."

"It's okay, Anna. I know Dr. Beasley and her temperament very well."

I narrowed my eyes at Declan. "Don't you dare belittle me by acting like I'm always flying off the handle."

"I do recall you kneed me in the balls a few weeks ago."

When I cut my eyes over to Anna, I caught her horrified, yet curious expression staring back at me. "Because of Declan's Main Street expansion, I've gone from little water pressure to zilch. I came out of spaying the Dunlop's Shih Tzu, and my vet tech and I couldn't even wash our hands," I explained to her.

As Anna nodded her head, Declan's brows furrowed. "You don't have any water?"

"No, genius, we don't."

Rising out of his chair, Declan came around the desk. "Peyton, I'm so sorry. I had no idea you were experiencing any structural issues at the clinic."

I rolled my eyes to the ceiling. "Sure you didn't."

"I know my word isn't much to you, but I can assure you I would never intentionally have my foreman tamper with your waterlines."

"You told me yourself you need my corner building to fully complete the development. What better way to drive me out than by sabotaging my business?"

Declan narrowed his eyes me. "Do you really think I'd do something so devious?"

"I think we're both aware of your track record."

"For Christ's sake, Peyton, that was *ten* years ago. I've apologized profusely for my callous actions while also trying to get you to understand I've changed."

"Excuse me for finding it hard to believe you."

With a frustrated growl, Declan turned to Anna. "Will you get Scott on the phone for me?"

"Yes, Mr. St. James." She wheeled around on her tiny stilettos and then clicked like a mad-woman out of the room.

Motioning to the chair, Declan said, "Would you like to have a seat?"

"I'm fine, thank you."

"You're welcome to use my private bath to wash up in."

"Once again, I'm fine."

Declan swept his hands to his hips. "You're fine? You have gunk all over your scrubs."

"I'm aware of that." I pointed to my pants. "And that isn't gunk—it's blood and tissue from Miss Bailey's uterus."

"Jesus Christ, Peyton."

When the phone on his desk beeped, Declan held up his hand. "I'm putting Scott on speaker, so you can hear for yourself what he has to say and can't blame me any further."

"Fine."

"Hey, Scott, it's Declan."

"Hey, man, what can I do for you?" Scott's voice echoed through the room.

"Listen, I've got a pretty irate business owner in my office right now. I need to know what's going on with the water lines adjacent to the vet clinic."

Silence echoed on the line. "Uh, yeah, boss, we kinda fucked up with those."

Both Declan's and my brows shot up. "Could you please clarify what you mean?" Declan prompted.

"My plumber had his kid working on the pipes, and he's fresh outta school. He doesn't have a lot of experience with antique pipes. Somehow he nicked a line yesterday, and this morning we've been working on the repercussions i.e. a shit-ton of flooding."

"I see." Declan's jaw clenched. "I'm going to need your assurance you will have the cleanup taken care of as quickly as possible, as well as the restoration of water service to the veterinarian clinic."

"Yes, sir. You have my word."

"Thank you. And I'll also ask that you find another plumber to complete the rest of the service."

"I'm already on it, boss."

"Bye, Scott."

After he hung up, Declan gave me an apologetic smile. "Fuck. Peyton, I'm very sorry this happened. It will be sorted." His frustrated sigh was evident of just how irritated he was. *Maybe I misjudged this... maybe I misjudged him.* "I'll cover the financial losses the clinic might incur today.

My mouth dropped unattractively open. Wait, what just happened here? Not only was Declan not the villain I had believed him to be, but he was appearing quite heroic. Although I'd heard it with my own ears, it was still almost too hard to fathom.

"Let me get this straight. You didn't sabotage the business, and you want to help take care of today's business losses?"

"That's right."

"Oh God," I murmured. I'd just totally and completely shown my ass in front of Declan for absolutely nothing. It'd been one thing to knee him in the balls after he smacked my ass, or to berate him for the way he treated me in the past. But I had just falsely accused him of being petty and unprofessional. I could almost see Papa's disappointed face at my behavior.

And that's when it happened. Something I would have never, ever in a million years wanted to happen in front of Declan St. James.

I burst out crying. Like snotty-nose, very unattractive crying.

The sight of my tears caused Declan's head to snap back like I'd slapped him. "Jesus, Christ," he muttered.

Hysterical laughter tore from my lips at both his words and expression. "You're right. At this point, I think he's the only one who can help when it comes to the effect you have on me." God, this was so ridiculous. *I'm not a child anymore.* And he deserves to be cut a break here. "This is hard for me, Declan. I don't want to feel this way. I mean, I've tried staying away, but that didn't help. Somehow, you fucked with every relationship I tried to have. I did therapy, and inevitably, I always kept coming back to you."

Turning my face into my shoulder, I swiped away some of the tears running down my cheeks on my scrubs. "And now I've finally come back home and faced my demon, and I still don't have any peace. In fact, I just appeared completely immature by falsely accusing you." I threw up my hands. "You want to know the true irony? Your mom and Rebecca told me how you've matured and changed, and I didn't want to believe them. But you know what? You really fucking have matured. But me? I'm still stuck in the past when it comes to you, and I don't know if I'll ever recover. That thought is fucking crippling."

Declan remained ashen-faced through my tirade. Now that I was finished, he rose out of his chair. As he came around the side of the desk, he appeared truly remorseful. "Peyton, I'm really sorry."

I bobbed my head. "I know you are. And so am I." And with a defeated heart and soul, I sprinted out of Declan's office.

Chapter Ten

After running out of Declan's office, I took the alley back to the clinic so no one would see my tears. When I slipped in the back door, I didn't announce my arrival. Instead, I made a beeline to the bathroom to try my best to clean up the mess I'd made of my face.

Every time I thought of what an enormous ass I'd made out of myself, I'd just start crying all over again. I fought the urge to throw my hands in the air and scream, "WHYYY?" to the heavens. I didn't know how being so upset over a water shortage had morphed into a nervous breakdown in front of the very man who had inflicted all my emotional duress.

Sylvia's voice at the door interrupted my self-deprecating tirade. "Peyton, honey, are you in there?"

Sniffling, I swiped my eyes before walking over to the door. I cracked it and peered out. "Did you need me?"

She gave me a sympathetic look. "A man from the construction company just came by and said the water would be back on in about two hours. I went ahead and canceled your appointments until two."

"Thank you, Sylvia."

"Don't worry about it. With the water situation, I also told Vernon Hornsby you could come by earlier to take a look at his horse's foot."

"Yes, that will be fine. I'll grab my bag and head out."

When I opened the door and stepped out of the bathroom, I unexpectedly found Sylvia's arms around me. I had to admit it was a nice feeling being comforted after such a hellish day.

Sylvia squeezed me tight before pulling away. Staring into my eyes, she said, "Don't be so hard on yourself, honey. You've had a traumatic couple of weeks losing your papa and then coming back here."

I furrowed my brows at her. Had news of my breakdown at Declan's traveled that fast? Or had Jaycee told her I'd gone on the warpath to annihilate Declan? "Did you hear about what I did?" I cautiously asked.

"Jaycee told me a little bit."

Groaning, I brought my hands over my eyes. "God, I'm such a basket case."

"You know, your reaction is completely understandable."

"I just falsely accused Declan of sabotaging my business. I think that's pretty far outside the realm of understanding."

"Once again, you've been under a great deal of stress these past few weeks."

"I wish it was that simple."

She patted my arm. "Just don't be so hard on yourself."

"I'm pretty sure the train has already left the station on that one."

"Then try to get it rerouted," she replied with a wink.

After Sylvia left me in the bathroom, I pulled myself together to go do my farm calls. When I returned, I found the water was back on. I didn't know whether to laugh or cry at the fact.

With my stress level out of the roof, I polished off a bottle of wine with my Lean Cuisine dinner and then passed out shortly before eight. I slept like a log until a bellowing clap of thunder sent me shooting straight up in bed. Disoriented, I peered around the bedroom. My gaze fell on the glowing blue numbers of Papa's archaic alarm clock. It was just after one. Before I could settle back down on the bed, a frantic banging came at the door. It was coupled with an incessant ringing of the doorbell.

"What the hell?" I muttered as I threw back the comforter. Staggering out of bed, I lumbered out of the bedroom and down the hall to the front door. I couldn't imagine anything good coming from someone banging at my door at one in the morning during a hellish storm, so I grabbed Papa's Colt out of the foyer table drawer.

After taking the safety off the trigger, I pointed it at the front door. "Who is it?" I called.

"It's Declan."

What the fuck? "Excuse me?"

"Please, Peyton, open the door. I need your help."

I let the gun drop to my side before taking a step forward. In that moment, I really wished I hadn't fallen asleep in my tank top and panties. Throwing a glance over my shoulder, I wondered if I had time to run back to the bedroom to grab my robe. "Peyton?" Declan shouted, his voice holding a desperation I wasn't accustomed to.

Fuck it. After furiously working the locks, I swung the door open. A gasp escaped my lips at the sight of him. It wasn't his drenched form that was so shocking, but it was more that his face and clothes were covered in blood. "Oh, my God! What happened?"

"Cam's dog, Moose, got out of the fence earlier tonight. Before I could find him, he got hit by a car. I'm afraid to risk taking him to the emergency vet hospital since it's an hour away."

At my momentary hesitation, he jerked a hand through the soaked strands of his hair. "Look, regardless of what's happened between us, could you please think about Cam? He loves that stupid dog more than anything in the world. It will kill him if something happens to him. And..." Declan winced. "Please, Peyton, I can't let him down anymore."

I shook my head at him. "My hesitation wasn't about not treating him."

"It wasn't?"

"Of course not. It's more about the fact I don't have an adequate trauma center at the office. He's more than likely going to need surgery, and I might not be able to save him."

"Just do whatever you can."

"Okay. I'll try." Not wanting to waste a minute, I spun around and deposited the Colt on the table before grabbing my coat off the hook. After I threw on my coat, I opened the closet door and grabbed one of Papa's medical bags. "Let's go," I replied after slipping on a pair of tennis shoes.

Declan and I sprinted down the porch steps and down the walkway to his car. Instead of climbing into the front beside Declan, I slipped inside the backseat. I grimaced at the sight of blood covering the leather seats. "Can you turn on the inside lights?"

"Yeah, one sec."

Moose was a chocolate lab whose sad, soulful eyes stared into mine. "Hey there, Moose. You can take it easy now because I'm going to get you all fixed up," I said as I gently patted his head. When I dropped my hand to let him smell me, he gave me a friendly lick.

As Declan pulled out of the driveway, I reached into my medical bag and took out my stethoscope. I needed to know as much about Moose's condition as I could before we reached the clinic. Whenever an animal was hit, time was of the essence. I had no idea how long it had been since he had actually received his injuries.

I slid the silver disc of the stethoscope onto Moose's chest. His lungs seemed to be expanding well. The fact he didn't have any shallow breathing was a good sign. Although his heart was beating faster, it wasn't racing. "Your heart and lungs sound good, Moosie boy," I pronounced to him and for Declan's sake.

When I met Declan's gaze in the rearview mirror, he cocked his brows at me. Any other time it might've been comical that he wanted confirmation in case I was lying for Moose's benefit. "Yes, they honestly do sound good, and it's a good sign for shock caused by internal bleeding."

A flash of relief came over Declan's face. After wrapping my stethoscope around my neck, I grabbed one of the pen sized flashlights out of Papa's bag. Once I pried open Moose's mouth. I peered at his gums to see if they had changed color. "His gums aren't pale or blue, so that's also a good sign."

I deposited the flashlight back into the bag. "Okay, Moose, I'm going to turn you over just a bit to take a feel of your insides."

Thankfully, Moose didn't whine or appear to be in pain when I palpitated his organs. Outwardly, there didn't appear to be a lot of internal swelling. Both of those meant he wasn't experiencing any dangerous hemorrhaging. When I got to his back haunches, I saw large, gaping lacerations that could've been made by the grill of a car. "Ah, that's the issue."

"What?"

"He has some pretty deep wounds on his back legs. The one on his right leg is a little too close to his femoral artery for my liking."

"What does that mean in layman's terms?"

Right. Sometimes I tended to lose myself in medical jargon. "If I don't get the artery closed, he could bleed out."

Declan banged his fist against the steering wheel. "Fucking hell."

"Hey now. I need you to keep it together for all our sake's. You are driving after all."

"Sorry," he gritted through his teeth.

We rocketed into the clinic's parking lot on two wheels. I guess I should have been grateful we made it at all considering Declan's erratic driving in the last ten minutes. He'd barely put the car in park before he was out the door. As he gently lifted Moose into his arms, I exited on the other side. I ran ahead to unlock the clinic and turn off the alarm. I then began flipping on lights as Declan swept through the door with Moose.

He fell in step behind me and followed me down the hallway through the door of the surgical anteroom. When we got inside the OR, I motioned to the table. "Put him down there."

After easing Moose down, Declan turned to me. "Now what?"

"I go to work, and you wait."

"Are you sure you don't need my help?"

I shook my head. "It wouldn't be good for you or for Moose."

With a reluctant nod, Declan bent over and kissed Moose on the head. "You're in good hands, boy. Just be strong and pull through, okay?" After scratching behind Moose's ears, Declan started for the door. When he reached for the handle, he stopped. Whirling around, he pinned me with a determined look. "Pey, no matter what happens with Moose, I just want you to know that tomorrow morning I'll pause the Main Street improvement. There are things I can't change, like with workers' contracts and whatnot. But I can halt what's happening in the building next to yours and eventually stop it."

My eyes bulged. "You will?"

He nodded. "I know my word probably doesn't mean much to you, but you have it."

With my throat constricting, I couldn't speak. It was too hard to find the words to describe the jangled emotions inside of me. There was elation and gratitude. Not to mention the extreme shock I was feeling. Instead, I merely blinked at him.

When I didn't respond, Declan said, "Right. Anyway, I'll let you get to work." He jerked a thumb at the door. "I'll just be out in the hallway."

"Okay," was all I could reply.

As soon as Declan was out the door, I mentally slapped myself to get my wits about me. I didn't have time to stand around pondering the implications of Declan giving up on the deal. I had a patient to care for.

After shrugging out of my coat, I threw on a pair of scrubs from the closet before getting down to business. Without a tech present, it was down to me to gather the necessary tools and supplies. Once that was done, I scrubbed my hands, donned my face and hair mask, and slid on my rubber gloves. Then I got down to business.

The first thing I did was knock Moose out. As soon as he was pain-free in la la land I started working on cleaning his wounds. With the beam from the operating room light, I could see where he had a slight nick in one of his arteries. Most likely, it accounted for a large part of the blood he had lost.

I sutured it up and then repaired the wound area as best I could. Moose would need a skin graft to properly close the area, but it would have to stay open until a tissue bed could form, which would take a few days.

With the surgery complete, I slid a blanket under Moose to help transfer him from the operating table to a gurney. After easing him into the recovery bay, I turned my attention to cleaning up. But then it hit me that Declan was probably about to have a nervous breakdown.

For once, I allowed myself to forgo proper procedures for the sake of a patient's family. When I opened the exam room door, I didn't see Declan in the hallway at first. My gaze dropped, and I found him slumped in the floor, his head in his hands. "Declan?"

At the sound of my voice, he shot to his feet. His wild eyes met mine. "Moose?"

"He came through just fine."

Pinching his eyes shut, Declan wheezed out a breath before falling back against the wall. "Thank God."

"Now he's not totally out of the woods yet. Since he lost a lot of blood, I'm going to need to get some of his type from the emergency clinic so I can do a transfusion. Because he needs a skin graft, there is the risk of infection, which could lead to sepsis. However, at the moment, I don't think there's any reason why he won't pull through."

When tears sparkled in Declan's eyes, I felt a tug in my chest. I couldn't remember the last time I had seen him cry. He'd sadly always subscribed to the toxic masculinity idea that men who cried were weak. I had to admit how much fatherhood had changed him if he was willing to weep over a dog.

After grinding the tears out of his eyes with his fists, Declan gave me a sheepish grin. "If I give you a hug, will you promise not to deck me?"

Oh wow. Declan wanted to put his arms around me. I wasn't quite sure if I was really ready for that. "Um, I'll try."

He chuckled. "Well, it's the best I could do considering I'd offer to buy you a drink, but this is Hayesville, not Atlanta, so everything is closed."

Holding up my hands, I replied, "It's okay. There's no need for any of that. I was just doing my job."

He quirked his brows at me. "We could grab breakfast at the Waffle House."

The one staple of twenty-four-hour dining in the South was the chain of Waffle Houses, and Hayesville actually had one. Although there were a million reasons why I should have told him no, I found myself nodding. Maybe it was because I always devoured a massive meal after surgery. I think the adrenaline had something to do with it. Tonight, or I guess I should say this morning was no different. Just the mention of food sent my stomach growling. "Um, sure. That sounds good. Moose should be pretty comfortable from the anesthesia for another hour or two."

Declan beamed at my agreement. I couldn't imagine why the simple act of buying me breakfast would make him so happy, but I was too tired and too hangry to question it. "Great. Can I see Moose before we go?" he asked.

"Sure."

Declan followed me through the door of one of the examining rooms and then into the kennel where I'd set up Moose in the recovery bay. While I cleaned up, Declan pressed his hands against the cage and spoke softly to Moose in a sweet sing-song voice. Although he was woozy as hell, Moose did thump his tail.

Glancing over at me, Declan shook his head. "When I first saw him collapsed in the yard, covered in blood, I thought he was a goner."

"I'm sure at first glance it did look that way. Thankfully for Moose, his injuries were primarily external in nature. Had he experienced a tear in his diaphragm or a broken back..." I sighed. "We might not have had the same outcome."

"Thank God for small mercies, huh?" Declan mused.

"Yes. Very much so."

He smiled. "And for talented vets."

Warmth flooded my chest at his compliment. I could read the true sincerity in both his tone and his eyes. "Thanks," I murmured.

Then it seemed the moment was broken. "Come on. Let's go get some artery clogging Waffle House food."

I laughed. "Okay."

Chapter Eleven

After turning on the alarm and locking up, I followed Declan to his truck. When I opened the door, I was surprised when the metallic smell of blood didn't hit my nose. Instead, it was the cloying scent of one of the cleaning products we used in the clinic.

Declan met my gaze across the front seat. "I hope you don't mind that I borrowed some cleaning stuff. I was about to lose my mind pacing around, so I decided I needed something to do."

"Of course, I don't mind."

I climbed up into the truck as Declan cranked up. Hayesville's Waffle House was just outside of town near the interstate ramp. We drove along the empty streets in silence. In my mind, I went back to the countless times I'd ridden shotgun in Declan's truck. My thoughts went straight for the gutter when I thought of the many times we'd had sex in the bed of his truck. Ducking my head, I stared out the window.

When we pulled into the parking lot of the Waffle House, it was pretty abandoned, which made sense since it was just after three in the morning. Just a few commercial trucks were scattered in the spaces. As we started inside, Declan rushed ahead of me to open the door. It was a nice and somewhat surprising gesture. Sure, he'd done the same thing when we were dating, but that was ages ago. Not to mention the fact we weren't still a couple.

After we slid into a booth, a waitress appeared with her notepad in hand to get our drink orders. "I'll take a large coffee, two creams, please," I said.

At Declan's grin, I furrowed my brows at him. "What?"

"Ten years have passed and you still order your coffee just the same."

"Some things never change when it comes to my coffee."

Tilting his head at me, he said, "What are the odds you're going to order a waffle, an order of extra crispy bacon, and hash browns with cheese?"

Damn him. How did he possibly remember my Waffle House order? Part of me wanted to get something differently just to spite him, but my growling stomach won out over me being petty. After I plopped my menu behind the napkin container, I said, "I like the same food. What's it to you?"

He shrugged. "Nothing. You always were a creature of habit."

The waitress glanced between us. "Y'all wanna go ahead and order your food?"

Somehow I'd forgotten she was standing there witnessing our exchange. "Yes, please," I said before repeating the foods Declan had rattled off earlier.

"Be right back with your drinks," the waitress said.

Declan grinned at me. "Remember how we used to always come here after the football games?"

I nodded. "I think the waitstaff ordered extra for Friday nights since they knew half of the school was going to be here."

"My favorite times were when we'd go back to my house after we ate for a midnight trail ride with the horses."

"Try an eleven o'clock ride. My weekend curfew was midnight, remember? And that was only senior year."

With a laugh, Declan replied, "How could I forget? Your daddy put the fear of God in me to always have you back on time."

"What did you expect from a minister?"

"That's true." A wicked look flashed in Declan's eyes. "Of course, he never would have dreamed what we managed to do before midnight. Especially that summer after junior year."

Warmth flooded me at his words and the memory of our nocturnal activities. But I didn't want Declan to know that. "I'm pretty sure he would have lost his religion if he'd known I lost my virginity that summer."

"It was more my fault since I finally wore you down."

Rolling my eyes, I replied, "You didn't wear me down. It was my decision, and I made it in my own time."

"Yeah, well, considering what a horndog I was, I'm sure I was an ass about it sometimes."

"Actually, you weren't."

Declan furrowed his brows at me. "I wasn't?"

"I always remember you being very patient with me and respecting that I wanted to wait until it felt right."

"And it did feel right that first time, didn't it?"

His words sent a rush of warmth over the top of my head and down to my feet. It seemed to pool between my legs. In spite of my physical reaction, I couldn't help feeling surprised he was bringing this up now, and it wasn't just because we were at the Waffle House. It was because of the emotional shit-show that had transpired between us. Regardless of what all went down, it didn't erase how special that first time was. I'd loved him and he loved me, and we'd sealed the deal by making love. I hated that he might doubt what my feelings had been like then.

Before I could respond, the waitress returned with our food. As I was pouring syrup onto my waffles, I felt Declan's stare on me. When I looked up at him, I smiled. "Yes. It did. Regardless of how everything else turned out, the first time was special."

Surprisingly Declan's expression was very tempered. I'd imagined he might go on a typical male ego trip with my comments. "I remember being nervous as hell."

"Why? You'd already had sex." At the remembrance of how he lost his virginity at fifteen to Shay O'Briant—who was a senior when we were freshmen, I wrinkled my nose.

"Still hating on Shay, huh?"

"No. I wasn't."

Declan chuckled. "Yeah, you were."

"You didn't answer my question."

"Why was I nervous? Because I wanted to make your first time amazing. All I ever heard was how important losing their virginity was for girls. That's why I didn't want it be skeezy like in the back of a car or at a motel or something."

"Sneaking off to Papa's hunting cabin wasn't skeezy?" I countered with a grin.

"If he had been there, yeah, it would have been."

"Thankfully, it was the off season, and we didn't have to worry about him or any of his buddies showing up to bag a deer."

In that moment, I was swept back in time to the summer I'd turned seventeen. When I'd packed my overnight bag, I still wasn't a hundred percent sure I was going to have sex with Declan. With our one-year anniversary coming up, it made sense. Besides, I was merely a technical virgin since we had partaken in everything but the full enchilada.

But when I'd stepped into the one room cabin that was basically one rung below glamping, I knew I wanted to be with Declan more than anything in the world. Yeah, it sounds totally romantic, doesn't it? Seriously, in that moment, it could've been a five-star hotel suite, and I would have felt the same way. And it was by candlelight in a way—the lanterns made it cozy and romantic.

But what had mattered most was what had transpired after we finished. As we lay there tangled in each other's arms, Declan had stared intently into my eyes. "I'm going to marry you someday."

My adolescent heart had almost exploded right out of my chest. "And I'm going to marry you," I'd breathlessly replied.

The sound of plate breaking jolted me out of the past. I stared past Declan to where our waitress was picking up the pieces. Shaking my head, I replied, "It was nice."

He stared intently at me. "Yeah, it was."

Under the heat of his gaze, I focused on the food on my plate. After a few moments of silence and chewing, Declan asked, "What made you save Moose?"

The scrambled eggs I swallowed lodged in my throat. I reached forward for my water and took a large gulp before replying. "I'm a veterinarian—it's my job."

Shaking his head, Declan countered, "Not in the middle of the night when you're off the clock and certainly not for a man who you've experienced past and present bad blood with. You could have told me to go on to the emergency clinic, and I would've deserved it."

I'd never imagined having to answer that question, least of all that Declan would've asked it. I narrowed my eyes at him. "Jesus, I know a lot of shit went down between us, but do you really think so badly of me that I would turn an injured animal away?"

"Fuck, Peyton, that's not what I meant. The last thing in the world I would want is to insult you." We were both tired, and I knew what he meant when I stopped to think about it. He looked so apologetic that I felt I needed to let him off the hook for that one.

"Moose didn't choose his owner," I replied diplomatically.

The corners of Declan's lips quirked up. "Touché."

"You're the one who asked."

"I know."

I slid my fork through the river of maple syrup. "In spite of my resolve to always care for injured and sick animals, I had other reasons to help you."

"What were those?"

Oh boy. I was really going to go there with him. "I know it was you who sent me all of those care packages in college."

Declan's smile faded. "How did you find out about that?"

"When your mom brought me a casserole the other day, I thanked her for sending the packages, and she had no idea what I was talking about. Then she told me it had to have been *you*."

"Yeah, I sent them."

"Why?"

He furrowed his brows at me. "Why? Because I felt like doing something nice for you."

An exasperated laugh bubbled from my lips. "After jilting me at the altar?"

"Can you think of a better time?" he countered.

"I suppose not. But why sign your parents' names? Why not just say it was from you?"

"Once again, I knew you too well. I wanted you to enjoy the stuff, but I knew there was no way in hell you'd ever accept the package if you thought it was from me."

He had a point. If I'd known the goodies were from him, I would have probably lit them on fire before sending the ashes back to him. "You're right."

"I think you forget I know you almost as well as you do."

Pinching my eyes shut in frustration, I shook my head. "I just don't understand how—"

"How I could be nice and thoughtful when you've always painted me as the worst villain ever?"

"Oh you *are* the worst, but that's not what I meant."

"Then what?"

"Why didn't you just try to talk to me?"

"For starters, you changed your number."

Well, he had me there. "Yeah, well, that wasn't my doing."

"Wait, what?"

"My parents changed my number. And no, it wasn't to keep you from calling me. It was about everyone else." I shook my head at the memory of the incessant ringing, and the overflow of voicemails. "Although their hearts were in the right places, there was no way in hell I was going to heal if I had to relive what happened over and over every day."

"I'm sorry you had to go through that. I'm also sorry I didn't try harder to get in touch."

Instead of letting him off the hook, I replied, "I suppose you could have written a letter or sent an email."

Declan exhaled a ragged sigh. "The truth is I really wasn't ready for all that."

"But you were ready to spend fifty or a hundred dollars a month shipping my favorite snacks to Georgia?" I countered.

"Like I've told you before, I was a stupid, immature kid. Somehow in my frame of mind, I saw the care packages as some sort of penance. Like it was worth more than just a few words."

In the end, it hadn't been worth it. Sure, I'd felt cared for believing they were from Pauline, but to know he'd sent the packages as a form of penance did nothing but make me angry. There was nothing he could have done to make things better. *Nothing.*

"No, Declan. You might think it was a form of penance for you, but it wasn't. You ran. You never attempted to face me and apologize. You could have at least tried to talk to me."

Declan quirked a brow at me. "Says the girl who spent ten years refusing to come home so she didn't have to see me."

With a scowl, I replied, "Touché."

"You're right, Pey. I should've moved heaven and hell to track you down to apologize. There's no excuse, and I can offer nothing more than my apology."

"And I accept it." At Declan's look of surprise, I replied, "I really do."

"I'm so glad." Tilting his chin at me, he asked, "What was the other reason you helped Moose?"

"Cam."

Declan swallowed hard. "You were thinking of him too?"

"I know how much pets mean to kids growing up. Then I also thought of what you said about how he had been through enough and you didn't want to let him down again."

Declan's expression saddened. "No. I couldn't bear the thought."

"How have you let him down?" I questioned softly.

"Because I couldn't keep Mommy at home with him—with us."

Oh God. My chest constricted in agony at both Declan's words and anguished expression. Shifting my plate out of the way, I leaned forward on the table. "From what I've heard, you aren't the one to fault for his mom leaving."

With a mirthless laugh, Declan replied, "I would've thought you of all people wouldn't be so naïve."

"I'm not."

"Come on, Peyton. I couldn't keep her happy or satisfied, so she left. How is that not my fault?"

"Was it my fault you jilted me at the altar?"

Declan winced. "Jesus, did you have to bring that up? I promise you I can't crucify myself for that anymore."

I shook my head. "That's not why I'm bringing it up. It wasn't my fault you didn't show up and marry me, Declan. It was *yours*. Just like your wife leaving for another man is all on her, not you."

"I wish I could see it that way."

"Give it a few years and countless hours of therapy and maybe you'll see things differently."

"Is that what happened with you?" he questioned.

"Yeah, it is. I should probably be pissed at the amount of money I spent to have someone get me to see the obvious."

Declan nodded. "It is the truth. There wasn't a damn thing you did that chased me away. It was all me."

"If you can see that, then maybe you'll see it's not your fault with Bailey."

"I wish it was that easy. Hell, when we started getting serious everyone told me she wasn't the marrying kind."

"Then why on earth did you marry her?"

"She got pregnant with Cam."

"Oh, I see," I murmured. Inwardly, my mind was screaming HOLY SHIT! For some reason, it was oddly comforting hearing Declan hadn't married Bailey because he was madly in love with her. It had been out of obligation. It was also incredibly frustrating since I'd wasted years wondering what it was about *her* that made him want to commit when he hadn't wanted to commit with *me*.

As if he could read my mind, Declan said, "Regardless of Cam, I did love her. In a weird way, I think I looked at her with some savior complex."

Oh. "You wanted to save her?"

He exhaled a ragged breath. "She doesn't come from families like we do, Peyton. She'd known nothing but upheaval and abuse. She was partying and drinking heavily when we started dating. I thought somehow I could be the one to get her to stop drinking and go back to college."

"That's an admirable way of thinking."

"It wasn't just about Bailey—it was about me. Somehow I thought by helping her I could atone for what happened with you."

Utterly stunned, I could merely blink at Declan. "You were thinking of *me*?"

"Yeah." A sad smile quirked his lips up. "Regardless of who I was with, I always thought of you."

This was the moment in an old movie the movie heroine might have dramatically rested her hand against her forehead while calling for some smelling salts. His admission had actually left me feeling faint. It still felt uncomfortable having him mention *who he was with*. But, I would have been surprised had he stayed celibate. Declan must've read my shock because he said, "Don't act so surprised."

"Trust me. I'm not acting."

"Come on, besides growing up together, you were my first love— the woman I planned to marry. How could I not compare other women to you?"

I shrugged. "I guess I just thought when you jilted me, you were done with me."

"No one who has ever met you could ever truly be done with you, Peyton. You're far too special for that."

Holy. Shit. He really was pulling out all the surprises. There was something to be said for middle of the night confessions. "Thank you."

Leaning forward in his seat, Declan tilted his head. "What about me? Did you think of me?"

Silly man, of course, I thought of you. I feared every single man I remotely cared about was just going to leave me in the end. I erected steel walls around myself that no man could possibly get through, which resulted in me being thirty and single. I've allowed myself to believe I would never find true love, and it's all because of you.

Those were all the things I wanted to say to him, but I didn't. Vocalizing that to him would have revealed my vulnerability, and I couldn't let him have that. Not again. "Yeah, sure."

My clipped response sent Declan's brows rising. "Why do I think that's your diplomatic response since we're in public?" he joked.

"Please. I would give you the same response regardless of where we are."

"Hmm, I call bullshit."

"Seriously? You do remember I kneed you in the balls at the funeral home."

Declan chuckled. "That's true." He wadded up his paper napkin and tossed it onto the table. "I think I'll refrain from asking just what you thought of me."

I grinned. "That's probably a good idea."

"I'm not sure you want to know where my imagination could go."

At the waggle of his brows, I rolled my eyes. "Rest assured there were none of those thoughts." Yes, I was totally lying through my teeth on that one, but he sure as hell didn't need to know that. He would never let me live it down.

"Fine. I won't tell you whether I had those thoughts about you."

An annoying part of me couldn't help being curious by his last remark. Considering I hadn't thought Declan capable of any kind thoughts about me post jilting, I certainly wasn't imagining him fantasizing about me. "I think I'll be okay with the mystery."

Shaking his head, Declan reached for his wallet. "Come on. I better get you home."

I threw a glance at my phone to check the time and groaned. "I'm going to be feeling this in the morning."

"You and me both." Grimacing, he replied, "We're getting old."

"Speak for yourself," I countered as I slid out of the booth.

"We're the same age, and we're both getting old."

"Thirty is hardly old."

"It feels like it somedays."

As I breezed through the Waffle House door, I threw him a teasing grin. "Some of us age faster than others."

"Are you trying to say I look old?"

"No. Not at all."

"You don't sound too convincing," he grumbled.

"Fine. Is this better? Declan, you don't look a day over twenty-nine," I mused.

"Always a smart-ass."

"Some things never change, huh?"

His scowl softened into a smile. "No. I don't suppose they do."

We made the drive back to my house in silence. Thankfully, it was more of an exhausted silence than an awkward one. So much had transpired since he had shown up on my doorstep hours earlier. It felt like a lifetime instead of a few hours.

After pulling into the driveway, he put the truck into park. "So, you think Moose is going to pull through, right?"

I nodded. "It'll be touch and go, but like I said before, I think he has a good chance. Then we have to wait and see how his body adjusts to the skin grafting process."

Declan ran a hand over his face. "What should I tell Cam?"

"The truth."

Shaking his head, Declan countered, "He's four for fuck's sake. How do I tell him there's a possibility Moose might die?"

"It's better than the alternative of lying to spare his feeling and then things going wrong." I gave him a pointed look. "How could he ever trust you after that?"

With a ragged sigh, Declan said, "You're right." He shifted in his seat. "You know when you decide to have kids, you only focus on all the good things you're going to do. Like how you'll teach them how to play football and swing a bat. Reading to them at night and taking them to Disney and to see Santa. You don't ever stop and think about the tough spots. Like how do you possibly begin to explain that dogs die and Mommies leave, but none of it is their fault?"

At the anguish burning in Declan's eyes, I averted my gaze to my lap. "I wish I knew."

A mirthless laugh bubbled from his lips. "I'm starting to get why Mom and Dad used to always say kids should come with instruction manuals. I sure as hell could use a parenting one."

"I think you're being too hard on yourself. At the end of the day, you're doing the best you know how to do." Turning in my seat, I once again faced Declan. "I know I only spent like two minutes with him at the funeral home, but he seems like a great kid."

Pride radiated in Declan's eyes. Probably not from my comment of his parenting abilities, but my compliment of Cam. "I appreciate that. Even if he is mine, he's pretty damn amazing. Smart as hell. Mom's been working with him on his sight words." At what must've been my blank look, Declan added, "The words that will get him ready to read."

"That's wonderful. He probably got a lot of his dad's intelligence."

Declan snorted. "Since when was I ever that intelligent?"

"You graduated with honors from high school remember?"

"I seem to remember someone else was valedictorian."

"We're not talking about my accolades right now, thank you very much."

"Fine. I guess I wasn't a total dumbass. Especially for a jock."

"Once again, you're not giving yourself the credit you deserve. You're a successful businessman in town with a gorgeous, smart kid." I nodded at him. "I know it might be hard, but you have a lot to be grateful for."

The intensity of his stare made me shiver slightly. I wished it was simply the air conditioning being on full blast, but it was much more than something so simplistic. It had been a long, long time since Declan had looked at me the way he was looking at me now. Although the years had changed me from the girl I was then, I still experienced similar feelings as I had a decade ago.

"Thanks, Peyton. That means a lot," Declan murmured.

"You're welcome." Motion caught my attention out of the corner of my eye. At the inquisitive glance of my neighbor in his running gear and headphones, I knew it was past time I got out of the car.

Peering through the windshield, Delcan asked, "Is that Bruce Daughtry?"

"Yeah, even though he's retired, he still gets up at four a.m. to run before going into work at five."

After throwing up his hand, Bruce jogged past us. I had the sneaking suspicion that by breakfast, most of Main Street would've heard that Peyton Beasley was sitting in the car with Declan St. James at five in the morning. The town gossips would have a field day imagining that we were coming home from some sexual tryst.

"Anyway, I'll talk to you tomorrow." When I realized what I had said, I quickly added, "You know, to update you about Moose."

Declan smiled. "I'll be waiting."

I momentarily fumbled with the doorknob before hopping down from the truck. As I started up the walkway into Papa's house, I felt Declan's eyes on me. Even though I was tempted to turn around, I kept my gaze firmly ahead. It was only after I slipped inside the house, that the truck began backing out of the driveway.

We hadn't fought.

That was the most prominent thought running through my head. We hadn't fought. In fact, we'd been civil. It reminded me of the many conversations Declan and I had before. Yes, we made out *a lot*. And yes, once we finally did the deed, we were at each other any moment we could get. But we were also best friends. He'd been the one I confided in about everything. And that was causing a riot in my head. I'd lost so much when our relationship had ended. I'd felt empty for so long without his friendship. *Bereft.*

With my emotions jangled and my mind spinning with Declan-centric thoughts, I pitched face forward onto the mattress before falling into a deep sleep.

Chapter Twelve

When my alarm went off the next morning, I groaned before burrowing deeper under the covers. After arriving home, I'd debated just staying awake since I'd need to be up at six. But exhaustion won out and I'd collapsed in the bed. Now two hours later, I wanted nothing more than to stay in bed all morning.

After dozing through one snooze alarm, I finally dragged myself to the bed. One quick shower and a quick cup of coffee later and I was out the door. Since I wanted to check on Moose, I skipped my breakfast stop at the Main Street Café and grabbed a totally unappealing protein bar out of my console.

When I got into the recovery bay, my heart leaped at the sight of Moose wagging his tail. "Hey buddy, I figured you might be whining to let me know it was time for more pain medicine."

He responded by licking my hand through the cage. "Why don't we try to get a little water into you as well as some drugs to keep you comfortable?"

I fed Moose some water with a syringe and then administered an injection of penicillin Once he was resting, I fired off a quick text with a picture to let Declan know how he was doing. With Moose sorted, I went to my office to see what was on the morning's schedule. "Two feline ball snips and some well checks," I murmured as I read the computer screen.

By seven-thirty, the office started coming alive with the arrival of Sylvia, the front office manager, Carly and Ansley the two vet techs, and last but not least, Hank Kisick. After briefing them on what had happened the night before with Moose, it was time to go to work with my patients.

The morning stayed slammed. When I finally had my first free moment of the morning, I plopped down in my office chair to update charts and reports. I'm not sure how long I was engrossed in my work before the phone beeped at my desk. "Dr. Beasley, you have an owner waiting for you in the lobby with a question," Sylvia said.

I furrowed my brows at the phone. Most owners addressed their questions at appointments, so I wasn't sure what it could be about. Fearing the worst, I braced myself for a potential dressing-down by an unhappy client.

When I opened the door to the lobby, I was shocked to see Declan standing there. It wasn't so much his presence as it was his son Cam's. Instead of staring shyly at me like he had at the funeral home, he wore a desperate, pleading expression.

Declan shot me a sheepish look as he stuffed his hands in the pockets of his khaki pants. "Hey Peyton, I'm sorry to interrupt you, but Cam has been insisting I bring him to see Moose." Tilting his head at his son, he added, "I told him it might not be possible for him to go back."

As I chewed on my bottom lip, I glanced from Declan to Cam. My heart ached at the sight of his tear-stained faced. "You're missing your friend, aren't you?"

Cam nodded. "I need to tell him hi."

At Blue Pearl, we didn't allow children under ten in the recovery area. But this was my clinic now, and I could bend the rules where I saw fit. "Okay, you can go back for just a few minutes if you promise to be very quiet. Moose needs his rest. The more rest he gets, the faster he can come home to you."

Cam's face lit up. "Really?"

I smiled at him. "Yes, you can."

Tugging on Declan's pants leg, Cam exclaimed, "Come on, Daddy! Let's go see Moose!"

"Easy now, Buddy. We need to listen to what Dr. Beasley says."

Rushing over from his father, Cam enthusiastically took my hand in his. "I'm listening, Doc."

The touch of his hand sent a jolt through me. Both the feeling and Cam's reaction took me by such surprise I momentarily froze. Cam tugged on my arm. "Come on, Doc."

Shaking myself out of my stupor, I replied, "Right. Yes. Let's go see Moose."

I led Cam through the waiting room door with Declan on our heels. As I started down the familiar hallway, Cam turned his head left and right, taking everything in. When I opened the door to the kennel, hearty yips and barks, along with a few meows, filled the air. "Why isn't Moose in one of those?" Cam asked as we passed by the boarding kennels.

"Well, Moose is a very special patient here, so we have him in a very special place."

"Oh. Okay."

When we entered the recovery bay, Moose's ears immediately perked up. He turned his head and pressed his nose against the front of the cage. Cam dropped my hand like a hot potato to race over to him. "Hi Moose, it's me, Cam," he said. Moose's tail immediately began thumping at the sight of his human. "How ya feeling?"

Declan joined me at my side. "He's looking a lot better."

"He really is. I think the blood transfusion is really helping as well."

Peering at me over his shoulder, Cam asked, "When does he do his crafts?"

I cut my eyes over to Declan. "Crafts?"

"I think he means the skin grafts."

"Right. Yes, that would make sense." Giving my attention to Cam, I replied, "Probably on Thursday."

Cam nodded. He then turned back to Moose. "You gotta get better, boy. Okay?"

Moose's response came in the form of licking Cam's fingers. "That tickles," Cam giggled.

"All right. You've seen how he's doing. Now I need to get back to work, and you need to get back to preschool."

Cam's face fell. "But I want to stay with Moose."

"We've talked about this, Cameron."

"No! I wanna stay!" Cam demanded.

"But you can't," Declan bit out through gritted teeth.

Trying to diffuse the impasse between father and son, I quickly said, "Moose has to get his beauty rest so he can feel good to come home to you. Why don't I send your dad several photo updates today of Moose? Maybe you guys can even Face Time this afternoon."

Excitement danced in Cam's eyes while Declan's brows shot up at my suggestion. "You'd really do that?" he questioned.

"Of course."

"That's really above and beyond," he replied, his voice choking off a little.

Wanting to lighten the tense emotions of the moment, I waved a dismissive hand at him. "Don't worry. I'll add a photography package to your bill."

Declan snorted. "I'll be sure to look for it." He held out his hand to Cam. "Come on, son. Let's let Moose get his rest and Dr. Beasley back to work."

"Okay." After taking his father's hand, Cam grinned up at me. "Thanks, Doc."

At his cheeky grin, I couldn't help smiling back. "You're welcome."

"Seriously, Peyton, I can't thank you enough for today, last night." Declan once again appeared to choke up. "For everything."

Although I could have argued I was just doing my job, I realized it was pointless. Even though he had hurt me badly, Declan knew my character. I would have reacted the same to attending to any pet if the same thing happened to someone else.

But, the feeling of rightness wouldn't have been present. The feeling that I wanted to make sure that *Declan's* little boy didn't have to face another heartbreak. Because I knew Declan's character. *He hated other people hurting because of his actions.*

Hence the care packages.

Hence the breakfast.

Hence his unrestrained appreciation.

It wasn't hard to look into that little boy's eyes and not feel some-thing. No words could adequately express what it had been like when he'd held my hand, looking up at me with such trust even though I was essentially a stranger. And right now, as Declan looked at me—*again* —as if *I was* someone remarkable, it was hard not to feel my heart softening toward him. *He was a good man.* He was a good man. And as long as it was only my head that thought that, my heart would remain completely safe.

Chapter Thirteen

I'd done a lot of things for my four-legged clients and their owners over the years. Holding up my phone to one of the recovery bays where Moose could both see and hear Cameron was a definite first. Of course, it was hard to discredit the positive effect it had on Moose. The sound of Cameron's voice had him immediately perking up before thumping his tail appreciatively.

Of course, FaceTiming meant talking to Declan. I'm not sure why things still felt slightly awkward, but they did. Maybe it was because I didn't know what to do with all my displaced anger. Maybe it was because we were blindly feeling along to rebuild and redefine who we were to each other. It couldn't have possibly been because I suddenly found myself attracted to him again.

After wrapping up the Face Time with Cameron, I closed up the office and headed down the street to the café. For the last few weeks, Becca and I had been meeting up for dinner a few nights a week when Anthony was on call. Most of the time we cooked, or I guess I should say she cooked, and then other nights we met at the café.

When I breezed through the doors of the café, Becca was waiting on me in one of the booths. I bypassed the hostess and headed over to sit down. "I'm glad you could finally join me," she good-naturedly chastised.

I held up my hands. "My apologies. I was just about to head out the door when Declan called for Cameron to Face Time with Moose again."

Becca pursed her lips at me. "You're Facetiming with Declan?"

Scowling, I replied, "No. Cam and Moose are Facetiming since he's going to be at the clinic for a few weeks for a skin graft. Declan and I are just facilitating the calls."

"Mm-hmm," Becca murmured.

I snatched up a menu. "What's that supposed to mean?"

"It just seems that you're seeing a lot of Declan lately."

"Well, duh, that's somewhat a necessity since I've been treating his dog."

"Mom said the other day the two of you were out to the wee hours of the morning together."

Shooting Becca an exasperated look, I replied, "Yes, because Moose was hit, and I had to operate on him."

"And then you went to the Waffle House with him."

I opened my mouth to argue but then closed it back when I realized she had me. "Surgery makes me hungry," I finally replied.

"Mm-hmm," she repeated.

"Would you stop with the 'mm-hmms' and just say what you really want to say?"

She grinned. "I think someone might've finally forgiven Declan St. James."

"Did Mom tell you that?"

She shook her head. "No. She only told me about you saving Moose, and that he took you to breakfast. I made the assumption you had forgiven him after you didn't inflict any bodily harm to him."

"Surprisingly, I haven't even been tempted."

Becca clapped her hands together before bringing them in front of her mouth. "Oh, Pey, you really have forgiven him, haven't you?" she said almost dreamily.

"Yeah, I suppose I have." As I said the words aloud, I realized it was the first I'd really acknowledged the momentous occurrence to anyone else. The last twenty-four hours had been such a whirlwind of emotion, and I'd been so busy that I hadn't had a chance to process it all.

"You know I'm going to need details."

With a shrug, I replied, "I'm not sure what there is to tell. We had a really good talk over waffles. Seeing him open and vulnerable made me remember the reasons why I'd fallen in love with him. At the same, he showed me the caring and compassionate man he's grown into."

"Took you long enough," Becca murmured.

Tossing my menu to the table, I replied, "Yeah, yeah, I'm a stubborn ass. The thing is I didn't just stop hurting overnight, so I think it's fair that I can't forgive overnight, too."

"Yeah, I know. I guess, I'm just proud you can admit it."

"Me too. It also didn't hurt that he's going above and beyond to cease the development next door to the clinic."

"Wow. That's huge."

"It is."

The waitress arrived and took our order. After she left, Becca placed both her palms on the table and leaned in. Her expression turned serious. "You can't imagine how thankful I am to hear you're moving on from all your Declan baggage."

Tilting my head at her, I replied, "After that last statement, I can't help thinking there's something pretty heavy you're about to say."

"You're right."

"And?" I prompted.

"There's someone I want to fix you up with."

My eyes bulged. "Yeah, I think that's going to be a big no."

Becca wagged a finger at me. "Oh no, you promised me when you first moved back to town you'd let me fix you up."

Shit. I had said that, hadn't I? At the time, I'm pretty sure I'd been okay with it, and I hadn't been uttering it under some sort of duress.

In my silence, Becca said, "You haven't been out one time since you moved back."

"I've been busy getting settled in here, not to mention taking over at the practice," I countered.

"You need to get out."

"I will. Just not now."

Shaking her head, Becca replied, "Nope. I'm not accepting that reply."

"Fine. I'll get out."

"But?"

"But what?"

"You'll get out but under what circumstances?"

"Look, when I really think about it, I don't need you to fix me up."

"I would disagree."

"No offense, Becs, but I've managed to do just fine all these years without your help."

"Okay, let's for a brief moment entertain the thought of you taking matters into your own hands. How are you possibly going to meet someone? You need to get out somewhere besides my house or the clinic."

"I come here every morning for breakfast. Does that count?"

Becca wrinkled her nose. "Not unless you're wanting to hook up with someone our parents age."

"It's more than just the senior set at breakfast."

"Come on, Pey. It's just a little set-up. If you meet him and hate him, you never have to see him again."

"That is such a lie in a small town. I will still have to see him—at the dry cleaners or the grocery store."

"Seeing someone socially is not the same thing as seeing them romantically."

"It can be just as disastrous if the date doesn't go well."

"Just work with me here, okay?"

My shoulders drooped in defeat when I realized Becca wasn't going to let this go. "Fine."

Her dark eyes lit up at my declaration. "I have the perfect person."

Oh, I'm sure you do. "Do tell."

"His name is Tripp, and he teaches sixth grade at the school. Not only is he really easy on the eyes, but he's knew to Hayesville so he doesn't know anything about your past."

Snorting, I replied, "My *past*? Way to make me sound like a whore or something, little sis."

"You know what I mean."

Sure, I knew it was Declan and not my alleged promiscuity she was referring to, but at the same time, it still sounded seedy. "Do I get to see a picture of this perfect Tripp who didn't grow up here?"

I'd barely finished my question before she was flashing her phone in front of my face. As I focused on the screen, a handsome blonde-haired, blue-eyed guy smiled back at me. "Cute," I replied.

"I know, right? If I wasn't married to Anthony, I would be all over him like a bad rash."

With a groan, I replied, "That has to be the worst analogy ever. Like, seriously, it sounds like you have an STD."

Becca waved her hand dismissively before taking her phone back. She gave Tripp one last seemingly lustful gaze before turning back to me. "When I told him about you, he was really interested."

"Did you show him a picture?"

"Yeah, but he was already interested before I did."

I'm sure he was. Considering how visual most men were, I could only imagine his interest hadn't been truly piqued until he saw my picture.

"Okay, he's cute, and I'll go out with him. Now what?"

"Great. Send him a text."

"Seriously? Like that won't seem odd or anything?"

"I told him I was meeting you for dinner tonight, and you'd text him if you were interested."

"All right. You can give me his number and—"

"Text him now."

"Can't I wait until later?"

Becca shook her head. "Nope. I want to see you do it."

"You're really pulling out all the stops to make sure I can't get out of this, aren't you?"

"Damn straight," Becca replied with a grin—the one I called Papa's Grin.

"Fine," I grumbled as I picked up my phone. "What's the number?"

"678-252-8643."

After typing in the digits, I scrolled down to the message box. My fingers hovered over the keys as I debated what to say. Nibbling on my bottom lip, I typed, *Hey Tripp, it's Becca's sister, Peyton. I'm just texting to see when it might be convenient for you to meet up.*

"Could you be more formal?" Becca asked.

I jerked the phone away from her area of vision. "This is not a booty call where I just put in an eggplant emoji. Besides, I've never been one of those people who can't text in complete sentences."

Becca snorted. "I'm surprised you managed not to use a bunch of pretentious words like you usually do."

At the mention of my vocabulary, Declan flashed before my mind. No one had ever good-naturedly teased me as much as he had. The thought made me smile. It also caused uneasiness to prick along my spine. Like I was doing something wrong thinking about Declan while I was texting another man.

The ding of my phone caused me to jump. "Ooh, he's texted back!" Becca screeched in my ear.

"You know it could be someone else," I replied as I tried scooting away from her to save what was left of my hearing.

"Oh, I just know it's him."

Peering at my phone, I clicked on the text bubble, which was Tripp. "*Ice House Fri Nite 4 drinks?*" I read aloud.

"See he knows how to be succinct."

"Nice word choice there."

She winked. "I learned from the best." Jerking her chin at the phone, she said, "Hurry up and reply."

As I stared at Tripp's response, I shook my head. "I'm not sure I like the suggestion of drinks."

"Why not?"

"It's too noncommittal."

"But it's still a date."

"Don't you remember that scene in *Sleepless in Seattle* where Tom Hanks is explaining how it's better to ask someone on a first date to drinks because you can get out of it easier if it's not going well?"

"If I remember correctly, he also says if it's going well you can ask them to dinner."

"What kind of dinner would it be at the Ice House?"

Becca winced. "True."

"Ugh, I'm not so sure about this."

"Look, even if it's just for drinks, you need to get out." She tapped the screen of my phone. "Text him back."

"Let me guess. I should just write, 'K'?"

Laughing, Becca replied, "Yes."

After typing in a lone k, I said, "There. It's done. Are you happy?"

"Deliriously so."

Although exasperating in the matchmaking department, I seriously loved my sister. She wanted nothing more than for me to be as blissfully happy as she was in her marriage. It was equal parts endearing and irritating.

My phone dinged with Tripp's eloquent reply of *C u Fri*. Smirking, I replied, "I certainly hope he'll be speaking in complete sentences by Friday. I'm obviously not fluent in text-speak."

Rolling her eyes, Becca popped a fry into her mouth. "Har, har." She rubbed her hands together. "Now let's plan on what you're going to wear."

I groaned at her suggestion. "Seriously? Are we back in high school? I haven't consulted with anyone on what to wear on a date since college."

"Yeah, well, you weren't here for me to advise you back then, so I think we need to make up for lost time."

"Way to give me the guilt trip."

The waitress returned to clear the plates. "Would you like any dessert?"

As Becca shook her head, I replied, "Yes, I'd like a slice of the chocolate cake please." I gave Becca a pointed look. "I'm going to either need chocolate or booze to get through the rest of this conversation."

"Then try the Kentucky Bourbon pie instead." She waggled her brows. "You get the best of both worlds."

Grinning, I said to the waitress, "Sounds good to me."

"I'll be right back."

As the waitress went to grab my pie, Becca tilted her head at me. "I bet you've got a few sexy numbers in your closet that you used to wear out in Atlanta."

"While I may have some, I don't think they'd be appropriate for the Ice House."

"Are you insinuating it's a backwoods establishment?"

I gave her a pointed look. "I grew up here, remember? While the

Ice House might've been after my time, I'm pretty sure I wouldn't wear
the same outfit there as I would somewhere in Atlanta."

"Fine. Just promise me you'll at least change out of your scrubs
before you go."

"I'll try."

"Somehow I'm afraid you really won't."

"Well, I can't make any promises."

"You know it might make Declan jealous if he was to hear about
you dating someone."

I straightened up at the mention of Declan. "What are you talking
about?"

"You know exactly what I mean."

"No. I don't think I do."

Becca pursed her lips at me. "Come on, Pey. Admit it. There's still a
part of you that has feelings for Declan, and I don't mean feelings of
revenge."

My eyes bulged at the very insinuation. "I most certainly do not."

"You do know there's nothing wrong with having feelings for him."

"Of course, I do," I muttered as I twisted my linen napkin in
my lap.

"You're single, and he's separated and about to be divorced. There's
really nothing stopping you."

"Except the epic baggage of our past."

Shrugging, Becca replied, "Everybody's relationship comes with
some sort of baggage. It's how the two of you choose to handle it is
what matters."

"I don't know, Becs. It's a lot to overcome."

"You don't know until you try. And I have a feeling you want
to try."

"The truth is I am feeling something for Declan—I just don't know
what. The way we were able to talk and laugh last night was just like
old times." The corners of my lips quirked. "It felt good."

"Then continue fostering the relationship. See where it goes."

"Fine. I'll be more open-minded."

"In the meantime, you can be focusing on some of the other fish in
the sea by going out with Tripp."

I tossed my napkin at her. "You just don't give up, do you?"

"Nope."

After the waitress returned with my pie, I waved my fork at Becca. "I was going to offer you some of this, but this conversation negates the need for me to consume the entire thing."

With a laugh, she replied, "You might need another slice after we tackle how you're going to do your makeup."

I speared a hunk of the pie onto my fork. Gazing at the gooey, chocolate goodness, I groaned, "I don't think there's enough pie in the world!"

Chapter Fourteen

On Friday, I left work around five-thirty and headed home to get ready. After showering, I stood before my closet door debating about what to wear. First dates were always tricky, especially blind ones. You didn't want to look like you were trying too hard while at the same time, you didn't want to look like you'd just peeled yourself off the couch after a Netflix binge.

I finally decided on a pair of dark skinny jeans, a dressy sweater, and some low heels. Once I was dressed, I did my makeup before putting a few waves into my hair with my straightening iron. After turning left and right in the mirror, I nodded my head in satisfaction.

When I got into my car, I turned on some thumping rap music to try to get me in the zone. I'm not exactly sure why I needed gangsta rap music before a date, but something about it always tended to put my mind at ease. As I made my way to the Ice House, I inevitably had to pass by the road where Declan grew up as well as Roy Wallace's pasture.

The close physical proximity to him caused my mind to wander to thoughts of Declan. Since it fit my fantasy better, I imagined him being with Cam. Maybe they were tearing down the trails on four-wheelers or riding through the overgrown grass of the pastureland. Afterwards, they'd sit down to a big Southern meal around the mahogany dining table at Robert and Pauline's.

Of course, my thoughts had to torture me with images of him on a date with someone who looked like his receptionist. They were probably at a beer tasting at a hip new brewery. Declan wasn't a fan of wine, but maybe for this chick, he would be truly selfless and take her to a winery. Then they'd have passionate, mind-blowing sex in front of a floor-to-ceiling fireplace.

Rolling my eyes, I muttered, "Would you get a fucking grip?"

I then shook my head and tried to free myself of any thoughts of Declan. I was heading to my first Hayesville date—my first post Declan's redemption date. My dating life had been shackled and chained by his memory for far too long. It was a new day, and Tripp was a new man.

After parking the car, I grabbed my purse and headed inside. The Ice House had come to Hayesville after my time in town. A lot of businesses had sprouted up during my absence. While it was styled in the same vein of a Taco Mac, it appeared more of the Southern staple of a honky tonk—pool tables, a bar, the potential for fist-fights, and parking lot sexcapades.

When I walked up to the hostess stand, a barely twenty-one-year-old coed with a Hooters-esque uniform, asked, "Can I help you?"

"Yeah, I'm here to meet someone."

"Peyton?"

"Yes."

The hostess nodded. "He's at the bar."

Well, alrighty then. I'm not sure what that said for Tripp that he couldn't wait for me in the lobby to arrive before he hit the booze. I hoped it was because he was nervous and not because he was a closeted alcoholic. Mind you, wasn't it basic courtesy to meet a date at the door rather than expect them to find you? Maybe backwoods manners were different than city manners. *Whatever. I'm here. Let's get to this date to get Becca off my back.*

As I walked towards the bar, my eyes scanned the occupants. There were a few couples along with a cluster of men watching ESPN. Finally, I spotted Tripp sitting at the end of the bar away from the crowd.

"Tripp?" I questioned.

He whirled around on the stool. After he did a quick head to toe appraisal of me, a megawatt smile curved on his lips. "Peyton. It's so nice to meet you."

Tripp thrust out his hand, and I shook it. He then motioned to the stool next to him. "Please. Have a seat."

"Um, sure." I would have much preferred getting a table or booth. *Stop being such a hard-ass and go with the flow.*

"What would you like to drink?"

"I'll just take a vodka cranberry for the moment."

He nodded before waving the bartender over. "Another Heineken for me and then a vodka cran for the lady."

As the bartender went to fill my order, Tripp leaned in closer on his stool. "You know, your sister didn't tell me how hot you were."

Um, okay, Mr. Skeezy. "No. I don't suppose she would have," I answered diplomatically.

"I mean, she showed me a picture on her phone, but I really didn't know if I could trust her. Especially after I couldn't find anything much about you on social media."

"I'm not much of a techie girl."

He waggled his brows. "Or you like to keep your dirty secrets offline."

Right. I now appreciated the fact it was just drinks and not dinner. Not to mention I had a feeling it was going to be a two or three drink night. Instead of worrying about staying sober, I would just call Becca so I could cuss her out in person for fixing me up with such a lowlife.

"How long have you been teaching?"

"Five years total, but this is my first year at Hayesville Elementary."

I smiled. "Like I tell Becca all the time, teaching is such a noble profession, and I totally admire the job you guys do."

"Yeah, I mainly went into education because I wanted summers off and to coach."

I didn't think Tripp's statement would go on any motivational teaching posters. "So, you're into sports?"

Tripp nodded. "I love them all, but I played baseball in college. I'm the new head baseball coach at the high school."

"Good for you."

"Thanks. I'm hoping some of the hags in the history department at the high school hurry up and retire so I can take one of their positions."

Oh, you charmer, you. "Are you a history buff?"

"No. I just hate how whiny and needy the younger kids are." *Jesus, Becca, did you even speak five words to this moron?*

"Uh-huh," I replied before downing a huge gulp of my drink.

"Enough about me. Becca said you're back in town from Atlanta because you're taking over as the town vet."

"Yes, I am."

His expression soured momentarily as he reached for his beer. "I honestly don't know how you do it. I've never much cared for animals myself."

What in the hell? What could have possibly been going through Becca's mind to fix me up with someone who didn't like animals? That was like the ultimate deal-breaker when it came to dating me. While being a vet was just my day job, there was also the fact I adored animals and questioned people who didn't.

"You don't like dogs or cats?"

"Not really. All the feeding and cleaning? It's just too much to put up with."

"Hmm, if you're not up for taking care of a domestic animal, I bet you're not down for having children, huh?" I teasingly asked.

His eyes bulged. "Who said anything about children?"

"Well, no one. I was just making a correlation between the two."

"That's a fucking huge leap to make, not to mention a major assumption to make about someone." Before I could argue that my intent hadn't been bad, he reached for his wallet and fished out a twenty. After tossing it onto the bar, he rose off his stool. "I think it's best for both of us if I go ahead and bounce. Have a lovely evening."

And with that, he stormed off, leaving me staring open-mouthed at his retreating form. I blinked a few times while fighting the urge to pinch myself to see if it had all been a dream. "What the fuck just happened here?" I muttered under my breath.

"A total prick," the bartender answered.

"You can say that again."

It took a few seconds to recover from the ridiculousness. Shaking my head, I reached into my purse to dig out my phone. After I dialed

Becca, she answered on the third ring. "You are so dead," I pronounced.

"Wait, what? Why are you calling me on your date?"

"I'm not on a date anymore because he just stormed out of here, which was probably a good thing considering it was the worst date humanly possible."

"Was he really that bad?"

"Becca, I love you dearly, but I'm not sure how you managed to so cluelessly fix me up with an animal loathing narcissistic douchebag!"

"Seriously? He's always so nice at school."

"Um, hello, narcissists have the innate sensibility to always deceive people."

"Are you trying to say I'm easily manipulated?"

"It's more like Tripp is very good at what he does."

"All my teacher buddies thought he would be such a good fit with you."

"Last thing I'm going to say about it is sleep with one eye open, little sis."

"Ugh. I'm sorry it was that bad. Anthony has a fellow cop he'd loved to fix you up with."

"Nope. Nada. Ain't happening. No more fix-ups. When I'm ready to date, I'll find someone myself."

"Fine. But you're missing out."

"I'm willing to take that chance."

"Where are you now?"

"I'm still at the bar finishing my vodka cranberry. The one I'm paying for myself because my shitty fix-up only paid for his before he left."

"No way. He didn't even pay for your drink?"

"Oh, I'm sure he would say it's my fault because I dared to bring up the c-word. Children."

"Well, he's not getting any more of my breakfast casserole at the weekly potluck."

"That's right, sis. Hit 'em where it hurts."

Becca laughed. "Hey now, you seriously underestimate the jackass's love of my casserole."

"The hash brown one or the spinach and egg one?"

"The spinach and egg."

"Yeah, that one is really good." The bartender came over and raised his brows at my almost empty drink. "No. I'm good, thanks," I told him.

"I should let you go and enjoy your drink. Maybe take a look around."

Groaning, I replied, "I know exactly where you were going with that statement."

"Can't blame me for trying."

"Good night, Becca."

"Night, Peyton."

After I ended the call, I picked up my glass. I'd just taken a swig when the sound of bellowing cheers caused me to almost fall off my stool. Glancing over my shoulder, I saw a group of men coming in from the poolroom. Their jovial expressions and celebratory nature made me think they were all together for a bachelor party.

When I turned back around, I waved the bartender over for my check. "I better get out of here before things get too crazy with the Bachelor Party."

"Actually, it's a divorce party."

"A what?"

"One of the guy's divorce was final today, so they're partying."

I rolled my eyes. Leave it to men to have to celebrate the severing of the old ball and chain. After paying my bill, I hopped off the stool. I threw one last wary glance at the crowd of thirty-something men. And then my heart stopped.

It was Declan.

Chapter
Fifteen

Christ almighty, could this night get any worse? Declan must've felt someone looking at him because he swept his gaze up and met mine. A warm smile curved on his lips before he threw up his hand in greeting. As I waved back, I debated whether I should walk over to speak to him. Before I could make the decision, he came to me.

"Good evening, Dr. Beasley."

"Good evening to you."

Sweeping his arm towards the bar, he asked, "May I buy you a drink?"

"That's very kind of you, but I think I'm the one who owes you a drink." I jerked my chin at the group he had just left. "Especially since you're here to celebrate."

"Yes. Bailey finally signed the divorce papers."

"I assume congratulations are in order since you're now a free man."

He grinned. "Yes, I am. Well, as free as one can be who has full custody of a four-year-old."

"But that's what you wanted, right? I mean, it's the best thing for you and for Cam."

"Yes, it is. Of course, I didn't want any of this for him, but I'm glad to know I'm the one calling the shots from now on out so I can make sure he's put first and everything is in his best interests."

"I'm sure you will do an amazing job."

"Really?"

Nodding, I replied, "I know I'm not a parent yet, but I can tell a good one when I see one." I smiled at Declan. "He's very lucky to have such a devoted dad."

Declan's jaw clenched and unclenched before he responded. "That means a lot."

"You're welcome."

Wanting a subject change, Declan asked, "What are you doing here?"

With a roll of my eyes, I replied, "Finishing up a blind date that will go down as the Top Five worst dates I've ever had."

"Damn. That sucks."

"You have no idea."

"Who was it?"

"Tripp Neighbors."

Declan winced. "You're joking, right?"

"Unfortunately not."

"Why in the hell would you want to go out with a douchebag like that?"

"I didn't. My sister, who I will be maiming later this evening, fixed us up."

With a shake of his head, Declan replied, "He's been living here probably five months, and he's already managed to make a name for himself."

"Apparently, Becca didn't get that memo."

"Oh, I'm sure she didn't. Neighbors is one of those smooth-talking pricks who snows most women. All the teachers at the school just worship him. I guess I should say all the female teachers. All the men know what he is."

"Women can be so stupid," I grumbled.

Declan laughed. "I would have to agree with that one." Winking, he added, "Present company excluded."

"Why thank you," I replied with a smile.

"So that the evening isn't a total loss, why don't you join us?"

My mouth dropped open in surprise. "You're inviting me to your divorce party?"

"Sure."

Glancing past him, I eyed the men in his group. "Somehow I don't think my presence would be appreciated." I gave him a pointed look. "It appears to be a dude thing."

"While it is predominantly male, it is my party, and I can invite who I fucking want."

"I suppose that's true."

"You'll get to see a few of the old crew."

I wasn't entirely sure I wanted to see any of them, nor would they be overjoyed to see me. The guys who were part of our crew were the same guys who were going to be groomsmen in our wedding. "Who is it?"

"Steve and Dustin. Josh said he might drop by later."

"Yeah, I haven't seen them in forever."

After throwing a quick glance at the group, Declan said, "I think they're the only ones you'd know. The other guys are friends from work."

"Not Hayesville peeps, huh?"

Chuckling, Declan replied, "No, they're from Adairsville."

"I see."

After taking me by the arm, Declan led me over to the men. "Hey guys, is it okay if someone else joins us?" Declan asked while I held my breath. When a riotous cheer went up over the crowd, I started to breathe again.

"She's not here for entertainment, is she?" a lanky guy asked while wagging his brows.

I gasped in horror as Declan's expression turned stormy. "Hell no. Why would you even suggest that?"

Lanky Guy shrugged. "It's a divorce party. I thought we might be celebrating with a stripper."

"This is the Ice House, not the Pink Pony," Declan argued.

Motioning to my attire, I replied, "Correct if I'm wrong, but do strippers usually wear this much clothing?"

"Just more to take off."

Turning to me, Declan said, "Ignore him."

"Will do."

A ripped guy with a shiny bald head jerked his chin at me. "Welcome to the party. I don't think I caught your name."

"I'm Peyton." At the admission of my name, silence echoed back at me. With all eyes on me, I shifted on my feet. I was starting to feel like Tripp wasn't going to be the worst thing about this evening.

Snorting, one of the other guys said, "Holy shit, dude. What are the odds you'd find another girl with the same name as your ex?"

Someone groaned while another guy said, "That is Peyton, you dumbfuck."

"Oh," he murmured.

"Guess my reputation precedes me, huh?" I quipped.

"It's nothing bad about you, I promise," Declan replied.

Smiling warmly, Baldy said, "Fuck no. We're all aware of what a giant prick he was to leave you on your wedding day."

The other guys all nodded in agreement, which caused nervous laughter to bubble from my lips. "Good to know."

Shifting on his feet, Declan said, "Right. Why don't I introduce you guys now?"

"Sounds great."

Lanky Guy was actually Bryan, and he was a mortgage specialist who worked with Declan on some of his business projects. Baldy was Neil, and he and Declan had met through an Equestrian club. I tried keeping up as he rattled off the rest of the names.

"And these two jokers need no introduction," Declan said as Steve and Dustin started coming towards us.

It was hard to remember a time when I hadn't known Steve Pappasian or Dustin Jones. We went all the way back to elementary school. When I started dating Declan, we'd shared the same lunch tables and hung out together almost every weekend. Dustin was the strong, silent type who had been a tight-end on the football team while Steve was the jokester who was always getting in trouble in class.

At the sight of me, their jovial expressions momentarily faltered. I could always see the WHAT THE FUCK blaring in their minds. But they quickly recovered to plaster on welcoming smiles. "Peyton, I didn't think we'd be seeing you here," Steve said as he reached over to hug me rather than shaking my hand.

"Neither did I." At his furrowed brows, I replied, "I just escaped a hideous fix-up."

Steve winced. "Those are the worst."

Not the touchy-feeling type, Dustin merely patted my upper arm in hello.

"Give me a minute to grab a drink, and then I want to hear what you've been up to the last ten years," Steve said.

"Um, okay."

"Can I get you anything?" Dustin asked.

"No, thanks. I'm good."

"Another club soda for you, D?" Steve asked.

When Declan nodded, I guess I couldn't hide my surprise because Declan asked, "What?"

"I'm sorry. I thought you were celebrating."

"I am."

"Then why are you not drinking?"

"I gave it up a long time ago."

Shock reverberated through me. Back in the day, Declan had been known to put more than just a few beers away. He was the first person I ever got drunk with. "You really don't drink anymore?"

"Nope. Not a drop."

"Then why the hell are you celebrating your divorce in a bar?"

Declan chuckled. "That's because of the crew. I was planning on spending tonight at home, watching crime dramas on Netflix after Cam went to bed, but they dragged me out."

"Okay, I know it's really none of my business, but I have to ask. Is it because of Cam you stopped drinking?"

"Actually, I quit because of what happened between the two of us."

The room began to spin slightly, and I had to fight to keep myself upright. It was almost unfathomable that I had somehow had a hand in him making such a monumental decision. "You did?"

He nodded. "I was drinking way too much in those days. I realized it probably attributed to my lack of good decision making. So, I walked away."

"Wow...I don't know what to say."

"Congratulations is always nice," he replied with a wink.

A nervous laugh bubbled from my lips. "You're certainly to be praised for having the strength to give up a vice like alcohol. I can't even begin to imagine how hard it's been dealing with all the divorce stress without drowning your sorrows."

"I won't lie that it's been hell. I find myself at the gym a hell of a lot more than I used to. Not only am I not drinking, but I'm in the best shape I've been since high school."

My gaze trailed down his incredibly cut body. *Oh my, yes, I can see that.* "That's a much healthier way to let off steam."

"Thanks."

We were interrupted when Steve reappeared. After plopping his empty solo cup on the table beside us, he cocked his head at me. "Peyton, would you do the honor of dancing with me?"

"I thought you wanted to talk about what I'd been up to all these years?"

"It's called multitasking. We can dance and talk."

I laughed. "I think I left my dancing shoes back in Atlanta."

"Bullshit. Besides, you totally owe me a dance from back in the day."

I furrowed my brows. "I do?"

"I know you promised me one or two, but instead, Declan selfishly kept you all to himself."

"Yeah, asshole. She was my girlfriend," Declan replied.

Steve rolled his eyes. "You act like I was going to spirit her away to some dark corner to seduce her when it was just a measly dance in the high school gym surrounded by our peers."

"That wasn't the point at all. I didn't want anyone dancing with her but me."

"Then why aren't you dancing with her now?"

Glancing between Steve and me, Declan sputtered for a moment before replying. "She's not my girlfriend."

"Exactly. She's free to dance with me."

As Steve waggled his brows, a laugh bubbled from my lips. "Fine. Let's dance."

"Jackpot!" Steve held out his hand to me. After I slipped mine into his, he dragged me out onto the small dance floor. The DJ was already in the middle of "Strawberry Wine" when Steve wrapped his arms around my waist and drew me against him. With my arms around his neck, we started swaying to the music.

Jerking his chin at Declan, Steve said, "He really doesn't like me dancing with you." When I glanced over his shoulder, I saw Declan's glowering face.

"I can't imagine why."

Steve grinned at me. "And I can't imagine why since he knows he has nothing to worry about."

"Because we were always just friends?"

Steve chuckled. "I know you've been gone a decade, Pey, but surely even you know I'm gay."

I gasped. "Wait, what?"

"Oh, come on. You're really surprised?"

"But you always said you were in love with me."

"And with you taken by Declan, I was off the hook about dating any other girl."

"Pretty ingenious."

With a wink, Steve replied, "I like to think so."

"Do you have a partner?"

"I do. We're getting married next year."

"That's wonderful. Congratulations."

"Thank you." Glancing past me, Steve blew a kiss at Declan. "You don't have anything to worry about, man," he called.

Declan glowered at him. "I didn't say I did."

"No, but you're going to need Botox if you don't stop wearing that frown."

"Fuck you," Declan called.

I shook my head with a smile. "Ten years later and the two of you are still giving each other shit. Some things really never change."

"You're right. They don't." Dipping his head, Steve whispered into my ear, "Just like Declan's still in love with you."

I jerked my head back to stare at him. "E-Excuse m-e."

"You heard me."

"Yeah, well, I hoped I was hallucinating...or maybe you were."

"Bullshit."

"What?"

He shook his head. "You want him to still be in love with you."

"Are you try to say I'm petty, and I want revenge on Declan by having him still in love with me?"

"That's not it at all."

"Then what?"

His breath tickled my earlobe. "You're still in love with him."

A cold panic pricked over my skin hearing the words come from Steve's lips. It was one thing to lie awake at night and have those thoughts running through my mind or ponder it with Becca. However, it was quite another to have someone else say it.

Overwhelmed, I wanted nothing more than to escape to the bathroom to try and get ahold of myself. As I started to push out of Steve's embrace, he tightened his hold on me. "What the hell are you doing?"

"Making you face reality."

"Let me go."

"Will you just hear me out? This is for your own good as well as his."

"I'm sorry, but how is holding me against my will good for me?"

"I don't want you trying to run away like you did ten years ago."

Scowling at him, I countered, "I didn't run away. I left for school and then I started a new life."

"You and I both know that's a load of shit."

"Okay, fine. You're right. I did run away from my life here in Hayesville."

"I'm glad you can admit it."

"Fine. Now will you let me go?"

Steve's expression grew serious. "He needs you, Peyton. You have no fucking idea the number Bailey's done on him."

He was right. I only saw the effects that Declan allowed me to see. But a best friend like Steve would be privy to far more. "I can't begin to imagine how hard it's been since she left him and Cam." I shook my head sadly. "No man could ever be worth leaving my child over."

"It wasn't just one man."

"What are you talking about?"

Disgust flashed in Steve's blue eyes. "She was fucking half the town behind his back."

Bile rose in my throat. "She was?"

"We told him not to marry her. I knew she was the kind of woman who was only out for what she could get. She played him not only for his money, but for his heart."

For years, I would've snapped back that Declan didn't have a heart after what he did to me. But that wasn't the truth. That was my anger talking. But it was part of why I had been so angry. Even when he was not yet a man, Declan had a good heart. He helped those who needed it by giving his time or his money. When I thought about it, I could see why Bailey had played him. But why did he fall for her in the first place? And what did she really get out of it—

"She trapped him, didn't she?"

Steve nodded. "She told him she was on birth control."

"She never really loved him," I stated more for me than for him.

"No. She didn't. I'm not even sure she ever loved Cameron either. He was just a means to an end to get the lifestyle she wanted."

Tears pricked my eyes at the thought. How could anyone not love that precious child? "God, she's a monster."

"So you see what I mean about Declan needing you."

"I'm not sure it's me who he needs."

"Come on, Pey. You were the only woman he ever truly loved."

He's the only man I've ever truly loved. "Of course, I'll be here for him." I stared pointedly into Steve's eyes. "As a friend."

"You are so full of shit."

"I am not!" I protested.

"Frankly, both of you are full of shit. You've already wasted ten years. How many more years is it going to be?"

"We just repaired our relationship two days ago. Give us a minute to catch our breath." *And just the thought of opening my heart to Declan again scares the ever-loving hell out of me.*

I jumped at the sound of Declan's voice. "Is everything okay?"

"Yeah, why?" I replied.

"You two seemed pretty intense."

Steve winked at me. "Just reliving some of the glory days." His arms dropped from my waist. "Maybe the two of you would like to relive some?"

"Oh, I don't—" Declan and I started to protest in unison, but Steve didn't give us a chance. Instead, he backed away from me. "Just take a turn or two around the floor."

The song changed over to Willie Nelson's "Help Me Make It Through the Night", and I inwardly cursed. I'd been hoping for a fast song, so Declan and I didn't have to get all hugged up. There was also the fact we had a history with the song. Or I suppose I should say his dad had a history. I couldn't remember a time when I hadn't been riding in Robert's truck where he didn't have Willie Nelson on.

As we stood there staring at each other, I nibbled on my lip. "We don't have to if you don't want to."

"No. I don't mind if you don't."

I shrugged. "Okay.

He reached out for me, but then his hands momentarily hesitated. Drawing in a deep breath, I took a step closer to him. The air whooshed from my body as Declan slid his hands around. His touch was electric and sent memories ricocheting through me.

"*I don't care what's right or wrong...*" Willie sang as my somewhat shaky hands swept around Declan's neck, my fingers curling through the hair at the base. I'd pulled and tugged on the silky blond strands many times in the past. I'd raked my fingernails through his scalp when he lay his head in my lap while we watched television.

We stood immobile for a moment as we stared into each other's eyes. I'd forgotten just how blue his eyes were. How the dimple in his cheek stayed out even when he wasn't smiling. How it felt to be pressed against the hard angles of his chest.

Everything and nothing had changed in the last ten years.

"*Let the devil take tomorrow. Lord, tonight I need a friend.*"

We began moving to the music. As I swayed to the song, I pressed my cheek against his face, tucking my chin to his shoulder. It seemed like we'd echoed this same posture dozens of times over the years. There'd been all the formal dances at school like Homecoming and Prom. We'd danced on the cruise together when he'd asked me to marry him.

"You know what this makes me think of?"

I jerked my head up to look at him. "High school?"

Declan chuckled. "Actually, I was thinking of those ballroom dance classes you made me take."

Right. I'd completely forgotten about those. Or perhaps it was my mind had expunged them since I had wanted us to learn to dance for our reception. Unable to look him in the eyes, I replied, "I remember."

Declan brought one of his hands away from my waist to cup my chin. He stared into my eyes with a forlorn expression on his face. "One day I hope I can mention our wedding without it causing so much pain. I don't flatter myself to say there will never be a time when the memory doesn't cause pain, but I hope someday it will lessen."

"It has. Time has helped. Finally letting go of the past and accepting your apology has also helped." I drew in a ragged breath. "It also hasn't hurt to see you aren't the black-hearted villain I once thought you were." And that was the truth. The last few days I'd felt lighter emotionally than I had in years. Somehow our talk at the Waffle House had finally unraveled the remaining painful tethers, and I was truly free.

"You don't know how happy that makes me to hear you say that. It's truly tormented me to have caused you so much pain over the years."

"In the end, I probably could've handled it better myself."

His brows shot up in surprise. "Really?"

"I should've talked to you sooner and not held on to my grudge. I let my past cripple me in the present for far too long."

"Trust me, I understand."

With a truly genuine smile, I said, "But the two of us being able to share a dance together after all these years? How amazing is that?"

"Pretty fucking amazing." Declan returned my smile. "I hope we can share many more moments together now you're back in town."

My breath hitched at his comment. What he saying? He wanted us to hang out as friends? Or was he trying to say he wanted us to be more?

"Yeah, that would be nice," I finally replied.

"You know, after our time at the Waffle House, I'd forgotten just how much I enjoyed being with you."

I'd felt the same thing. It had reaffirmed to me once again why I'd fallen in love with him in the first place. Sure, time had changed and matured us, but that familiar spark was there. "I know what you mean."

Declan slowly shook his head. "Even after all these years, no one holds a candle to you, Peyton. No one ever has and no one ever will."

Oh God, I couldn't breathe. One minute I was fine and the next minute Declan had totally annihilated me with his words. As I inwardly screamed at my lungs to work, I stared hopelessly at Declan. I didn't know what to say...or maybe it was I didn't know if I could say what I needed to. Instead, I just pressed my face against his cheek again and held him tight.

When the last chords of the song came to an end, it was like the magic had been sucked out of our moment. The harshness of evening was back, including the fact we were at the Ice House surrounded by Declan's buddies celebrating his divorce.

Taking a step back, I let my arms drop from around his neck. "Thanks for the dance."

"My pleasure."

As we started back to his group, a voice stopped me in my tracks. "Well, well, if it isn't Peyton Beasley."

Ugh, it was Carson Hayes. If there was one way to describe him, it was smarmy. He was the epitome of Steff in *Pretty in Pink*. Not only had the town been named for his so many great-grandfather's, but his family was the richest in Hayesville. Even though we were the same age, he'd gone to boarding school over in Dalton. But on the weekends, he and his other prep school friends had hung around town.

To say he and Declan had a rivalry would be a mild understatement. I can't quite remember how it exactly started. Maybe it was before high school or maybe it started during. I just remember once Declan and I started dating, Carson always hit on me, which enraged Declan.

"Hey, Carson. Good to see you again," I lied.

An "I'm undressing you with my eyes" smile spread across his lips. I'm sure some women would've found it sexy, but it was just downright creepy to me. "The pleasure is all mine. It's been what—" He paused as his gaze flickered between Declan and me, "Ten years?"

I stiffened at the jab. "Yep. A decade."

With his eyes trailing over my body, he replied, "You've aged like a fine wine."

"That's sweet of you to say."

He flashed me a wicked grin. "I'm always sweet. You just need to get to know me better."

"I'm not sure how that would be possible considering we run in very different circles. I mean, I wouldn't have dared to assume you hung around places like this," I said.

"Shows what you know. I'm usually here every weekend."

Declan crossed his arms over his chest. "I think you forgot to mention you're the financial backer behind the Ice House."

With a smirk, Carson replied, "What can I say? There's good money in providing booze and entertainment to the masses." Lowering his voice, he added, "I suppose I should say the lower class."

Ugh, see what I mean? A pretentious bastard. "Right. Well good seeing you."

Before I could walk away, Carson reached out for my arm. With his gaze flickering between Declan and me, he said, "I didn't know you two were seeing each other again."

"We're not," Declan replied to my surprise. If anything, I expected him to be vague towards Carson about our relationship status or lack thereof. Anything to continue having one up on his old nemesis.

Carson's brows quirked. "Then what is it you're doing together tonight?"

With a shrug, Declan replied, "Hanging out."

"Is that what you call it?" He wagged his brows. "You looked pretty cozy out there."

"Fuck. Off," Declan growled.

Carson held his hands up. "Hey man, I'm happy for you. I can't imagine it's been too easy these last few months." He tilted his head. "Pretty lonely for you...and your bed."

"Excuse me. I need some fresh air."

As Declan started to walk off, Carson said, "Don't miss out on your theme song." When Declan froze, Carson said, "It makes sense a song about cheating would get under your skin considering what Bailey did."

"Wow, way to be an asshole, Carson," I bit out.

Slowly, Declan turned back around to face Carson. "Do you know the song?" When Declan didn't reply, Carson said, "It's *I Hope She Cheats*. I asked the DJ to play it just for you."

Out of nowhere, Steve and Dustin appeared at our side. Throwing an arm around Declan's shoulders, Dustin said, "Forget him, man. He's not worth it."

"Oh, but Bailey was worth it."

I gasped as I glanced between Carson and Declan. The agonized look on Declan's face told me he'd had no clue Bailey had screwed around with Carson. I'd never hated Bailey more. How? Why would she do that to Declan of all people? *Such a bitch.*

Pursing his lips, Carson said, "She was a hell of a piece of ass. Of course, married bitches usually are."

Carson's comment sucked the air out of the room. As my hand flew to my mouth in horror, Declan's fist connected with Carson's chin, sending him staggering back. When he righted himself, Carson wiped the blood off his mouth. "All right, motherfucker. You want a piece of me? You can have it."

That was all it took for Declan to launch himself at Carson. Grabbing him around the waist, Declan shoved Carson until they tumbled onto a pool table. They rolled over the top before falling to the floor. Their fists flew wildly, but it seemed Declan had the upper hand.

Steve grabbed me by the arm. "Let's get you out of here."

I jerked away from him. "I'm not leaving without Declan."

"You could get hurt."

"Oh please. I wrangle animals for a living." With those same animals in mind, I whirled away from Steve and sprinted over to the bar. "Quick. Get me a pitcher of water."

Thankfully, the bartender appeared to be on the same wavelength I was. "You better hurry up and get them to stop. The owner just called the cops."

"Seriously?"

"Do you known how much a bar fight can cost in damages?"

He slid the pitcher over to me. "Thanks," I muttered. I grabbed the pitcher and then hightailed it back over to where Declan and

Carson were fighting. Raising my arm back, I sloshed the water on the two of them. It immediately had the effect I was going for since they scrambled apart and stopped hitting each other.

As they lay there with their chests heaving, I narrowed my eyes at Carson before chucking the pitcher at him. Steve scrambled around me to grab Declan's arm. "Come on. They've called the cops."

With an agonized grunt, Declan pulled himself to his feet. As we scattered out the door to our cars, I couldn't help feeling like I was back in high school and fleeing another melee Declan and his group had gotten themselves into. Usually it was a shouting match in the parking lot of an opposing school after a football game. Just like then, I had no idea what we were doing or where we were going. All I did was blindly follow Declan.

He surprised me by leading us over to my car. As we fought to catch our breath, I glanced up at him. "You're bleeding," I lamely announced.

"No shit. I just kicked Carson's ass," Declan grumbled.

I motioned to his bloodied brow. "That looks pretty deep. I'm afraid you might need stitches."

He grimaced. "I don't have time to sit around all night at the hospital. I promised Cam I'd pick him up before bedtime tonight."

Once again, Declan was only thinking of his son, and it was so damn endearing. "You won't have to wait around all night." At his questioning look, I replied, "I'll take care of you."

"You will?"

"I can get you patched up at the clinic."

Declan nodded. "All right."

Peering into my purse, I fished my keys out. "Why don't I drive you over?"

"I can drive myself."

I rolled my eyes. "Would you stop trying to be a macho man and just let me help you?"

With a scowl, he replied, "I'm being practical, not macho."

"Just get in the car."

"Fine," he grumbled.

Chapter Sixteen

After I unlocked the doors, he slid into the passenger seat. As I was hurrying around the front of the car, the wail of a police siren pierced the air. I flung the car door open and hopped inside. I gunned the engine before stomping on the accelerator, which sent us flying out of the parking space.

Declan cut his eyes over to me. "It's a measly cut, Peyton. You don't have to drive like I'm hemorrhaging."

"Didn't you hear the police siren? I have to get you out of here."

Chuckling, Declan replied, "Aiding and abetting a fugitive, Dr. Beasley. Whatever will this do to your reputation."

"I don't care about any of that." Truthfully, I did, but I cared more about Declan's safety.

"They're not going to arrest me."

"You and Carson did a lot of damage—"

"Which I'll pay for."

My gaze flickered from the road over to his. "That's it? We just ran for our lives when all you ever had to do to avoid jail was write a check?"

He grinned. "Did you really think you were helping me evade the law?"

"Maybe."

"The place has cameras everywhere, Pey. Not to mention I just left my car in the parking lot for them to run my tag," he replied with amusement vibrating in his voice.

"Shit! I didn't even think about that."

"No, because you're a nurturer, not a law breaker."

I laughed. "I suppose I am."

"I wouldn't have it any other way," Declan mused.

When I cut my eyes over to him, my heartbeat thrummed wildly at the affection burning in his eyes. I quickly focused my attention back on the road. When we got to the clinic, I pulled around back.

As I hurried to unlock the door and turn off the alarm, Declan lumbered behind me, rubbing his side. "Nothing is broken in there, is it?" I asked as he swept past me into the clinic.

"Probably just some bruising." With a mirthless grin, he replied, "Carson is too big of a pussy to inflict too much harm on me."

"Such a man thing to say," I muttered as I started up the hall. When I realized Declan wasn't behind me, I turned around. "Where are you going?"

"To peek in on Moose and see how the graft is going."

I pointed my finger at the exam room door. "Oh no, mister. You know exactly how the graft is healing since I briefed you this morning just like every morning. Moose is going to be on the mend for a while. Once you're cleaned up, you can see him."

Grumbling under his breath, he smacked his palms against the door before pushing it open. I followed close on his heels. After turning on the lights, I motioned for Declan to sit on the examining table.

"You're joking, right?"

"Why would I be joking?"

"Because I'm not a fucking animal."

"One might argue that you are considering your behavior tonight," I teasingly replied.

"Har, har."

"Look, just humor me and have a seat, okay?"

He nodded before hopping up on the table. As he got comfortable, I got to work gathering the supplies I needed. Silence permeated the room and made me wish we were in the OR where I could at least have some music pumping in.

I rolled my supply tray over to Declan. As I slid on my gloves, I glanced warily at Declan's thunderous face. "Normally this would be where I offered the person a drink, but that's out of the question with you."

"Just sew me up, Pey, so I can get the hell out of here."

I bit my tongue to keep from snapping at him not to boss me around. I knew the pain was causing him to be less than civil. Using the antiseptic, I cleaned the blood away from the wound. "How did he get you so deep?" I couldn't help asking.

"He wears this jacked up ring on his right hand."

In my mind, I could see exactly what he was talking about. Carson had started wearing it in high school. It had a raised version of their family crest. "Yep. That would do it."

Once the area was clean, I threaded the suture through the needle and prepared to sew Declan up.

When the needle pierced his skin, Declan hissed. "Motherfucker."

"Sorry," I murmured.

"No, I'm the one who's sorry for being a pussy."

I wrinkled my nose. "Ugh, I hate that word."

Declan chuckled as I continued threading the sutures through his eyebrow. "Some things never change, huh?"

"I suppose you're alluding to how I always hated when you wanted to talk dirty about what you were going to do to my..."

"*Pussy*," Declan slowly enunciated.

"Yes, that."

"I seem to remember in the heat of the moment, it never bothered you if I talked about what I wanted to do to your pussy."

Oh, good lord. Was he seriously referencing not only my pussy, but our previous sexy times? "Seriously, if you don't stop using that word, I'm going to lose my focus and plunge the needle deeper into your skin."

"Like a dick plunging deep into a pussy?"

With a shriek, I released the needle and stepped away from Declan. "Enough!"

Grinning, he held up his hands. "Fine. I'll stop."

"Thank you." As I stepped back over to him, I pushed the thoughts of *his* dick plunging into *my* pussy out of my mind.

Changing the subject, Declan said, "Bet you never thought you'd be cleaning me up after another fight, huh?"

"No. I thought those days were over."

"For a hothead like me, they're never over."

"Who said you were a hothead?"

"Seriously, Peyton? I just went apeshit on Carson in the middle of a bar."

"Yeah, well, he deserves a lot worse for what he said to you."

Declan clenched his jaw before cutting his gaze away from mine. "The bitch of it is he was telling the truth," he bit out.

My hand stilled against his brow. I thought about what Steve had said about Bailey screwing most of the men in town. "It doesn't matter whether it was true or false. He had no place bringing it up in front of you and everyone else, least of all throwing his and Bailey's affair in your face." I snipped the remaining thread. "Talk about not changing. Carson's the same prick he was ten years ago."

"Of all the men Bailey could've fucked, why the hell did it have to be him?"

"She was a fool to cheat on you."

Regret flickered on Declan's face. "Maybe. Or maybe I wasn't giving her what she needed."

"I find that hard to believe. It's true you have your faults, but when you love someone, you love them completely."

"I'm talking about in the sack."

"Oh," I murmured.

"I mean, it would seem I wasn't satisfying her if she had to fuck half the men in town."

"I know it's been ten years, but I still remember how good the sex was between us."

Declan's eyes flared at my declaration. "You do?"

Damn me and my big mouth. "Yes."

"What do you remember?"

The look smoldering in Declan's eyes could've melted the panties right off of me.

"You always took your time and made sure it was good for me."

"How did I do that?" he prompted, his voice deep and sultry.

"For starters, you loved going down on me."

"Mm- hmm, your pussy tasted amazing." Declan's arms encircled my waist, drawing me closer to him. "What else do you remember?"

"Unlike a lot of men, you always made sure I came." Shuddering at the illicit memory, I replied, "Multiple times."

"I can still remember the way you sounded when you came—the little cries and moans."

Holy shit. Who turned the heat on in here? Sweat broke out at the base of my neck while every inch of my skin felt afire with pure lust. It felt like an inferno between my legs. I couldn't remember the last time a man had ever had me this turned on just from his words and from the way he looked at me.

My tongue darted out to lick my lips, and Declan's eyes flared. The next thing I knew he was launching himself off the gurney at me. His hands grabbed the sides of my face before he crushed his lips to mine. Ten years melted away in an instant. The moment his mouth covered mine I was back in the time before he jilted me—a time when we were blissfully in love and lust.

When he plunged his tongue into my mouth, I wrapped my arms around his back. I fisted his shirt in my hands as he massaged my tongue with his. Declan dropped his hands from my face to wrap around my waist, pulling me closer against him. From there, they continued south to cup my buttocks. As he kneaded the globes of my ass, he drove my pelvis against his crotch, grinding his need into my core. I moaned at the exquisite feeling of him even through my jeans. God, I'd missed this man. He knew every button to push on my body.

As he moved against me, I gripped his waist, pulling his shirt out of his pants. I slipped my hands under the hem of the shirt, desperate to feel more of him. I raked my nails across his spine, causing Declan to groan into my mouth.

Everything felt familiar yet new. His lips were still just as smooth as velvet like I remembered. His back was broader, and the muscles that tensed beneath my fingertips, were more defined.

Declan kissed a warm trail across my jawline as his hands dove underneath my sweater to cup my breasts over my bra. "God I've missed these."

I laughed. "Seriously?"

"Hell yeah. They're my favorite pair ever."

With a roll of my eyes, I replied, "Sure they are."

"I'm serious." His fingers delved inside my bra, cupping my bare breast. When his thumb flicked back and forth across my nipple, I gasped and arched into his hand. His lips came back to mine as he continued palming my breasts and tweaking my nipples. Although his hands were nice, I wanted his mouth on my skin.

I broke our kiss to whisk my sweater over my head. As Declan's expression darkened with lust, I reached around my back to unhook my bra. When my breasts fell free, Declan bent his head and brought his mouth over one of my nipples. My head lolled back as he suckled it deeply before flicking and swirling his tongue across it.

"Fuck, Pey. Taste so good," Declan mumbled into my breast.

He was not wrong. It felt divine. His hand kept stroking my other breast as his tongue worked the nipple in his mouth into a hardened pebble. Crying out with pleasure, my fingers automatically went to his hair, tugging and grasping at the strands as the pleasure washed over me.

Declan licked a wet trail over to the other breast before claiming the nipple. The ache between my thighs grew. As if he could read my mind, Declan snaked a hand down my stomach. His fingers feathered across my belly teasingly, causing my hips to buck. He hesitated before finally dipping them between my legs. I widened my thighs to allow him to cup my pussy. As Declan worked my clit over the fabric of my jeans, my hips arched involuntarily. I rubbed myself against his hand for more friction, soaking my panties with my need.

"Fuck me, Declan," I murmured against his lips. With frantic hands, I reached to unbutton his pants.

When I palmed his cock, Declan tore his mouth from mine. "Wait, stop."

"What's wrong?"

Easing me back, he shook his head. "We can't."

"Yes, yes, we can," I panted.

"Not like this."

"Do you want to go to my house or yours?"

Declan shook his head. "It's not about where we're doing it."

I furrowed my brows at him. "What are you talking about?"

"We shouldn't be doing it anywhere."

"I don't get it. Don't you..." *Want me?* "Don't you want this?"

His fingers gripped my chin. "I want you and this more than anything in the world. But we need to slow down a minute."

"I don't want to slow down. I want you inside me."

With a groan, Declan said, "This is not the way I want us coming back together."

I blinked at him. "You want us to get back together?"

Declan tilted his head at me. "Don't you?"

Not wanting to hang myself out to dry, I countered, "I asked you first."

Chuckling, Declan replied, "Yes, Peyton. Hell yes."

"Really? Like since I came back to town?"

"If I were honest, it would be long before then."

My heart was beating at a full gallop and threatened to burst right out of my chest. "I want to get back together with you, too. But more than anything, I want us to have sex right now."

Grinning, Declan replied, "Trust me, I know."

"Then let's go back to my house."

He took my hands in his. "Babe, I want to do this the right way."

"You always did it the right way," I teased. And the smile that graced his face was one I'd known well. *Smug.* And I wasn't lying. He really did. No other man had come close if I was really honest.

"Just hear me out for a minute."

Pouting, I replied, "Okay."

"We both know I made a lot of mistakes in the past. This time I want to do everything right. I can't help but think that taking it slow and honorable is the right way to do it."

Any other woman would find his ideals endearing. It was like he was suggesting some old-fashioned courtship. But tonight I was a horndog who desperately needed the D. "I'm thirty years old, Declan. I'm way past caring about my purity."

"It's not just about being honorable." He swept a strand of hair out of my face. "I want to romance you."

I blinked at him. "You do?" We both knew he had never been much of a romantic. It just hadn't been his thing. With his looks and popularity, he'd never had to try hard to get female attention.

Declan nodded. "I want nothing more than to show you just how much I've changed."

Although I wanted nothing more than to fuck him ten different ways to Sunday, I realized the depth of what he was saying. We'd first come together as kids. A decade had passed, and we'd become different people. It was time we got to know those people to see if we could love them as much as we did the older versions of ourselves.

Holding up my hands in defeat, I replied, "You win."

"It wasn't about winning or losing, Pey," he argued.

"Tell that to my vagina. It's feeling like a pretty big loser right now."

With a grin, Declan replied, "My apologies to your pussy."

Shrieking, I pinched my eyes shut. "Do not go there."

"Oh, but I eventually will."

My lids flew open to see his cocky smirk. "It better be sooner and not later."

"How about we wait until it feels right?" When I started to protest that everything had been feeling right, Declan placed a hand over my lips. "When it feels right *emotionally*."

"When it's right emotionally," I repeated.

Declan nodded. "Come on. I need you to take me to my car, so I can get home to Cam."

After our sexual melee, I'd completely forgotten that Declan was trying to get home. Hopping down from the table, I started furiously straightening my clothes. "Shit. I can't believe I'm going to make you late to get Cam."

"It's okay."

"No. It's not okay. He's the most important person in your world. I can't be the reason why you're letting him down."

Declan smiled. "Stop worrying about it."

When I froze adjusting my sweater, Declan eyed me curiously. "What's wrong?"

Everything and nothing. Just the mention of Cameron had sent my mind reeling with out-of-control thoughts. It was no longer just about me and Declan. Another person had been added to our relationship equation.

"You're a dad."

"Yes, I am," he said slowly like he was worried I'd suddenly lost my mind.

"We want to get back together, but it's not just about what we want. We have to consider what's best for Cameron."

Declan's brows furrowed. "Why wouldn't it be best for Cameron?"

"I don't know. Maybe he needs more time to get used to his mom being gone before a new woman shows up on the scene?"

"She's been gone almost a year, Peyton."

"Okay, but what if he doesn't like me?"

The corners of Declan's lips quirked up. "I think after you saved Moose, you're his favorite person in the whole world."

"As a vet, sure, but what about his dad's love interest?"

"My love interest? I'm pretty sure he doesn't he know what that is."

"I bet he would surprise you."

Declan cupped my face in his hands. "Would you please stop worrying? I'm pretty sure I know my kid well enough to know he isn't going to be threatened by you or not like you."

Nibbling my bottom lip, I replied, "I hope so."

"If anything, he'll be thrilled to have a mother figure around again."

"Or he could hate me because he sees me as the reason why his mom isn't coming back."

"Bullshit. His mom left and has barely seen him for eight months now."

"I just don't want to hurt him." And that was the honest to God truth. To be four years old, he'd already been through enough trauma. I couldn't bear the thought of adding any more.

"And you won't. The fact that you're putting his needs first proves that, Pey." When I started to protest, he added, "Not unless you tell him he can't have ice cream for dinner or won't let him stay up past his bedtime."

I laughed. "Oh no, I'll defer all of that to you so you can be the bad guy."

"Thanks a lot."

"That way I can stay the wonderful lady who saved his dog and never tells him no."

Declan threw his head back with a laugh. "Yeah, we'll have to work on that one."

Chapter Seventeen

When I woke in the morning, my thoughts immediately went to Declan. I couldn't help wondering if the two of us getting back together had all been a dream. I was debating pinching myself to see if it had been real when my phone dinged. Rolling over, I grabbed it off the nightstand.

It was Declan.

A smile curved on my lips as I read his words. *Good morning, beautiful.*

My fingers flew furiously over the keys as I typed back *Good morning.*

Hope you got a good night's sleep and have a great day.

My heart started beating erratically. While I was charmed at his words, it was the fact he texted in full sentences just like me that really got me. *How's your war wound?*

Nothing a little Motrin won't take care of.

Hope you feel better soon.

Thanks. Talk to you later.

Bye.

After I finished texting, I hopped in the shower to start getting ready for work. When I arrived at the café, I half expected to see Declan waiting on me, but he wasn't there. As I ate my usual morning pancakes, I kept throwing an expectant look over my shoulder.

"He's already been in, honey," Cissy said as she refilled my coffee.

Shit. Had I been that obvious? "Oh," was all I managed to reply.

With a wink, Cissy said, "He had an early morning meeting over in Helen, but he left me with strict instructions to cover whatever you wanted to eat."

My brows shot up. "He bought my breakfast?"

"Yes, ma'am. He sure did."

At the tingly feeling in my belly, I fought the urge to roll my eyes. *For fuck's sake, Peyton, it's breakfast, not a diamond ring.* "That was sweet of him," I nonchalantly mused to Cissy.

"Wasn't it? I sure wish I had a young, handsome man buying me breakfast."

"Lucky me," I replied.

With a waggle of her brows, Cissy left me with my pancakes as well as my growing feelings for Declan.

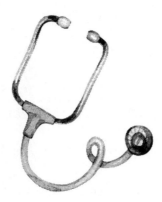

The rest of the morning was slammed with back-to-back wellness checks for some four-legged patients. It was almost two before I had a moment to sit down in my office and nibble on my lunch.

At the sound of Declan's booming voice, I jumped out of my skin, sending my salad container flying. "Good afternoon."

Rubbing my chest, I replied, "Good afternoon." I whirled around on my stool. At the sight of his face, I winced. "Ouch. That turned into a worse shiner than I thought."

"At least he looks worse."

"I'm sure he does." Winking, I added, "He didn't get my expert care last night."

"Or your sexual healing."

With a shriek, I bolted off the stool before jerking Declan inside the room. Once I closed the door, I jabbed my finger at him. "Excuse me but what happened last night was *not* sexual healing."

"Only because I stopped it."

Damn him. Scowling, I replied, "Are you constantly going to throw it in my face that you took the moral high road?"

Declan grinned. "I would say hell yes considering I'm usually in the hole when it comes to morality."

"I won't argue with that part."

Declan's expression turned serious. "You're not having second thoughts, are you?"

I eyed him curiously. "No. Are you?"

"Definitely not."

"Good." Sliding a hand around my waist, he drew me closer against him. "I would take you to dinner tonight, but I have a late meeting over in Adairsville."

"That's okay."

As his fingers drew circles at the base of my spine, he dipped his head to where his breath warmed my cheek. "Tomorrow?"

"Yes, tomorrow sounds good."

I closed my eyes in anticipation of his kiss, but then Declan abruptly pulled away. My eyelids popped open, and I stared up at him in confusion.

With a wink, he said, "I figured it was best to keep things chaste between us. I didn't want things getting out of control like they did last night."

I smacked his rock-hard bicep. "Asshole."

He chuckled before bending over to place a chaste kiss on my cheek. "I'll talk to you later."

"Don't bother if you're just going to keep being a vagina tease."

"I think you mean *pussy* tease."

Wagging a finger at him, I replied, "Oh no. Don't you dare go there."

"One day soon, I am going to go there. I'm going to jerk off your panties, spread your legs, suck your clit until you're shaking with need, and plunge my tongue deep inside your pussy. While you're screaming your orgasm, I'll be licking and sucking every drop of your arousal."

My mouth literally went dry. After fumbling for my water bottle, I took a long sip as I nodded my head at him. "Yes, you should totally do that."

With a shit-eating grin, Declan replied, "And when I finally do, you'll thank me for the exquisite foreplay of us abstaining."

"Yeah, those are *your* words. Mine would be more like, 'Why the hell did you make me wait so long for this magnificent oral attention'?"

"We'll just have to see about that."

"Sooner than later, okay?"

He grinned. "I'll try."

"You're insufferable," I replied as he started to the door. At the same time, I couldn't hide my smile. He might've been insufferable, but he was mine. Were there tiny voices asking if I was wise? Yes. But I had known Declan for a long time, and what I knew about this adult version, I truly liked already. I didn't doubt him . . . and I didn't doubt us.

Chapter Eighteen

I didn't hear from Declan again until bedtime. He called as I was watching a true crime drama on Netflix.

"You weren't asleep, were you?" he asked.

"No. I was just watching TV in bed."

"It's only eight-thirty."

"Way to make me feel old."

He chuckled. "Sorry. I thought Cam was the only one who went to bed at eight-thirty."

"I have an early morning slammed with neuters from the Humane Society."

"Poor guys. They have no idea they're spending their last night with their balls."

"Hopefully, they realize how much trouble they get into because of what's dangling between their legs," I countered.

"True. But it does make life worthwhile."

"Whatever," I laughed. "Are you home?"

"Nope. I'm stuck in the car for another half hour."

"And you thought you'd call me as a means to pass the time?"

"Way to cheapen me wanting to talk to you."

"I'm terribly sorry."

"What are you wearing?"

I shot straight up in bed. "Excuse me?"

"I think you heard me."

"Yes, but I was thinking that asking about my attire could be construed as sexual, and you have curbed anything sexual between us."

"I didn't take everything sexual off the table."

"You wouldn't even kiss me this afternoon," I countered.

"I didn't want to tempt you."

"Me? Why is this all about me?"

"I know you're more about wanting to be physical with me than cultivating a relationship."

"That's not true. I very much want to *cultivate* with you."

Declan laughed. "You know what I mean."

I blew a frustrated sigh out of my lips. "Yes, I know what you mean. The rational side of me thinks you're very wise to insist we take it slow. However, the side of me that is teetering close to my sexual prime says you're a bastard."

"I'm sorry you're frustrated. Want me to help you out with that?"

"Are you going to come by my house?"

"No. I was going to talk you through an orgasm."

I gasped as a tingle shot straight to my nether regions. "How is us having phone sex not against the rules?"

"Because we're not actually touching."

"Sounds like a bullshit excuse to me."

"Hey, I was just offering to help you blow off a little steam."

"What are you going to be doing while I'm pleasuring yourself?"

"I planned on pulling over."

Was I really going to have phone sex with Declan? It's not like it would be the first time. We'd certainly dabbled in it back when we'd gone off to separate colleges.

"Peyton?" Declan asked, drawing me out of my thoughts.

"What?"

"Are we doing this?"

"I am if you are."

"Are you touching yourself?"

"Not yet."

"You're still in your clothes, right?"

"Yes."

"Strip down to just your bra and panties."

"I'm wearing pajamas so I don't have on a bra."

"Fuck, I like that visual. Then strip down to just your panties."

"Um, okay. Let me put you on speakerphone."

After I lay the phone down, I whipped my pajama top over my head. Lifting my hips, I then shimmied out of my shorts. "Okay, now what?"

"Touch your tits." Just as I was told, I brought my hands to my chest, cupping their fullness. Although I'd touched myself countless times since my times with Declan, there was something illicit in doing it now.

"What are you doing to them?"

"I'm palming them in my hands."

"Squeeze them."

"Yes, sir."

"Does it feel good touching yourself while I'm talking to you?"

"Mmm, yes."

"Are your nipples hard yet?"

"Yes. But now I'm pinching them to make them even harder," I murmured

"God, I wish it was my hands on your tits right now."

"So do I." Shifting in the bed, I asked, "Are you touching yourself?"

"Yeah, I have my cock out."

"Are you stroking it fast or slow?"

"Slow and then tugging on the tip. I'm imagining you sucking my dick into your warm mouth."

A shudder went through me at his words as the dull ache between my legs began to grow.

"I'm slipping a hand into my panties now."

"Is your pussy wet?"

"Yes. My panties are damp."

"If I was there, I'd have them soaked."

"I know you would," I panted.

"Stroke yourself nice and slow."

"I am."

"Is your clit getting bigger?"

"Mm-hmm," I murmured as I started to speed up my pace.

"Don't go fast yet."

"It feels too good not to," I moaned.

"Are you fingering yourself?"

"No."

"Slip two fingers into your pussy."

He didn't have to tell me twice. As my middle and index finger slid inside, my arousal coated my fingers. Rubbing my thumb against my clit, I pumped the fingers in and out of me. When I sped up my tempo, I couldn't help gasping with pleasure.

"Oh baby, that's right. Let me hear you."

"I want to hear you, too."

Pinching my eyes shut, I focused on the image of Declan sitting on the side of the road with his cock in his hands, pumping his hand up and down as he thrust up his hips. With my fantasy came the sounds of him jerking off, which turned me on even more.

"Are you close to coming?"

"Yes. Oh fuck, yes."

"Fuck yourself harder," he commanded.

As my fingers pumped frantically in and out of my pussy, I began raising my hips in time. With my free hand, I rolled and pinched my nipple between my fingers. The sounds of Declan's grunts and groans fueled me on. My body tensed as I went over the edge. "Oh Declan!" I screamed as my walls convulsed around my fingers. God, that felt good. *I want him here. I want him right now.*

"Did you—"

"Almost. Fuck, Peyton. I almost blew my load listening to you."

"If I was there, I'd let you finish in my mouth."

"Fucking hell."

"Are you close?"

"Yes."

"Tug your balls with your free hand." I knew he had with his gasp. "Now pump your cock harder."

"Fuck. I'm coming." His loud groan of pleasure echoed through the bedroom and made me hot all over again.

It was a few seconds after his last curse that Declan spoke. "I can't believe I just jerked off next to a cow pasture on Hwy 140."

Giggling, I replied, "At least your only witnesses were cows."

"That's true. All I need is for it to get out in town."

"I think your secret is safe with them."

"What about you? Feel better?"

"Yes. Of course, it would be even better if I was sore from your dick."

"Your dirty mouth is something that has certainly changed since we were together."

"You aren't complaining, are you?"

"Fuck no. I love it."

"Good. What about you? How are you feeling?"

"I'll feel better when I can get home and clean up. I'm afraid to turn on the light and see I have fucking cum on my steering wheel."

Snickering, I replied, "It wouldn't be the first time."

"Oh yeah, those good old days in the front seat of my truck."

"Maybe we can reenact some of those soon," I suggested.

"Mm, I'd like that a lot."

"How's tonight?"

He groaned. "Would you stop?"

I huffed out a frustrated sigh. "Now you know how I felt back in the day."

"You have my apologies."

"Well, you don't have mine now. It was one thing being a sixteen-year-old virgin with a minister for a father. It's quite a different thing being a thirty-year-old independent woman."

"Come on, Pey. You and I both know sex complicates things."

Although I hated to admit it, he did have a point. When you jumped in too quick, it clouded your judgement. If the sex was really good, it was like slapping on a pair of rose-colored glasses to read the relationship. With sex as my only focus, I'd used Kieran as a fuck boy, so there was no hope for anything between us. I didn't want that happening with Declan. "While it pains me to admit it, you're right. It does complicate things. It certainly did the last few times for me."

"And me." His ragged sigh echoed through the phone. "Oh fuck me!"

"What's wrong?"

"A cop just pulled up behind me."

Although it was horrifying, I couldn't help busting out laughing. "It's not funny, Peyton," Declan chided.

"I know. I'm sorry."

"What in the hell am I supposed to tell him? I sure as hell can't say I pulled over to have phone sex with my girlfriend."

The word girlfriend gave me a momentary pause. It still seemed so strange to be Declan's *girlfriend*. "Do you have something to eat in the car?"

"Wait what?"

"Like a granola bar or even a sandwich wrapper?"

"Yeah, why?"

"Tell him you're diabetic and pulled over to eat something because you were feeling lightheaded."

"Damn, that's pretty good."

"You're welcome."

"Okay, he's at the window now."

"I hope you've put your cock away."

"Shut up," he said, laughing.

"Good luck. I'll feel really special if you spend your one phone call on me."

"Smart-ass," he muttered before hanging up."

Chapter Nineteen

After our phone sex, I fell into a satiated sleep. Well, I did after Declan called me when he'd gotten home safely and hadn't been arrested for lewd behavior. The next morning I hit the sleep button twice on my alarm before I finally dragged myself out of bed. I wanted to stay there, rolling around in my semi-sex sheets.

I didn't stop at the café because I was running late from being lazy. I was between back-to-back kitten neuters when Sylvia came to the door of the operating room. "The florist just delivered this."

She held out a vase with just one red rose and a sprig of baby's breath. The sight of it caused my pulse to accelerate because there was only one person who would send me one red rose.

Declan.

As I reached for the vase, Sylvia winked at me. "I think I know who sent this."

I cocked my brows at her in surprise. "You do?"

With a knowing look, she replied, "I've seen the two of you getting back together for a long time."

Well then. I picked off the card to read the inscription. I couldn't hold back my smile as I read the words.

Poking her head out the door, Jaycee asked, "Just one rose? Is Declan teasing you or something?"

At the somewhat disgusted look on her face, I busted out laughing. "Let me guess. You're thinking Declan is a cheap bastard for not popping for a whole dozen?"

Pink tinged her cheeks. "Um, maybe?"

"Don't feel bad. I would think the very same thing." I grinned before handing her the card. "Declan knows from back in the day how I think its wasteful to spend money on flowers, so he would always just give me one red rose and then spend the rest of the money on something else."

Jaycee's eyes widened as she jerked her head up from the card. "To thank you for caring for Moose, he gave the money for *ten* dozen roses in your name to the College of Veterinary Medicine at UGA."

Sylvia swept a hand to her chest. "Oh, my, that's so romantic."

"It is, isn't it?" Tilting my head, I said, "Slightly excessive on the donation, but at the same time, I'll take it."

"I'm sure the school is happy to take it as well," Jaycee remarked as she handed me the card back.

As I slipped it into the envelope, I said, "I'll have to call and thank him after we finish up with the next neuter."

With an impish gleam burning in her eyes, Jaycee said, "You know, you could go down and thank him in person."

"Oh, I could, huh?" I replied with a grin.

Jaycee nodded. "For a gift like that, I think you should express your gratitude thoroughly and completely in person."

When she waggled her brows, I laughed. "I'm not giving Declan a mid-morning delight."

While Sylvia gasped in horror, Jaycee countered, "Why not?"

Because he's withholding his fabulous cock from me so we can rebuild our relationship based on emotional intimacy. "Well, for starters, I have patients to see."

"Oh please, like Bubba the barn cat can't wait fifteen minutes more to lose his balls."

"Yes, I'm aware that he would probably welcome more time with his manhood."

"Then what's the problem?"

As diplomatically as I could, I replied, "We only just started seeing each other again, and we aren't to the physical level yet." *You're such a liar.*

Jaycee's expression told me she thought I was completely bullshitting her, and I couldn't blame her for thinking that. It only made sense you would rekindle an old relationship with sex. God knows I tried the other night.

Sylvia nodded. "I think it's good the two of you are rebuilding your foundation first before becoming physically intimate."

Okay, she was starting to get a little creepy with how well she knew Declan and me. "Thank you." I stared pointedly at Jaycee. "I'm glad one of us can see that."

Jaycee laughed. "I suppose after everything the two of you went through, it's the right thing to do."

"I appreciate that." I jerked my thumb towards the door. "I'll go sit these down in my office, and then go thank Declan."

Waggling her brows, Jaycee replied, "Yeah, you go do that."

With a roll of my eyes, I headed out of the operating room to go to my office. After depositing the vase on my desk, I slipped out the back door to head to Declan's. When I swept through the door to his office, I inwardly groaned at the sight of Receptionist Barbie aka Anna. After my performance here last week, I couldn't blame her for eyeing me warily. I forced a smile to my lips. "Good morning, Anna. I was wondering if I might speak with Declan for just a minute."

"He's actually between meetings at the moment. But have a seat while I check if he wants to see you."

I didn't miss the subtle jab. Apparently, Declan hadn't made her aware that the two of us were together again. She was merely going off the spectacle I'd made of myself the other day.

Before she could buzz his phone, Declan appeared in the hallway. At the sight of me, his face lit up. "I thought I heard your voice."

"I had a few minutes between patients, so I thought I'd come down in person and thank you for the rose."

With Receptionist Barbie's wide eyes on us, I swept around the desk before throwing myself into Declan's arms and slamming my lips down on his. When his mouth opened in surprise, I slid my tongue inside, which caused him to groan in pleasure. I poured all my gratitude into that kiss. I knew I was really hitting it out of the park when I felt Declan's appreciation growing against my thigh.

Unfortunately, he came to his senses and broke the kiss. When I opened my eyes, he was grinning at me. "I would say after that kiss, it was worth every penny."

"And from your reaction, I'd say I'm even closer to wearing you down."

Declan snickered. "I feel like we're role reversing from when we were teenagers."

With a giggle, I replied, "Yes, I'm the horndog now trying to steal your virtue."

At Receptionist Barbie's sharp intake of breath, Declan said, "Do you have a minute to come back to my office?"

"It depends on what you plan on doing in that minute," I teased.

Declan rolled his eyes. "In that case, I'll just ask you out here."

"Ask me what?"

"I wanted to invite you to dinner. Are you free tomorrow night?"

"If I say I am, do I sound too forward?"

"I think you'd sound like you live in a small town with limited entertainment."

I giggled. "Then yes, I'm free." Batting my eyelashes, I asked, "Where are you planning on taking me, Mr. St. James?"

"To my house." Okay, I certainly wasn't expecting that. I was extremely curious about what his house looked like. In a way, it was like seeing what would have been between the two of us if we'd built the house we'd always talked about.

"Are you planning on ordering in?"

"No. I'm going to cook dinner for you."

My brows shot up in surprise. "You cook?"

"As a matter of fact, I do."

"Color me surprised. Back when we were engaged, the only thing you liked to do was marinate and grill."

"What can I say? I've evolved since then."

"I would say so." The fact the man wanted to cook for me had my pulse racing. Call me crazy, but there was something so sexy about a man preparing you food. And it wasn't because he might be doing it shirtless...or naked. It was the level of care that went into the process. Yeah. I know. I'm not believing myself either.

After licking my lips at the thought, I asked, "What are you cooking?"

"It's a surprise."

"Oh, I see. What time would you like me?"

"How about seven?"

"That will be great. I can run home and shower before coming over."

"You can always shower at my house."

"Will you be showering with me?"

Declan groaned. "No. But thanks for the imagery."

"You're welcome." I dipped my head to give him a final kiss. "I'll see you at seven."

"I'll be looking forward to it."

When I glanced past him to Anna, her shock was evident by the fact her eyebrows had practically disappeared into her hairline. "Have a lovely afternoon, Anna," I said as I started around the desk.

"Uh, yes, thanks. Same to you."

I started back to the clinic with the goofiest grin on my face.

Chapter Twenty

Anxiety pricked its way along my spine as my car's GPS directed me towards Declan's house. I'd spent most of the day on edge, and then the closer it got to seven o'clock, the more I felt like I was going to come out of my skin. I could only chalk my anxiousness up to the fact it felt like I was going on a first date. In this case, it was a first date with a man I'd once been engaged to.

Everything seemed to be transpiring at warp speed, which didn't help matters. It had only been forty-eight hours since our post Ice House make-out session. Since then, we'd gotten back together—something two months ago I would have said was completely and totally impossible. Like to the same level as hell freezing over. And now I was driving to Declan's house where he was preparing dinner for me.

Yeah, it was epically surreal.

Turning on Declan's road, I wondered why in the hell he thought it was a good idea for us to be alone together when we were abstaining from getting physical. It seemed like we were setting ourselves up for failure. Or I suppose I should say Declan was setting us up. It felt just like we were teenagers again and had the house to ourselves while our parents were out. Of course, I wouldn't have dared to turn down his offer to cook for me. He was really going above and beyond to show me how much he'd changed, and I had to say I was loving every minute of it.

As I neared his street number, I couldn't help leaning forward in my seat. Since I'd been back, it had taken everything within me not to stalk by Declan's house. Although my curiosity had been at a fever pitch, I had managed to temper it with the worst-case scenario of being caught by Declan. The last thing my pride would have allowed was that to happen.

When the GPS announced I'd reached my destination, my mouth dropped open. In my mind, I had imagined something modern with sharp edges and a cold, soulless look. Of course, that had been based on my previous attitude towards Declan. Now it made total sense his two-story farmhouse looked like something out of a Norman Rockwell painting. It wasn't exactly the house we'd planned on building, but it was still gorgeous.

I inhaled a deep breath to fortify my strength before exhaling it as I made my way up Declan's front walk. I climbed up the steps of the wide front porch filled with rocking chairs. Before I could reach my hand out to ring the doorbell, the door jerked open, and Cameron's grinning face stared back at me. "Hiya, Doc!"

After a few ridiculous moments of my mouth opening and closing like a fish, I finally said, "Well, hello there."

Tilting his head at me, Cam asked, "Wanna come in?"

"Yes, please."

As I stepped into the foyer, my gaze flickered around my surroundings. Not only had Declan hired an amazing architect to design the house, but it looked as though Joanna Gaines had personally done the decorating. Everything was farmhouse chic, and I was in serious love.

"Is your dad home?"

"He's upstairs changing his clothes."

"I see."

Declan's voice floated down from the upstairs landing. "Cam? Was that the door?"

"Yeah, it's the Doc."

I caught a flurry of movement before Declan came pounding down the stairs. While he looked positively delectable in his white button-down shirt with the sleeves rolled up and khaki pants, his expression was somewhat flustered. "I'm sorry. I didn't hear the doorbell."

"That's probably because someone anticipated me before I could ring it," I replied with a grin.

"He got pretty excited when I told him you were coming over." Declan ruffled Cam's hair. "Didn't you buddy?"

Cam bobbed his head emphatically. "Hey, Doc, you wanna see my new nerf gun Daddy got me?"

"Um, sure."

After Cam sprinted off, I cocked my brows at Declan. "I see it's going to be a party of three, not two, for dinner."

Wincing, Declan put his hands out in front of him. "I'm so sorry. Mom and Dad are puking their guts out with some sort of stomach flu, and every other babysitter I tried was busy tonight."

"It's okay. If you'd called, I would've taken a rain check."

He shook his head vehemently from side to side. "After everything we have been through, there was no way in hell I was going to cancel on you."

My heart fluttered at the thought he was willing to go through so much to keep his word. "I'm glad you didn't."

He grinned. "You might rethink that response later."

I laughed. "I doubt that."

Motioning me with his hand, Declan said, "Come on in. As soon as the bread is finished, we can eat."

As I sniffed the air, a delicious tomato smell filled my nose. "Did you make spaghetti?"

"Homemade lasagna."

"Wow, like really homemade or you 'took it out of the box and put it in the oven' kind of homemade."

Declan gave me a withering look. "No, smart-ass, I didn't take it out of a box."

"My apologies and color me impressed," I mused as we walked into the kitchen. The moment I saw the quartz countertops and distressed cream cabinets, I was in love. "This is gorgeous."

"You really like it?"

"Like it? I love it."

The farmhouse kitchen table was set with fine china and crystal water goblets. Although it was beautiful, I couldn't help wondering if the place settings were part of his and Bailey's wedding china. Ugh, it seriously sucked being in a house of Declan's ex-wife. Just how many touches and elements were because of her? I felt that scratchy skin feeling working its way up my back. *I can't undo time or his marriage.* So, it was time to pull up my big girl panties.

"Would you like some wine while we wait on the bread to come out?"

I gave him a quizzical look. "You have wine?"

He grinned. "For you."

"Seriously, you didn't have to do that."

"It's okay." With a wink, he added, "I was never a fan of the taste anyway."

Although I could have used some wine to calm my nerves, I decided against it. I wasn't going to tempt Declan's sobriety even if he wasn't a fan of wine.

When Cam reappeared with his nerf gun, he asked, "Daddy, is it a holiday?"

"No. Why do you ask?"

"Cause Grammy only uses the candles on holidays."

When Declan's face somewhat flushed at being called out by Cam, I had to bite down on my lip to keep from laughing. "Sometimes you use candles for company."

"And she"—Cameron pointed to me—"is our company?"

"That's right."

"I like having company."

"And I like being your company," I replied.

Tugging on my hand, Cam asked, "Hey, Doc, you wanna see my fish Mr. Blue?"

"Her name is Peyton, or you can call her Dr. Beasley," Declan corrected.

Cam rolled his eyes. "Okay, Pey-ton, you wanna see Mr. Blue?"

With a grin, I replied, "I would love to see Mr. Blue. I don't see too many fish in my practice."

"Let's go!" Cam jerked me over to the stairs. He pulled me up the steps at a frantic pace. When we got to the landing, he hurried us down the hallway. Although they were somewhat of a blur, I eyed the framed pictures lining the wall. I had a feeling they'd been arranged by Bailey in happier years. A pang entered my chest at the sight of what I imagined were the perfect family images.

Cam's room was done in a John Deere theme with a mural of farm-land and tractors painted on one of the walls. Even Mr. Blue's aquarium had a small tractor in it. "Now that is a handsome fish," I mused.

Beaming with pride, Cam replied, "He was the biggest at the pet store."

"I bet. He sure looks fierce."

"We had to put him on the second shelf because Moose kept trying to jump up and knock the bowl over."

I laughed. "I can only imagine he thought Mr. Blue looked tasty."

"That's what Daddy said."

Cam pointed to an oversized green and yellow dog bed. "That's Moose's bed." Cupping a hand over his mouth, he whispered, "He's supposed to sleep there, but I always let him sleep in bed with me after Daddy closes the door."

I bit down on my lip to keep to from laughing. I had a feeling Declan probably knew Cam's secret but wasn't saying anything because of everything going on with Bailey. "As good as Moose is doing, he should be coming home within the next week."

Cam's face lit up as he danced around his room. "Moosie's coming home!" He cocked his head at the wall. "Did you hear that Mr. Tractor? Moose is coming home!"

It felt wonderful to be able to give him that happiness. Gazing around the room, I eyed the tractor and farm mural painted onto one of the walls. "Wow, this is a really cool wall you have here."

"My mommy painted it."

Shit. I'd walked right over that potential landmine without even trying. I cut my gaze over to Cam to see if my gaffe had reduced him to tears. Thankfully, he appeared unfazed by my reference to his mom.

"She's very talented."

"She doesn't live with us anymore." He peered curiously up at me. "What does *bitch* mean?"

Oh sweet Jesus, this just continued getting worse. Glancing past

Cam, I debated whether I should make a run for it. Maybe I could feign the need to use the bathroom to get out of answering his question. After a few agonizing seconds of Cam staring at me, I replied, "Uh, I think you might need to ask your daddy about that one."

"Granny called my mommy that to Daddy."

I don't blame her. "It's just a word grown-ups use. You shouldn't use it though."

"Okay."

The sound of the smoke alarm going off interrupted us. We hurried out of Cam's room and then down the stairs. When we got to the kitchen, smoke billowed from the oven. "Motherfucker!" Declan bellowed as he fanned the smoke with a magazine.

I couldn't help giggling. "What happened?"

"I burned the f—" He clamped his mouth shut at the sight of Cam. "The lasagna."

Sweeping a hand to his hip, Cam waved a finger at Declan. "Daddy, I told you not to cook. You always burn everything."

Once again, Declan's face turned scarlet. "I didn't the last time I tried." He gave me a knowing look. "There was too much pressure tonight."

I smiled. "I'm sorry."

"It's all good. I should have known better than trying to put it back in to reheat it.

"If it helps, it really smelled good when I got here."

Declan laughed. "Thanks." Sweeping his hands to his hips, "We can always go out or order in pizza."

Cam danced around me shouting, "Pizza, pizza, pizza!"

I nodded at Declan. "That sounds good to me."

Reaching into his back pocket, Declan produced his phone. "Pizza it is."

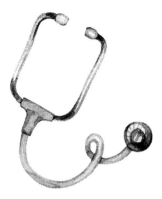

As we waited on the pizza to arrive, Declan walked me and the burned lasagna to the edge of his property while Cam ran along ahead of us, shooting off his nerf gun. After throwing the contents of the dish over the fence, he mused, "At least the possums and raccoons might get some enjoyment out of that."

I giggled. "That's kind of you to think of all the woodland creatures."

"Or torture them."

"I'm sure they'll appreciate your culinary delight."

When we started back to the house, I admired his property. "You have a gorgeous place here, Declan."

"Thanks."

"How many acres?"

"Ten."

"Really? But we were only going to have—" I snapped my mouth shut.

"Five acres," Declan interrupted.

"Right."

"I acquired five more acres from my parents before I built." He gave me a knowing look. "I decided to build on the other end of those five acres and not the ones where we were going to live."

An ache burned through my chest at what could've been. Robert and Pauline had gifted Declan and me the five acres as a wedding present. We'd decided to wait to build until Declan finished his under-grad degree. That way we could afford it more with me in vet school. That discomfort was back. *Instead he built his home with his actual wife.*

"That's understandable," I replied staring down at the grass. I'm sure he hadn't wanted to start a new life on the property where we were supposed to live. I certainly wouldn't have wanted to. I couldn't even start a life anywhere near him, for goodness sake.

Cam interrupted us by running up to me. "I'm going to get you, Peyton."

I held my hands up. "I surrender. Don't shoot."

The next thing I knew a nerf bullet was momentarily stuck to my boob with a suction cup before it fell to the ground. "I got you!" Cam shouted before running away to shoot something else.

When Declan started snickering, I rolled my eyes. "You would find this funny."

"He has a good aim. I mean, he got your nipple, didn't he?"

"Like he was aiming for that," I countered.

"You never know. He could be a closeted boob man."

"Like his father."

With a wink, Declan replied, "Could be."

"Men," I muttered.

We got back to the house and sat outside on the back porch that overlooked a small pond. When the pizza arrived, Declan brought it back outside with him. While it might not have been gourmet food or an expensive location, I loved each and every minute of it. Conversation flowed easily between myself and Declan, not to mention the sweet and funny things Cam said.

After we cleaned up from dinner, Declan asked, "Want to watch a movie?"

"Sure. What would you like to watch?" I replied.

"*Toy Story!*" Cam interjected.

While Declan rolled his eyes, I laughed. "Do you like *Toy Story*?"

Declan groaned. "More like he's obsessed with it. I bet we watch one of the three movies at least once a day."

"Let's watch the second one, Daddy, with Jessie."

"*Toy Story 2* it is," Declan said resignedly.

"Can we have some popcorn?" Cam asked.

"Sure. Why don't you two go get settled in while I make it?"

"Okay," Cam replied. He took my hand and led me back into the living room. While I sat down on the couch, he started playing with some of his toys. Declan appeared a few minutes later with the popcorn. After turning on the TV, he sat down next to me before placing the bowl between us. "Ready, Cam?"

"Yep." After abandoning his toys, Cam hopped up on the couch. Instead of sitting beside me or Declan, he wiggled between the two of us.

I grinned at Declan over Cam's head. "Are you comfy?" I asked Cam.

"Uh-huh," he replied, not taking his eyes off the screen.

As we sat there watching *Toy Story*, I couldn't help feeling like I was experiencing a real family life. Although I shouldn't have, I imagined for a moment what it would be like if this was my normal Friday night nestled between the two men in my life as a wife and mother. I liked the idea more than I probably should have. While Declan and I were dating again, there were no guarantees it would last. The thought of that made me incredibly sad.

Halfway through the movie, Cam's body slumped over against mine. When I glanced down at him, I saw he was fast asleep. "Aw, little guy's out," I announced.

"I'm surprised he made it this long. He's usually wiped out by seven-thirty on the days he has pre-K." He grinned at me. "Let me get him to bed."

"Sure."

Declan slid his hands under Cam's body and then brought him into his arms. As he started over to the stairs, I couldn't tear my eyes away from them. After our years together, it was so foreign seeing Declan in the role of a father. I couldn't lie that it was incredibly sexy. At the same time, it was very endearing.

"Do you want to help me?" Declan asked.

"Do you want me to?"

He chuckled. "There you go with that habit of answering a question with a question."

I rolled my eyes. "I just wanted to make sure you were sure."

"I am."

Right. But was *I* sure I wanted to help put Cam to bed? Talk about your next level intimacy. Declan was giving me even more access to his son's world. Like everything with us getting back together, it was moving at warp speed.

In the end, I merely nodded. I then crossed the living room to the two of them. Declan motioned for me to go ahead of him up the stairs.

When we got inside Cameron's bedroom, Declan asked, "Will you grab his pajamas out of the top drawer?"

Turning around, I eyed the armoire and the chest of drawers. "Um, which top drawer?"

"Left drawer in the chest of drawers."

"Got it."

When I opened the drawer, I couldn't help smiling at all the neatly folded sets of pajamas. I had to wonder if they were Declan's doing, or since Bailey had been gone so long, it was Pauline's. Of course, it was amusing thinking of Declan doing laundry—he'd always claimed that was woman's work when we were dating, which I'd told him was utter bullshit.

After grabbing the red pair of Thomas the Tank Engine pajamas, I joined Declan by the bed. With Cam being deadweight, Declan worked to wriggle him out of his shirt and pants. Since he was occupied with Cam's top half, I reached for the button on his pants and worked those off. While Declan got his pajama top on, I slid on his pajama pants.

"Great teamwork," Declan whispered with a smile.

The comment tugged at my heart. What we had just done was the teamwork that parents usually did. As I watched Declan smooth down Cam's hair and kiss his forehead, an ache burned through my chest. One I hadn't experienced in a long, long time.

The ache for motherhood.

Maybe it was because I was thirty that my clock had started ticking louder and louder. Maybe it was because with Papa's death, my own mortality was more evident, which in turn added to the need to procreate. It certainly didn't help my ovaries to be in the presence of a gorgeous father and an adorable son. While the idea of having a baby had always been on my mind, I'd never given much thought to being a stepmom. When I thought about Cam's case, it was more like being his mom.

Gazing down at his sleeping face, I wondered if I could be enough. Would Cam want that? Me stepping into his life? What if he was happy it was just him and his dad? *Getting a little ahead of yourself there, aren't you? You and Declan have barely started dating again and here you are inserting yourself not only into the role of wife, but as mother.*

"Peyton?" Declan questioned.

I snapped my gaze from Cam over to him. "What?" I whispered.

"I said let's go downstairs."

"Oh, okay. Sure."

After Declan eased Cam's door closed, we headed down the hallway and back downstairs. "Want something else to eat or drink?"

"No. I'm good, thanks," I replied as I sat back down on the couch.

With a beaming expression, Declan said, "You made a big impression tonight on Cam."

"I did?"

He nodded. "He normally takes a long time to warm up to people outside our family."

"He just likes me because I've been taking such good care of Moose," I replied with a grin.

"Oh, it's more than that, trust me."

"He's a great kid, D. You've done an amazing job."

"Thanks. But it wasn't all me. Bailey could be a very good mom when she wanted to be."

"When she wanted?" I repeated softly. Even though I wasn't a mom, I knew it wasn't about turning your maternal instinct on and off when it served your purpose. From my own mother, I'd seen what complete and total sacrifice looked like. As we were growing up, it was rarely ever what she wanted and more about what Quinton, Becca, and I wanted.

Declan ran a hand over his face. "Yeah, that's pretty fucked up, isn't it? Jesus, I don't know how I was so blind for so long."

"Because you loved her."

He exhaled a ragged sigh. "I'm not so sure I actually loved her for her."

"Because you wanted to save her?"

"That was a huge factor. There was also the idea I was in love with the idea of her." He grimaced. "She put on a good front when we were dating and first married. Then when she had Cameron, I started loving her because she gave me such a perfect little human." Shaking his head, he said, "And then all went to shit."

"I'm so sorry."

"It's not your fault."

"Neither is it yours."

"We'll have to agree to disagree on that one."

As I drew my bottom lip between my teeth, I debated about what to do. I wanted more than anything to take his mind off his troubles. Since he couldn't drink, that only left me with one other vice to work with, even though it was allegedly off-limits. But times like these called for drastic measures.

When I brought my hand to cup his crotch, he jumped. "Whoa, what the hell are you doing?"

As his dick came alive to my touch, I replied, "Just getting reacquainted with an old friend."

Warily, he said, "We talked about getting physical too soon."

"You need a little stress relief. You don't drink, and the gym is closed."

"Ah, is that what you call this?"

"Aren't you feeling relieved?"

"Slightly."

"Hmm, let me try something else." I unbuttoned his pants before sliding the zipper down. My fingers delved inside his briefs before encircling his cock. The way it felt against my palm was a truly déjà vu moment. "Better?"

His head collapsed back against the couch. "Getting there."

"Do you remember the first time I gave you a hand job?"

Declan groaned as my fingers began to pump around his cock. He swallowed hard. "After the homecoming bonfire our junior year," he grunted.

With a smile, I replied, "You do remember."

"I remember every time we fucked."

I lifted my brows in surprise. "You do? I don't remember every time."

As I worked his cock faster, a lazy grin slunk across his lips. "Maybe I don't remember every time, but I remember the creative ones."

"Creative?"

"Like that time we hid out in the laundry room, and I fucked you on the washing machine."

The memory of that, coupled with Declan bringing his hand to knead my breast, caused wetness to pool between my legs. "It's been twelve years, and I can still remember what the vibrations felt like on my bare ass," I replied.

"They made your pussy vibrate, which was amazing around my cock."

I grinned. "Maybe we can do laundry together sometime?"

"I'd fucking love that." He squeezed my nipple through the fabric of my dress, causing me to gasp. He then made quick work unbuttoning the top of my dress. Jerking the cups of my bra down, his fingers tweaked my already hardening nipples. All the while I kept pumping my hand up and down his cock.

"I want you to come with me," his deep voice rumbled.

"Yes, please."

Declan snaked his hand under my dress. His fingers skimmed along the skin of my thighs. As he grew closer to my pussy, I spread my legs, widening myself for him. At the feel of his knuckles brushing against my sensitive flesh, I moaned.

As the pre-cum grew on the head of his cock, he slipped two fingers into my wet core. "Oh God," I murmured as his fingers began to pump inside me. He dipped his head to bring his mouth over my breast.

"Daddy?"

"Oh God!" I cried. This time my exclamation was from horror and not pleasure. As I scrambled away from Declan, I jerked the hem of my dress back down from where it had been circling my equator before fumbling with the cups on my bra.

"What is it Cam?" Declan choked out as he stuffed his dick back in his pants.

Thankfully, Cam had remained on the bottom stair and hadn't come close enough to see anything traumatizing. In a wavering voice, Cam replied, "I've been calling you over and over and over but you didn't come."

Well, hello, guilt trip. I would now be known as 'the mean woman who took Daddy's attention away by distracting him with sexual favors'. Maybe I was the one who Pauline should be calling a bitch rather than Bailey.

"Sorry, buddy, I didn't hear you." Declan hopped off the couch and hustled over to the stairs.

"Was it another nightmare?"

Sniffling, Cam replied, "She was hurting me and saying I could never see you again."

I could only imagine who *she* was in Cam's nightmare. It made me want to track down Bailey and beat the hell out of her for inflicting so much pain on Cam. He wasn't even my child, yet I ached for him and what he was going through. How could she possibly turn her back on her own flesh and blood just for a dick...or dicks?

Declan gathered Cam into his arms before turning around to face me. "I'm sorry, Peyton, but I—"

I held a hand up as I rose off the couch. "You don't need to apologize. You go take care of Cam, and I'll let myself out."

"You could stay," he suggested, his voice cracking a bit.

I didn't know if we were ready for that yet. Sure, we were officially back together not to mention we were just heavy petting like a bunch of horny teenagers in his living room. In the vast scheme of things, it was all pretty innocent. If I stayed, it meant a whole new level of commitment, and I wasn't sure I was ready for it.

But when I stared into his agonized eyes, my heart ached with grief, and I wanted to do everything within my power to ease his pain. "Yeah, sure, I can stay."

Both relief and gratitude flashed in his expression. "Good." Turning his attention back to Cam, Declan said, "Come on, buddy. Let's get you back to bed."

When he started upstairs, I fell in step behind him. At Cameron's bedroom door, he turned around. Jerking his chin down the hall, he said, "Go on in and make yourself comfortable. I'll be back in a minute."

I nodded. After he dipped into Cameron's bedroom, I glanced down the hallway with slight trepidation. For a moment, it felt like that scene in *The Shining* where the hallway stretched on infinitely. It was just Declan's bedroom. No biggie. No potential for anything to go wrong.

When I stepped inside, I froze at the sight of the huge four-poster bed. Declan and Bailey's *marriage* bed more precisely. I'm not sure why I found it so repugnant. It wasn't like I hadn't slept on the same mattress as my boyfriends' other girlfriends had. Maybe it was because none of them had been married.

At least there weren't any pictures of her in the room. Of course, she was all around in the interior design of the room—the specially made curtains that coordinated with the bedspread. The high-back chairs and ottoman in the corner. None of those things appeared to be Declan's doing. *It wasn't fair. Why did she get all this? Him? Cam? She was so . . . undeserving.* I didn't want to step into *their* space.

Standing in the middle of the room, I tried not to imagine their life together in this room. It wasn't so much the sex I didn't want to think about, although that was horrific enough. It was more the other aspects of intimacy.

Declan reappeared still wearing a battle worn expression. An agonized sigh rumbled through his chest as he dropped down on the bed beside me. After rubbing his hands over his face, he shook his head. "Bailey's effect on Cam is killing me."

I reached over and took my hand in his. After giving a reassuring squeeze, I said, "As Papa always said, 'what doesn't kill us only makes us stronger.'"

A mirthless laugh escaped Declan's lips. "Then I must be at Hulk-level by now." With his jaw clenching, tears shimmered in his eyes. "When it comes to making it easier for him, I don't feel strong. I feel so fucking weak."

"There's not a weak bone in your body, Declan St. James. You are doing the best you can, and that's all that matters. One day down the road, Cam will reflect on how you got him through this difficult time."

He scrubbed the moisture from his eyes with his fist. "I sure as hell hope so. I don't want this to be the part he talks about later in a prison-organized therapy session."

I shook my head. "That's not even a possibility."

"I hope not." Cutting his eyes over to me, Declan shook his head. "This all has to be so terribly romantic—my traumatized son and me blubbering. I'm surprised you're not running for the hills."

I understood what he was saying, and a lesser woman might've bailed. But we'd been through too much together over the years for anything like that. "This is life, D. It isn't always pretty. God knows I've had my own unattractive moments over the years." Of course, those "unattractive moments" usually involved me being unable to commit out of my fear of being left again. I'd never waited for the men to bail—I had to be the first to leave.

"It's not what I wanted right at the start of us rebuilding our relationship."

"You forget I already *know* you. There isn't anything you have to pretend to impress me." I reached out to run my hand over his cheek. "I know you, and I like what I see."

It appeared he didn't have words because instead of agreeing or arguing with me, he brought his mouth against mine. I deepened the kiss by sliding my tongue against his. When I started to slide my hand down his chest, he stopped me. "No. I don't want to finish what we started."

"Because you don't want us being physical yet?"

Pain flickered in his eyes. "Bailey tried to solve all of our problems with sex."

Both regret and disgust filled me that I'd done something like her. Would that always happen though? Would he always compare things I did with his *ex-wife?* Can I deal with that? "I'm sorry. I didn't know."

"It's okay."

"I . . . um, can I use the bathroom?"

"Sure. It's through there," he said, pointing toward the en suite bathroom that I hadn't noticed before then.

I hopped up hoping he didn't pick up on my . . . well, what did I feel? My heart ached because getting back with Declan seemed fraught with obstacles and challenges.

Even though Papa was an old-fashioned man in so many respects, it was these confusing moments when I often talked to him. He had that older-person wise discernment that was rarely affected by emotion. I missed him. *Terribly.* An avid reader, he often communicated with quotes from people he respected. Two came to mind as well as when he said them to me. Both times had been when I'd felt confused or unsure of a decision. Even vet school. Robert Frost had written, "In three words I can sum up everything I've learned about life: it goes on." *Life goes on. Even in death.*

What would he recommend here? I do want the man, Declan St. James. That's an easy truth. His son? Too adorable to not want. But the baggage they came with, the history made difficult because of another woman? Was I actually strong enough to take that on? As well as all the changes I was currently going through? *"Peybug, remember what Eleanor Roosevelt said, because you are just as strong as she was.* 'In the long run, we shape our lives, and we shape ourselves. And the choices we make are ultimately our own responsibility.' Make wise choices, Peybug, and never blame someone else for how those choices turn out."

Did that mean I had to look beyond the challenges toward a future *with* Declan and Cam? To understand and appreciate what things had shaped *their* lives, how moving away had shaped *my* life, and together make choices for us? I didn't have the answer, but I did want to comfort a man who had been dealt an extremely shitty hand.

So, I left the bathroom, and returned to the man who needed me. Not sex. *Me.*

He gave me a reassuring kiss. "You want to make me feel better?"

"More than anything."

"Just hold me."

My brows shot up in surprise. When we were together, Declan had never been one for cuddling. "Really?" When he nodded, I replied, "Yeah, of course." We rose off the edge of the bed and walked around the side. I climbed up first and slid over to the middle of the bed.

Once I was on my back, Declan's weight bore down on the mattress. He spread out on his stomach before curling up next to me in the crook of my arm. After lying his head on my chest, I wrapped my arms around his back.

I didn't bother asking him how it felt. His contented sigh as the tension unfurled from his body told me everything I needed to know. It wasn't just good for him—I loved the feeling of him so close to me.

It didn't take long for my eyelids to grow droopy and for sleep to come. I don't know how long I was out. As I started coming into consciousness, I realized someone was rubbing my cheek. Fluttering my eyelids, I tried taking in my surroundings. My gaze focused on a pair of deep blue eyes. But it wasn't Declan staring back at me in the dim light—it was Cam.

Shit. We were so busted. "Cam? What's the matter?"

"I need to snuggle," he stated, his voice wavering.

"Um, are you supposed to get in bed with your daddy?" I whispered.

Cam's chin trembled. "Pwease."

I figured that was a no since he'd turned on the epic pitifulness. Glancing over my shoulder, Declan still slept like the dead, and I hated to wake him up. I was going to have to make an executive decision. "Okay. Just this once."

Holding my arms out, Cam dove into them. With the high bed frame, I wondered how in the hell he'd managed to get up here. I peered over the side to see where Cam had brought what appeared to be his bathroom stool. The little guy had been on a mission.

For the second time tonight, I'd snuggled one of the St. James men to my chest. As I rubbed circles across Cam's back, I whispered, "Did you have another nightmare?"

"No. I just woke up sad."

God, he was breaking my heart. "You don't have to be sad. Daddy's here. And, well, so am I." Even though I wasn't really supposed to be.

"Are you going to be my mommy now, Doc?"

My hand froze midway across his back. "Uh, no sweetheart."

"Why not?"

"Well, you already have a mommy."

"But she never comes to see me."

Because she's a selfish, heartless bitch. "Well, that doesn't mean she isn't your mommy." Part of me wanted to lie and say she loved him very much and wanted to see him. I didn't know what it could possibly hurt to reassure him that she did care in spite of her apathy. At the same time, I felt it was somehow disrespectful to Declan's plight.

"But I want a better mommy." He patted my shoulder. "You'd be a good mommy."

Oh God. Had he actually just said that? In that moment, the room started closing in on me, and I struggled to breathe. I'd never expected such a vote of confidence from him. "I don't know about that," I choked out.

"You took good care of Moose, so you'd take good care of me."

His simplistic reasoning sent an ache through my chest. "We'll have to think about that, okay?"

He nodded. "I'll tell Daddy. He usually gets me what I want."

Hmm, usually it's your daddy getting what he wants. "I don't know about this time."

Yawning, Cam said, "Grandma says I'm too cute for my own good."

I laughed. "I think she's right." After squeezing him tight, I said, "Now go back to sleep, Mr. Cutie."

"Okay, Doc."

As we lay there in the silence, I continued rubbing Cam's back. When his breathing became labored, I knew he'd fallen back to sleep. I turned my head on the pillow to check on Declan. To my surprise, I found he was staring at me. I threw him an apologetic look. "I'm sorry."

"For what?"

"Letting Cam in the bed."

He smiled. "I always let him, too."

I exhaled a relieved breath. "Good." When he continued staring intently at me, I asked, "How much did you hear?"

"Everything."

"Oh."

He scooted over to where we were touching again. The look in his eyes told me there was so much he wanted to say but couldn't. Instead, he covered my mouth with his. He poured out all of his emotion into that kiss. When he pulled away, I was breathless not from passion, but from the depth of what he was feeling. He then lay his head down next to mine.

With Cam on my left side and Declan on my right, I fell back into a contented sleep.

When I woke up the next morning, both Declan and Cam were gone from the bed. As I stretched my arms over my head, I winced. My body felt like it had been through a marathon the night before. While it had gone through the emotional wringer, I'd slept in crazy angles, and my muscles were telling me about it.

As I rolled over on the mattress, an ache pressed in on my chest. It was one of loneliness and despair. I knew it wasn't just because of waking up alone or what I'd experienced with the St. James men last night. It had been building all week as I grew closer to a particular date on the calendar.

Papa's birthday.

Last year, we'd celebrated at his lodge in Helen. There had been catered in BBQ while my mom had baked one of her legendary cakes. We'd sat outside on the porch talking, eating, and watching the river stream by.

After using the bathroom, I swigged some mouthwash and tried to tame my out of control bedhead. Once I was somewhat presentable, I padded down the stairs. I found Declan in the kitchen with his head buried in his laptop while nursing a cup of coffee.

"Good morning," I said.

He jerked his gaze up to mine. With a smile, he replied, "Good morning."

Glancing around the kitchen, I asked, "Where's Cam?"

"Bailey's dad came to get him earlier this morning to go fishing. It's their Saturday morning thing."

"Oh, he sees her parents?"

"Just her dad. Her mom stays high most of the time," Declan replied, his face clouding over.

"I see." Leaning in on the counter, I decided a subject change was imperative. "Cam must get his love of fishing from your dad. I remember how much he loved to fish."

Declan grunted. "Tell me about it. Every Saturday morning when I was a kid he wanted to drag me out at the crack of dawn to go down to the lake."

"Hey, we had some good times fishing and water skiing on his boat when we were teenagers."

"Yeah, in the afternoons."

"Still not a morning person, huh?"

"Nope. I'm still a bear until about eight in the morning."

"I'll have to remember that."

With a smile, Declan rose off his stool to come over to me. After wrapping me in his arms, he kissed me. Pulling away, he said, "It sure was nice waking up to you this morning."

"I'm glad."

Declan furrowed his brows at me. "What's wrong?"

"Nothing."

"Bullshit. I can see it in your eyes." His thumb rubbed along my jawline. "You're not having regrets after last night, are you?"

"God no."

He exhaled a relieved breath. "Thank goodness."

Leaning in to his hand, I replied, "It's nothing about you."

"But it is something. I can tell."

A part of me didn't want to tell Declan about Papa's birthday. It was the part of me who often retreated from people during times of grief and depression. "Today is Papa's birthday."

Declan's expression saddened. "Oh Pey, I'm so sorry."

"It's okay."

"No, it's not. It's the first birthday without him. It has to be agonizing."

I did love how much he got me. Most men would have been clueless of my pain, least of all acknowledge it to the level he did. I know it helped that he knew Papa. "You're right. It is pure agony."

"What can I do?"

"It's sweet of you to offer, but really there's nothing." And that was true. Grief was so very isolating.

"What about some breakfast? I can try cooking for you again," he suggested with a smile.

I laughed. "While tempting, I think I'm okay. I'm just going to go home and have a quiet day by myself."

Declan shook his head. "You don't need to be alone."

"It's fine really."

"No, it's not." When I started to protest again, Declan said, "Why don't we do something to honor Harris?"

I scrunched my brows at him. "What do you mean?"

"We could take some flowers to the cemetery. I mean, I know you've never been a fan of spending money on flowers, but I do remember Harris always had fresh flowers in his office."

My heart melted at the suggestion. "That would be lovely."

"Then we could do something he loved and go horseback riding."

Tears pricked my eyes. If there was one thing Papa loved, it was horses. In spite of his age, he still rode once a month. His will had stipulated his horse be donated to an equine therapy for kids.

For a moment, it was hard for me to speak. "I can't imagine anything more wonderful."

"Good. It's settled. You go home and get a shower. I'll come by and get you around noon."

After kissing Declan appreciatively, I replied, "Okay. I'll see you then."

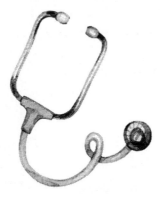

I walked across the cemetery with an armload of wildflowers, Papa's favorite. Declan had picked me up promptly at noon and driven me straight to the florist. He'd insisted on purchasing the flowers. He was really going above and beyond, and I loved him for it.

I was starting to think I was in love with him again. While we had started dating again, I wasn't quite ready to love him again. It wasn't so much the past continuing to cripple me as it was learning how to feel for the new Declan.

Although I tried holding my emotions in check, the tears began the moment I saw Papa's headstone. Guilt flooded me that I couldn't remember the last time I'd been out here. After I'd moved back, I'd come every other day. But then as the weeks flew by, I couldn't seem to find the time. Or maybe it was I didn't want to find the time.

"Happy Birthday, Papa," I murmured, as I arranged the flowers at the base of the monument. "I wish . . . I wish I'd had more time with you." *God, this was so hard.* "I thought I'd give you a quick update on some of the animals at the clinic. I always bring Ollie Parsons's horse carrots because you always did. Of course the first time, they didn't want to take them because they weren't from you. And Mrs. Covington's parakeet till cusses like a sailor when she brings him in just like he always did for you." I exhaled a ragged breath. "Most of them are getting used to me, but I know they miss you just like I do. Just like we all do."

After I righted myself, my emotions overcame me, and my shoulders crumpled with my sobs. Declan immediately wrapped me in his arms, his hand rubbing comforting circles across my back. "Shh, he wouldn't want you to cry. He loved you so much."

Pulling away, I swiped my eyes with the backs of my hands. "I shouldn't have been such a spoiled brat about coming back here."

"If anyone should feel guilty, it's me. I'm the reason why you didn't come home."

"But you weren't his granddaughter. And I should have swallowed my pride and gotten over it. I made it hard on him to see me."

"He understood your reasons, and I don't think he ever went without seeing you."

"I'm sure it hurt him when I didn't come back here to practice with him."

"Did he ask you?"

"No."

Declan shook his head. "Then there was nothing you could do. You made him so very proud by following in his footsteps and then practicing medicine in the big city."

Deep down, I knew what he was saying was true. It just seemed I would forever be crippled by guilt. Nodding, I extricated myself from him. Without another word, I dug into the bag he'd brought for the cleaning supplies.

With only the sounds of the birds in the background, Declan and I cleaned some of the bird poop off Papa's monument before washing it off. When we were finished, I stepped back to admire our work. "It looks great."

"It sure does," Declan replied. He held out his hand to me. "Come on. Let's go ride."

Although reluctant to leave, I knew it was the right thing to do. On the drive over to Robert and Pauline's, silence echoed around us. I felt too emotionally spent for words, and Declan respected that. Holding my hand in his, he occasionally gave it a squeeze.

When we got to his parents' barn, Declan had already saddled up two horses for us. Although I'd been an urban dweller for most of the last decade, I still rode horses whenever I left the city. Everything had been so crazy since I'd arrived back in Hayesville, so I hadn't had the chance to saddle up again.

After I climbed on the brown filly, I took the reins in my hands. "Where to, Trail Master?" I asked Declan.

He grinned. "Are you really going to allow me to lead?"

He was right. He always teased me about reining me in from taking control of the ride. But that was a long time ago, and the familiar trails were foreign to me now. "I'm officially in the rear today and leaving you in charge."

"I promise you're in good hands."

"I'm sure I am."

Declan took us along all the familiar pathways from my youth. We crossed over his property into several other owners. I would've gotten lost many times had it not been for him. We'd been riding about thirty minutes when we came to a small cabin. At the sight of it, my heart began beating out of my chest.

It was Papa's hunting cabin where I'd lost my virginity to Declan. My gaze snapped from the cabin to Declan. "Did you—"

"Yes, I meant to bring you here." He slid off his horse and came around to mine. "Come inside."

"But it's locked up." In Papa's will, the hunting cabin had been left to my brother because he was an avid hunter. Considering it was hunting season, I was surprised not to find him here.

"I called Quinton and got the key."

"You did?"

Nodding, Declan held his arms out to help me off the horse. I hopped down and into his embrace. "I can't believe you planned this."

"I have a few tricks up my sleeve."

As I made my way up the path with Declan, my heart began thrumming wildly. When we got inside, I gasped. Rose petals littered the floor, and there were fresh flowers in vases on the table.

I whirled around to look at Declan. "You came out here and decorated this?"

He nodded. "I thought you needed something to take your mind off things while reliving something positive from the past."

My brows shot up in surprise. "You brought me here to have sex and not reminiscence our early days?"

"I was shooting more for making love, but you can call it what you want," he replied with a smile.

"What about waiting?"

"I think after last night, we've waited long enough, don't you?"

He was right. Being with him and Cam last night had taken our relationship to a whole new level in my eyes. "Yes, I do."

"And this isn't about just getting your mind off the importance of today."

"I know." Crooking my finger, I beckoned him closer. "Now make love to me."

He smiled and being the wonderful man he was, he came right up to me. "Pey, there has never been anyone else inside my heart or my soul. That's why I brought you here. I want us. I'm offering myself to you." I smiled, because how could I not? The man was more thoughtful and incredible than I could have ever imagined or hoped for.

"And me to you. Now make love to me, Mr. St. James. I'm long overdue." I didn't have to ask twice. Declan closed the gap between us to slam his lips against mine. Declan didn't give me a moment to catch my breath before his tongue thrust into my mouth, dancing along with mine. Grabbing my arms, he lifted them above my head and placed them against the wall of the lodge. His fingers raked down the under-sides of my arms, causing me to shiver. When he reached my shoulders, his hands dipped behind my back to jerk my shirt out of the waistband of my jeans. After he pulled my shirt over my head, he unhooked my bra and freed my breasts. As he took them in his hands, I frantically worked my fingers down the buttons on his shirt. Once they were all undone, I flattened my palms against his chest before running them down his perfect abs.

With his hands on my waist, Declan pulled me over to the bed. He eased us down on the mattress before his weight came on top of me. My head lolled back when Declan's mouth closed over my nipple. He suckled it deeply before flicking and swirling his tongue across it. His hand kept stroking my other breast as his tongue worked the nipple in his mouth into a hardened pebble. Crying out, my fingers automatically went to his hair, tugging and grasping at the strands as the pleasure washed over me.

Declan licked a wet trail over to the other breast before claiming the nipple. The ache between my thighs grew. As if he could read my mind about needing attention to my pussy, Declan's hands came to the button on my jeans. He rose up to slide my jeans off before my thong went down my thighs as well. After he tossed them on the floor, his hand snaked down my stomach. His fingers feathered across my belly teasingly, causing my hips to buck. Gripping my thighs, he pushed them wide apart.

When his head dipped between my legs, I pinched my eyes shut in ecstasy. As his fingers entered me again, his tongue swirled around my clit, sucking it deep into his mouth. I fisted the sheets in both hands. "Oh Declan!" I screamed, and my hand immediately flew to cup my mouth. Considering it was hunting season, I didn't know who might be out in the woods to hear me. *God, it's been so long since I screamed in bed. He sure hasn't lost his oral touch.*

As he kept up his delicious assault on my clit, he pumped his two fingers in and out of me, stopping sometimes to curl them inside me to hit my G-spot. It was so intense I was tugging the strands of his hair and crying out his name. My hips kept a manic rhythm, rising and falling with the plunging of his fingers inside me. As I climbed higher and higher, I didn't know if I could stand any more, and then a burst came from within me followed by a locomotive charging through my abdomen. As I started falling back to the earth from my intense orgasm, I couldn't remember when I'd come so hard. I wasn't sure I ever had before except with Declan.

When I came back to myself, I glanced down to see Declan staring up at me, his tongue still lapping at my center. Heat bloomed inside of me again, and I wanted nothing more than to repay the favor he'd given me.

After scooting up in the bed, I rose onto my knees. "Your turn for some oral attention."

Declan's brows rose. "It is?"

"Oh yes."

"I won't argue with that," Declan mused with a smile as he lay back on his back. After I pushed his legs apart, I ran my hands up and down the inside of his thighs, my fingernails scraping against his sensitive skin. "Please, Pey," Declan murmured.

I smiled up at him as I pulled down the waistband of his underwear and freed his erection. Taking him in one hand, I licked a slow trail from root to tip. My tongue flicked and swirled around the head. I suctioned just the tip in my mouth and then released it. Declan groaned. "Babe, don't tease me. It's been too long."

I continued my slow assault on him, feeling him grow even larger with my ministrations. I blew air on his glistening tip, which elicited a low growl from Declan. When he started to protest again, I slid him into my mouth. Declan gasped and bucked his hips, causing me to take him deeper. I slid him in and out, sucking hard on the rim of his head while gripping him with my hand. Each time I did, he moaned in pleasure. "Oh Peyton, oh fuck!" I sped up the pace as his fingers tangled into my hair. "I'm going to come if you don't stop," he warned.

I let him fall free of my mouth. "I want you to come inside me."

"My pleasure. Let me suit up first."

Reluctantly, I let him pull away and reach over the bed to dig into his pants pocket. After fishing one out of his wallet, he tore open the wrapper with his teeth. Kicking off his boxer shorts, he then rolled the condom down his length.

As he eased back down on the bed, I widened my legs to allow room for him between them. When he rubbed his cock against my slickened core, I moaned. "Please, Declan."

"Patience," he murmured.

"I've waited long enough."

Declan bent his head to kiss my eyelids, the tip of my nose, and my cheeks. He stilled the movements of his cock rubbing against my slit. Staring intently into my eyes, he took my face in his hands. "Before we do this, I have to tell you something."

My breath hitched as I braced myself for the news. "W-What is it?"

"I love you," he murmured, holding my face in his hands.

A gasp of shock slipped from my lips at his declaration. Blinking a few times, I stared up at him. "You do?"

He nodded. "Even after all these years, there's never been anyone else for me. You've always been the one. You and only you."

My heart beat wildly in my chest as tears pricked my eyelids. Smiling up at him, I cupped his cheek in my hand. "I love you, too, Declan, and you're the only one for me."

With our declarations of love hanging in the air around us, Declan thrust inside me. His eyes locked on mine as he kept his movements tediously slow at first. I swept my fingertips up and down the corded muscles of his back. I thought of the times in the past when my nails had dug into his skin during some hardcore fucking. But there was no place for that tonight. We were making love together.

After a few delicious minutes, I squealed when Declan rolled us over to where I was riding him. He lay still, buried deep inside me, waiting for me to take the reins. Tentatively, I rocked against him until I slowly started speeding up the pace. Leaning back, I rested my palms on his thighs as I rode him hard and fast, grinding against him until I found just the right spot to send me over the edge again. "Yes, Declan! Oh God!" I cried.

Declan rose up into a sitting position. He took one of my swaying breasts in his mouth and sucked deeply while gripping my hips tight. He changed the rhythm to work me against him, pulling me almost off his cock and then slamming me back down on him. I felt him go deeper and deeper each time, and as much as I was enjoying the feeling, Declan was grunting in pleasure against my chest.

"Yes, harder, Declan!" I cried.

Just when I thought I might come again, Declan pushed me onto my back and brought my legs straight up against his chest so my feet rested at his shoulders. I whimpered when he rammed himself back inside me. He grinned down at me with satisfaction, and I knew I was in for it. I'd told him I wanted it harder, so he was going to really give it to me.

As he pounded into me, his balls smacked against my ass. He groaned as the position took him deeper again. My cries of pleasure seemed to fuel Declan on as he thrust again and again. I felt the tension in his body and realized he was getting close. Suddenly, he spread my legs and brought them back to their original position; we were now face-to-face and wrapped in each other's arms, and I went over the edge.

When my last orgasm tightened my walls around Declan's cock, he thrust one last time and then let himself go inside me. "Oh, fuck, Peyton!" he cried before collapsing on top of me.

We lay there entangled in each other's arms and tried catching our breath. Seconds turned to minutes as we just lay there. As we stared into each other's eyes, we said all the things we wanted to say but couldn't find the words. All the hurt, the pain, the love, the happiness, the hope for the future swirled around us in that moment.

No matter how many years had passed or where life had taken me, nothing compared to the feeling of being wrapped in Declan's arms.

He was home.

But even better, I was home, too.

Finally breaking the silence, Declan said, "I was hoping after all these years together and after everything had happened, it would be just as good as before." He smiled as he ran his thumb across my jaw. "But I think it was even better."

"Me too," I replied as I ran my hands up and down his back. "Seriously the best I've ever had has been with you."

"I can say the same thing." A few moments passed before a self-appreciative smile curved on Declan's lips.

"What are you grinning about?"

"I still have it, huh?"

"Don't ruin the moment by being so cocky."

"Hey, that cock just gave you lots of pleasure."

I giggled. "That is true." Wagging my brows, I replied, "Do you think it'll be up to pleasuring me again in a little while?"

Declan chuckled. "It's not as young as it once was, but it'll rise to the occasion if you give it a few minutes."

"I'm good at waiting."

"I would argue differently, but I'm willing to give you an orgasm or two while we wait."

"You'll get no complaints out of me."

Chapter Twenty-Two

Four months later

Forcing a smile to my face, I rose out of my office chair. "Thank you so much for coming. I'll be in touch with my answer within the week."

After showing today's fifth interview out my office door, I exhaled a defeated breath. Fifteen prospects had passed through the clinic in the last week. So far, none of them felt like the one. Some male, some female, some middle-aged, some fresh out of school. All brought different skills and talents to the table. Under different circumstances, each and every one of them would have made an excellent partner.

But Papa's clinic was an exception.

Regardless of how defeated I felt, I knew the right person was out there. The one who would respect the enormous shoes they were stepping into. The one who would understand the importance of a family run clinic.

Until then, I was overworked and slightly overwrought since Dr. Kisick's retirement a week ago. Easing back down in my chair, I unlocked my iPad to finish up the notations on today's charts. At a gentle knock on my door, I called, "Yes?"

Sylvia stuck her head in. "Any luck?"

I shook my head. "Lots of great candidates. Just not the *one*."

She smiled. "I get it. I haven't felt that spark with any of them either."

"Does that mean you don't think I'm crazy for not hurrying up and hiring someone?"

"Of course not. It's a big decision you're undertaking. Not only do you have to find the right one to work with you, but it has to be a good fit with the techs as well. After all, this is a family."

"Thanks, Sylvia. You don't know how much I appreciate that."

"You're more than welcome." Nodding at my phone, she said, "I came in to tell you Roy Wallace is on line two."

"Got it. Thanks." Picking up the phone, I pressed the button for line two. "Hi there, Mr. Wallace. What can I do for you today?"

"Well, Doc Beasley, I think I have another heifer with a breech calf, and I'm just getting too old for this."

I laughed. "It's okay, Mr. Wallace. You're in luck today because my calendar is clear. I'll be there in ten minutes."

After hanging up with Roy, I made a quick supply run before heading out the door. When I pulled up at his house, I had a slight feeling of déjà vu since it was here where I saw Declan again. Of course, my feelings towards him then were a complete one-eighty from now. I would have never fathomed a future with Declan that day. I only wanted to tell him off—to somehow make him hurt the way he had hurt me.

But now things were amazing. Outstanding. Glorious. *Right*.

When I got out of the car, Roy was waiting on me. "It's good to see you again although not under the circumstances," he said.

With a smile, I replied, "I would have to say the same thing."

Pointing out to the pasture, he said, "You can find the heifer where the last one was."

I couldn't help feeling surprised that Roy wasn't going to walk me out there again. There must've been a lot of truth in him saying he was getting too old. "I'll go take a look," I replied.

After grabbing my bag out of the backseat, I started toward the pasture. Today I was sporting my own pair of Wellies, not an old pair of Papa's. It made it a lot easier making my way across the muddy terrain.

When I crested the hill, I gasped. Below me Declan stood on a carpet of what appeared to be multicolored roses. A sea of flickering candles littered the grass around him. The one thing absent from the area was the cows.

My mind screamed at my feet to pick themselves up and started walking. Finally, after what felt like a small eternity of being frozen, I started down the hillside. The closer I got to Declan, the faster my heart began beating. I was afraid it was going to explode out of my chest before I could reach him.

As I slowly walked up to him, he gave me a beaming smile. "You made it."

"Under false pretenses, but yes, I did."

"Roy was a real trooper when it came to helping me with this."

"And what exactly is all *this*?"

"I'm commemorating the place where we reconnected six months ago today."

"Wow. Has it really been that long?"

"Yes, ma'am." He pursed his lips at me. "I thought women were supposed to be methodically good at remembering relationship dates."

Sweeping my hands to my hips, I countered, "Call me crazy that I didn't remember to draw a heart around that day. Maybe it slipped my mind because I was occupied with telling you off."

A wicked grin slunk across Declan's face. "And then you fell in a pile of cow shit."

With a roll of my eyes, I replied, "Yes, thanks for reminding me of that."

"You know I'll always be the first person to laugh at the absurdity of the moment when it comes to you."

"How gallant of you."

"I thought it was quite gallant, as you say, of me to try to make something beautiful out of this day."

Although I hated to admit it, he was right. After ten years apart, the anniversary of that day would always be important. "Yes, it was nice of you to do this."

"Just nice?"

"Fine. It was extremely thoughtful and endearing of you."

He grinned. "Much better."

After gazing around the pasture, I said, "The flowers and candles are gorgeous, but you could have done the same thing at home."

"That would have been too easy." He closed the gap between us. "You of all people should appreciate the fact our history will never be cookie-cutter perfect. It's messy and complicated. That's what makes it special." He brushed his hand across my cheek. "I want to spend the rest of my life righting the wrongs of the past. Painting this pasture where we reconnected in a better light is just one small step of many."

I couldn't help but swoon, which caused my knees to buckle. When I pitched forward, it appeared I was going to do a repeat of my epic face-plant from six months ago. Fortunately, Declan reached out to right me before I could fall. "Thank you," I said in a breathy voice.

"I'm starting to think there's something about this pasture that makes you klutzy," Declan teased.

I playfully smacked his arm. "The last time I was nailed in the thigh by an irate heifer's hoof. This time I was knocked off guard by your words," I argued.

An impish gleam burned in Declan's eyes. "Just wait. You haven't seen nothing yet."

Furrowing my brows at him, I asked, "What do you mean?"

When Declan knelt down in front of me, one of my hands flew to cover my mouth. "Oh. My. God. You're on your knees. You're..."

He smiled. "That's right, Peyton Elizabeth Beasley. I'm proposing. *Again.*"

Oh God. This was really happening. Declan wanted to marry me. Again. My head swirled with a trippy, lightheaded feeling. In the midst of my dreamlike state, it hit me. "You're proposing to me in the middle of a cow pasture?"

"Why not?"

"Oh, I don't know. Maybe the off chance you might be kneeling in manure?"

"That's not possible since I had this hillside cleaned this afternoon." With a wink, he added, "Besides, I'd roll around in cow shit if it meant spending the rest of my life with you."

While my heartbeat thrummed wildly in my chest, I shook my head. "Please don't."

Declan chuckled. "I promise." After a moment passed, his expression grew serious. "Look, I've spent the last few weeks wracking my brains about how I should do this. I knew I wanted it to be something completely different than the first one."

At the time, the day we got engaged was the happiest day of my life. I'd gone on a cruise with his family to the Caribbean and stayed in a room with Danielle. On our last day beside a gorgeous waterfall, he'd dropped to one knee. As a nineteen-year-old girl, it was the most romantic thing I could ever imagine, and at thirty, I had to say it appeared epically more romantic than Roy Wallace's cow pasture.

"After all this time, that one still holds up as being pretty magical."

"I know. But hear me out for a minute."

I grinned. "Trust me, I want to hear you explain this one."

"I knew a trip out of the country or even out of town was out of the question considering everything you have on your plate with Hank's retirement. I thought about a day trip to Atlanta and proposing there." He shook his head. "But while Atlanta was part of you, it's never been part of me. More importantly, it's not a part of *us*."

"You're right." When I thought about it, I wouldn't have wanted a proposal in Atlanta. The city didn't just represent the life I'd created post-jilting, but it was also a physical manifestation of my continued running from my problems or more precisely from Declan.

"For years, I hoped there would come a day when I would see you again. A day when I could tell you how sorry I was and how wrong I'd been. I'll never forget what it felt like to come out of the woods and see you standing there."

"With my arm up a cow's ass?" I teasingly asked.

Declan scowled at me. "Would you let me finish?"

I held my hands up. "Fine, fine."

"Everything in my life had gone to shit, and I was looking for a sign that things were going to somehow get better not just for me, but for Cam. And then I saw you. Even though I didn't know how I was going to make it happen, I just knew things were going to be better. You were the key."

I fought to breathe. "You really thought that?"

"I did. Of course, I never expected life to throw more obstacles in my way."

"Like me still hating your guts?"

He laughed. "While that was a problem, I was thinking more about how Harris's will gave you yet another reason for you to despise me. I realized redemption was going to be an uphill battle." He stared intently at me. "But you were worth the fight."

Tears stung my eyes at his words. Before I could swipe them away, Declan took my hands in his. "Peyton Beasley, would you do me the honor of being my wife?"

A decade after first uttering, "Yes! Oh yes!", I said it once again before diving into Declan's arms.

We then proceeded to cement our second engagement by taking a roll in the hay, or I guess I should say a roll in the grass. I sincerely hoped Roy Wallace wasn't looking. I'm pretty sure our actions would have scarred him for life.

"So, what happens now?" I asked.

"Besides us picking pieces of grass out of dark places where it should never be?"

I laughed. "Well, that. But I meant more along the lines of a wedding."

"You don't want to waste any time, do you?"

"Newsflash, ace. We're not getting any younger."

"You're right about that one."

Propping my head on my elbow, I grinned at him. "There's also the fact with your track record, I need to lock you down ASAP."

"Ha, ha," Declan grumbled as he sat up on the blanket.

"Seriously, though. What did you have in mind?"

"Well, after what happened the last time, I figure you might not want another big church wedding."

The truth was I'd never really given it much thought. Maybe it was because I'd always had such a hard time picturing myself marrying anyone else. Because I could barely envision the groom, I'd never actually considered the place. "You're right. I really don't." I smiled up at him. "All I care about is marrying you and being your wife."

"In that case, I have your father on standby. He can be at the church in ten minutes to marry us."

My eyes bulged at Declan. "You're joking."

He shook his head. "I'm totally serious."

"Dad agreed to marry us?" Yes, that was the part I was focusing on instead of the fact I could be Mrs. Declan St. James by the end of the night. Sure, my dad had come to embrace my renewed relationship with Declan, but at the same time, he still harbored some doubts.

"I went to speak with him yesterday."

My chest constricted slightly. "You did?"

"Even though I had asked for your hand ten years ago, I felt like I needed to officially apologize to him. We had a long talk, and thankfully at the end of it, he gave me his blessing." My dad was, in some senses, a softie. But when his baby girl was hurt, I actually doubted he'd ever forgive Declan, even though his life revolved around speaking forgiveness into people's lives. In the end, Declan St. James was an incredible man to have spoken to Dad. It made me love him even more.

But to propose in a cow pasture . . . "I can't believe you went to all this trouble." Gazing around the pasture, I added, "I mean, some of it is kind of odd, but at the same time, you really thought all this through."

"Of course, I did." He brushed his hand against my cheek. "You're worth it, Peyton. This and ten times more."

"Although it's incredibly tempting to take you up on your offer, I can't help but feel someone very important would be missing."

Tears shimmered in Declan's eyes. "Cam."

I nodded. "I can't imagine a wedding without him being there."

Nodding, Declan replied, "I can't either."

The look on his face . . . pride. That little boy, that precious, darling boy had entered my life in a rush, and I had to say, I felt like the luckiest woman in the world. He was cheeky, funny, gave the best snuggles, and every time he reached up to take my hand when we are out and about, my heart nearly exploded with joy. He'd simply accepted me into his home and into his heart as if it was always my place to be there. And he was so freakin' cute. And that's why, as much as I loved the idea of having my dad involved in the ceremony, I actually wanted to do something for our new family. Do things *our* way.

"What do you say when Spring Break rolls around, we fly to Orlando, and let Cam stand beside us as we get married at Disney World?" I suggested.

"You want to get married at Disney?"

"Cam's been wanting to see Buzz Lightyear for as long as I've known him."

"I like your way of thinking."

"Besides, it's infinitely better than a cow pasture."

"I wasn't insinuating we get married here," Declan scowled.

With a grin, I replied, "I know you weren't." I bent my head to kiss him. "If push came to shove, I'd marry you right here."

After Declan kissed me back, he stared into my eyes. "We're really doing this?"

My heartbeat broke into a wild gallop in my chest. "Yes, we're really getting married."

"God, I love you," Declan murmured.

"And I love you."

"I think on every anniversary we should come back to this pasture and make love," Declan said with a twinkle in his eye.

"Think again."

He chuckled. "But what a story that would be. We met again here in Roy Wallace's cow pasture, we got engaged here, and then maybe we conceived our first child together here."

I rolled my eyes. "What a shitty complex to give a child. Pun intended."

"There are worse places to conceive a baby."

Jabbing a finger into his bare chest, I replied, "Let's get a few married months under our belt before you knock me up. I don't need any of the town gossips flapping their jaws that the only reason why you married me this time was because I was pregnant."

"Oh, but I would love to give them something to talk about."

"If we don't hurry up and get dressed, Roy Wallace will be giving them ample talking points about seeing us half-naked."

"Considering how much I've been working out lately, I know he would have to be complimentary."

"I think you're suffering from delusions of grandeur," I muttered as I threw on my shirt.

Jerking me against his perfect pecs, Declan rolled his thick thighs against mine. "Oh really?"

With my mouth running dry, I found it hard to speak. "Okay, it's impressive."

"That's what I thought." He dipped his head to kiss me. "We're getting married."

"Finally," I corrected.

He laughed. "Yes. Finally."

And with those words, we walked hand and hand back through the pasture to our happily ever after.

Epilogue

A Year Later

"Okay, Scooby, let's try to stay out of the trash next time," I instructed to the hulking Great Dane on the exam table. He'd had to stay overnight for fluids and anti-diarrhea medication after eating something that hadn't agreed with him. Since he'd torn through most of the trash bag, his owner had had a hard time deciphering what the offending food was. Considering the shit-show he'd experienced both at home and here, it must've been something positively corroded.

With a wave to Scooby's owner, Mrs. Demarco, I then headed out of the exam room, leaving Jaycee to go over the aftercare instructions. Glancing at my watch, I grimaced. I was going to have to haul ass to make it to the school on time.

When I got out into the hallway, Sylvia had anticipated me like usual and was waiting with an enormous tray full of Halloween-themed cupcakes. I grinned as I gazed down at the green, orange, and black iced cupcakes with their little witch and ghost toppers. "These are amazing. Cameron is going to love them."

Sylvia beamed. "I hope he does."

I'd spent the last year trying to adjust to being a mom. The one area I still struggled in was cooking and baking. I started turning to Sylvia to provide the confections Cam's class needed for parties and festivals. Since she loved to bake, it was a win-win for both of us.

"I'll be back in time for my next appointment."

Nodding, Sylvia replied, "Have a good time."

"Thanks. I will."

When I arrived at Hayesville Elementary, I found the parking lot packed. It made sense considering they were hosting the Halloween carnival that evening, not to mention all the class parties taking place this afternoon. While Declan was forgoing attending the class party, he was going to be coming back with us that evening to the carnival.

Blowing through Cam's classroom door, I found the other mothers in a flurry of last-minute party prep. "Sorry I'm late," I said to Sally, the head room mom.

"You're fine. We still have about five minutes before they come back from recess."

"Here are the cupcakes."

Sally's blue eyes lit up. "These are gorgeous. You did an amazing job."

I merely nodded rather than giving myself away. I already felt like Cam was at a deficit for his real mom to not be involved in school. I didn't want to make things worse by him having a stepmom who was baking challenged. Smiling, I said, "What can I help you guys do?"

"You could set up the pin-the-tail on the werewolf," Sally said handing me the package.

"I'm on it."

After I finished putting up the game, I heard the shrieks and laughter of the kids coming back. When Cam came through the door with his friends, he made a beeline over to me. "Hey Mommy," he exclaimed as he threw his arms around me. Before Declan and I married, Cam had asked to call me mom, and I had happily accepted.

"Hey, sweetheart."

Craning his neck at the table, he asked, "Did you bring the cupcakes?"

"I sure did."

He leaned in to whisper in my ear. "I won't tell anyone you didn't make them."

I laughed. "Thanks, baby."

"Are we still going trick-or-treating tonight?"

"Of course. As soon as the clinic closes, I'm going to pick you up at Grandma's and then we'll go home and meet Daddy."

There wasn't much Cam asked of me and Declan, so when he requested we have family costumes this year, it was hard to say no. That's how I'd ended up with a Bo Peep costume while Declan was going to be Woody. Obsessed with *Toy Story*, Cam had wanted to be Buzz Lightyear. Even poor Moose hadn't escaped from a costume—he was going to be Slinky Dog.

"I'm going to go sit with my friends now, okay?"

"That's fine."

He gave me a squeeze. "Love you, Mommy."

My heart swelled in my chest each and every time he called me that. "I love you, too."

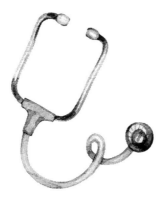

After the party, I had a few minutes to spare before my next four-legged client arrived. I had something special I wanted to give Declan before we were consumed with trick-or-treating, so I texted him to see if he had a moment. He did, so I headed down the sidewalk to his office. When I walked through the front door, Anna smiled at me. "Good morning, Mrs. St. James."

I waved a hand at her. "When are you going to learn to call me Peyton?"

"I'm working on it."

"He's expecting me."

"Go right on in."

As I walked down the hall, I couldn't help laughing when I thought about the day I'd stormed in here on the warpath to give Declan a piece of my mind. So much had changed in my life since that day. I'd found peace of mind through my forgiveness of Declan. That peace had led to contentment in other areas of my life.

Just like the other time, I didn't knock on the door. I just went right on in. Sitting at his desk, Declan looked positively edible in a pink long-sleeved shirt. I'd encouraged him to branch out with some pastels because they brought out his eyes. He hadn't been too convinced at first.

Declan had the phone cradled to his ear while he held a manila folder in front of me. Instead of sitting down in one of the chairs across from him, I walked around the side of his desk. When I made the motion for him to turn his chair around, he cocked his eyebrows at me. Once he was facing me, I eased down onto his lap. Suddenly, he couldn't get off the phone fast enough.

After hanging up the call, he brought his arms around me while he nuzzled his head against my chest. "It's been forever since you came in for an afternoon delight."

With a laugh, I replied, "I'm not here for sex."

One of his hands snaked up to cup my breast through my scrubs. "Can I change your mind?"

I wriggled out of his grasp. "Sorry. I don't have time."

"I can be quick."

Running my fingers through his hair, I pulled his head up to meet my gaze. "Not today."

"Fine. How was the party?"

"Wonderful. Cam loved the cupcakes. He was going for his third, but then he offered it to Ansley."

Declan's lips quirked up. "Does he have a crush?"

"I think so. He certainly followed her around the whole time."

With a grunt, Declan replied, "We'll have to work on his player skills. He should have the girls running around after him."

Rolling my eyes, I replied, "Yeah, let's not do that."

"It seemed to work well for me."

"Excuse me?"

"I'm talking about when you used to chase me around the playground."

"I did no such thing."

"Oh yes, you did."

Wagging a finger at him, I countered, "I seem to recall *you* chasing *me*. You even got in trouble for not letting me pass on the slide when you kissed me."

Declan tilted his head in thought. "Hmm, maybe I do remember that."

"So excuse me for being grateful my son isn't an elementary school player."

I thought Declan might protest about his player status, but he surprised me when tears sparkled in his eyes. "Did you realize what you just said?"

"That my son isn't a player?"

He shook his head. "You said Cam was *your* son."

"Oh," I murmured.

"It's the first time you ever said that," Declan said

"It is?" Wow, I'd just had a parental moment and hadn't even realized it. Over the past year, I'd never claimed Cam as mine even though he had often felt that way. After our marriage, Bailey had moved to Savannah with a man she'd met online. We hadn't even heard from her in the last few months.

Declan's lips grazed mine in a tender kiss. "Thank you."

"But I didn't do anything?"

"You love our son. You're the best mother he could've ever have hoped for."

Now it was my turn for the waterworks when tears pricked my eyelids. "I can't imagine not loving him or being his mom."

"Maybe one day we'll be able to convince Bailey to terminate her rights, and you'll be able to adopt him for real."

"I don't have to have a piece of paper to tell me Cam's mine. I know it now."

Declan kissed me again. "He's ours, and you're mine."

"Always." The mention of Cam and adoption made me think of my purpose in coming. "Listen, I have to be getting back to the clinic, but before I go, I have a treat for you."

"After denying me an afternoon delight, I hope you plan on giving me a treat later when we're alone." He waggled his brows.

"We'll see." Bending over, I fished the candy bar out of my purse. I handed it over to him. "Open it."

"Is there some sort of prize inside?"

"There might be." Once he had it open, I said, "Now read it aloud."

"Man, you're bossy this afternoon."

His eyes focused on the message in the wrapper. "Congratulations. You're going to be a father again." His eyes snapped up to mine. "You're pregnant?"

I smiled at him. "Almost eight weeks. I'm due in May."

"How long have you known?"

"I took a home test this week, but I saw the doctor this morning."

A beaming smile lit up his face. "I'm going to be a dad again."

"Yep. You are."

He brought his hands to cup my face. "I love you so much."

"I love you so much, too. And I love Cam." I brought my hand to my abdomen. "And I love this little nugget, too. You've given me a happily ever after I'd never thought possible."

"It took me long enough," Declan mused.

"Trust me. It was worth it."

And it was. All the hurt and pain made me truly appreciate what a wonderful gift I'd been given in my second chance with Declan. If we'd married when we were kids, I'm not sure I could have appreciated the love we had. I now knew what we had was something special. Something forever.

All it took to achieve such happiness was Declan finally reining me in.

After catching her husband in a compromising position, the last thing that Finley Granger wants is to enter the insanity that is the dating world. She's dealing with enough upheaval: she's quit her job as a journalist in Atlanta to start over as a librarian in the backwoods town of Green Valley, Tennessee. But her grandmother has other ideas. When GramBea teams up with her sister, Dot, and their best friend, Estelle, Finley finds herself surrounded by a trio of well-meaning yet incredibly bumbling matchmakers.

In spite of their efforts, there's only one man she's curious about, and that's Zeke Masters, the library's volunteer IT specialist. Sure, he's 6'4", impossibly built, ridiculously good-looking, and gets her nether regions tingling. However, it's the tingle of her journalist spidey-senses that holds her attention most as she wonders why he's on sabbatical from Seattle. Is he on lam, or on the run from a bad relationship? As Finley finds herself reluctantly drawn to the gorgeous IT guy, she can't help but wonder: should she indulge in a little rebound fun with the mysterious Zeke – or has she finally met her match?

ABOUT THE AUTHOR

Katie Ashley is a New York Times, USA Today, and Amazon Top Five Best-Selling author of both Indie and Traditionally published books. She's written rockers, bikers, manwhores with hearts of gold, New Adult, and Young Adult. She lives outside of Atlanta, Georgia with her daughter, Olivia, her rescue mutts, Belle and Elsa, and cat, Harry Potter . She has a slight obsession with Pinterest, The Golden Girls, Shakespeare, Harry Potter, and Star Wars.

With a BA in English, a BS in Secondary English Education, and a Masters in Adolescent English Education, she spent eleven years teaching both middle and high school English, as well as a few adjunct college English classes. As of January 2013, she became a full-time writer.

Although she is a life-long Georgia peach, she loves traveling the country and world meeting readers. Most days, you can find her being a hermit, styling leggings, and binging on Netflix whenever her young daughter isn't monopolizing the TV with Paw Patrol or Frozen.

CONNECT WITH KATIE

➜ NEWSLETTER: https://bit.ly/2BHeOyI. ➜ FACEBOOK: facebook.com/katie.ashleyromance

➜ FACEBOOK READER GROUP (ASHLEY'S ANGELS): facebook.com/groups/ashleyangels

➜ WEBSITE: www.katieashleybooks.com

➜INSTAGRAM: Instagram.com/katieashleyluv

➜ TWITTER: twitter.com/katieashleyluv

➜ PINTEREST: pinterest.com/katieashleyluv